How to Knit a Murder

Also by Sally Goldenbaum

Murder Wears Mittens

How to Knit a Murder

Sally Goldenbaum

KENSINGTON BOOKS
http://www.kensingtonbooks.com

KENSINGTON BOOKS are published by

Kensington Publishing Corp.
119 West 40th Street
New York, NY 10018

All Kensington titles, imprints, and distributed lines are available at special quantity discounts for bulk purchases for sales promotion, premiums, fund-raising, educational, or institutional use.

Special book excerpts or customized printings can also be created to fit specific needs. For details, write or phone the office of the Kensington Special Sales Manager: Attn. Special Sales Department. Kensington Publishing Corp., 119 West 40th Street, New York, NY 10018. Phone: 1-800-221-2647.

Kensington and the K logo Reg. U.S. Pat. & TM Off.

Library of Congress Card Catalogue Number: 2018944167

ISBN-13: 978-1-4967-1105-2
ISBN-10: 1-4967-1105-X
First Kensington Hardcover Edition: December 2018

eISBN-13: 978-1-4967-1107-6
eISBN-10: 1-4967-1107-6
First Kensington Electronic Edition: December 2018

10 9 8 7 6 5 4 3 2 1

Printed in the United States of America

To Don, for nearly a half century of love, life, and friendship.

Cast of Characters

The Seaside Knitters

Endicott, Nell: Retired nonprofit director; married to Ben
Halloran, Cass (Catherine Mary Theresa): Co-owner of Halloran Lobster Company; married to Danny Brandley; mystery novelist
Perry, Izzy: (Isabel Chambers Perry): Former attorney; owner of the Seaside Knitting Studio; Nell and Ben Endicott's niece; married to Sam Perry; toddler daughter, Abby
Favazza, Birdie (Bernadette): Sea Harbor's wealthy, wise octogenarian

The Men in Their Lives

Brandley, Danny: Mystery novelist; son of Archie and Harriet Brandley; Cass's husband
Endicott, Ben: Nell's husband; Izzy's uncle
Favazza, Sonny: Birdie's [deceased] first husband
Perry, Sam: Izzy's husband; award-winning photographer

Friends and Townsfolk

Anderson, Mae: Yarn shop manager
Babson, Josh: Artist in Canary Cove Art Colony
Bianchi, Anthony: Recently deceased friend of several Sea Harbor old-timers
Brandley, Archie and Harriet: Owners of the Sea Harbor Bookstore; Danny's parents
Brewster, Jane and Ham: Artists and cofounders of the Canary Cove Art Colony

Chopra, Rose Woodley: Newcomer to Sea Harbor; works at Palazola Realty

The Fractured Fish band: Andy Risso (drummer); Pete Halloran (guitarist, singer); Merry Jackson (keyboard, singer)

Garozzo, Harry and Margaret: Owners of Garozzo's Deli

Gibson, Esther: Police dispatcher

Halloran Family:

Mary, Pete and Cass's mother; secretary at Our Lady of Safe Seas Church;

Pete, Cass's brother; co-owner of the Halloran Lobster Company and singer in the Fractured Fish band;

Sister Mary Fiona Halloran, Mary's sister-in-law; Pete and Cass's aunt

Jackson, Merry: Owner of the Artist's Palate Bar & Grill; singer in band

McGlucken, Gus: Owner of McGlucken Hardware Store

McGlucken, Robbie: Gus's twenty-five-year-old son

McIntosh, Bree: Artist; married to Spencer Paxton

Northcutt, Father Lawrence: Pastor of Our Lady of Safe Seas Church

Palazola, Annabelle: Owner of the Sweet Petunia Restaurant

Palazola, Mario: Owner of Palazola Realty

Palazola, Stella: Annabelle's youngest daughter; Realtor

Paxton, Spencer III: Owner of Paxton Development; married to Bree McIntosh

Pisano, Mary: Newspaper columnist; owner of a B and B

Porter, Tommy: Police detective

Purl: The yarn shop's calico cat

Risso, Jake: Owner of the Gull Tavern

Sampson, Ella and Harold: Birdie's housekeeper and groundskeeper/driver
Santos, Liz: Manager of Sea Harbor Yacht Club
Stuber, Patricia: School principal
Thompson, Jerry: Police chief

Chapter 1

"Great bones," Spencer Paxton III said. "And look at these amazing grounds. We could have an extravaganza for two hundred here easily."

Spencer didn't look at his wife while he talked. Instead his deep-set eyes traveled over the wide lawns, the low winding wall that defined the property, a small guest cottage nestled in a clump of woods to the side. He looked at the sturdy stone foundation and sides of the mansion, the dozens of long mullioned windows. His eyes went back and forth, up and down, hungrily combing every inch.

One of Sea Harbor's finest.

Bree leaned back and looked all the way to the top of the three-story seaside villa. The fading light of early evening fell on the gabled roof, throwing shadows across the lawn and the flagstone walkway. The ocean wasn't visible from where they stood, but the sound of crashing waves behind the house and the feel of salty air heralded its presence. She pulled her hoodie tight.

"It's enormous," she said. "Twenty families could live in this house." She thought of the three-bedroom house in which her parents had raised their family of six. She had loved every inch of it.

"Yeah. Huge is good. We'll fill it." Spence walked his fingers up and down her back. "Rugrats. Maybe we'll get us some. Who knows? Things can change."

Bree was silent. No, contrary to what her husband thought, some things wouldn't change. Ever.

"I called a Realtor last week," he said, still not looking at her. His eyes were checking out the visible details—quality of materials, walkways, the grounds.

"You called a Realtor?" She looked at him in surprise. "Why?"

"That's how you buy a house, babe. I went to school with this gal—way back when." He laughed. "Stella Palazola. She was an upperclassman, but flirted with me like crazy. She had this big crush on me. I ran into her at the Gull one night. She fell all over herself wanting to help me out." He stopped and pointed. "Look at that balcony up there, the wrought-iron work. Amazing."

"The house we're renting is fine, Spence. It has wonderful light. I'm comfortable there. You won't be here forever."

Now he looked directly at her, his gaze sharp. "In the middle of that old art colony? My dad would roll over in his grave. Shove my face in it. No more. Canary Cove is a place for hippies and starving artists. Those knitters you hang around with would fit in there. Not a Paxton."

Bree smiled as his comment took form. *Those knitters you hang around with—those plain people. Ordinary.*

Wise, wonderful Birdie, who could buy and sell all the Paxtons without a blink of an eye. Elegant Nell, who'd once single-handedly run a large Boston nonprofit. Smart, gorgeous Izzy, with her law degree tucked away in some drawer of her successful yarn shop. And clever, dark-haired Cass, owner of a lobster company. Attractive, sassy, and exuberant.

Spencer had no idea of whom he spoke. And that was fine with Bree. Instead she said, "The home on Canary Cove is cozy. I like it."

"Not for me, babe. Doesn't fit the plan."

The plan. She looked sideways and caught the familiar odd smile that lifted the edges of his mouth, the lift of one dark brow. The set of his strong chin and the face that her own mother had compared to her favorite soap opera star the first time she'd brought Spence home.

"My old man wanted to buy this house when I was a kid. Did I tell you that? He wasn't fast enough, not savvy enough, and he lost out to an old Italian. Anthony Bianchi. It's my turn, babe. And I'll get it. They're doing some work on it now, fixing a few things. And then it'll be mine."

And it would be his, Bree knew. *What Spencer Paxton wanted, Spencer Paxton got.* She started to turn back toward the street, scattering leaves with the toe of her boot.

"Hey, where're you going? I'm not ready to leave yet. Come on," Spence said. He nodded toward the walkway circling the house. "Let's look around back."

"That's trespassing."

Spence laughed, and cupped her elbow roughly, prodding her along the flagstone path toward the back of the house.

Bree shook off his hand and put distance between them. She peered through the thick windows as they walked, but she saw nothing inside. Heavy black curtains held the dark tightly inside. Closed shutters protected smaller windows above.

When they reached the back of the house, a blast of damp ocean air lifted Bree's platinum hair and whipped it across her cheeks, stinging her fair skin. She pulled it back with one hand, bunching it as she looked out at the ocean. The surf was just yards from where she stood, down a terraced lawn and a footpath to a sliver of beach. Dark waves leapt in the air, then crashed against a graveyard of granite boulders, foam spewing in all directions. A small boat, moored nearby, rolled with the motion, tossing and turning in the cold air.

She breathed it all in, the air cold and bracing, until she felt she would burst. The ocean was magnificent.

She felt Spence's presence next to her, tall and dark and self-assured, his body shadowing her own. He had raised his binoculars and was scanning the horizon, as if waiting for a whale to perform, a fleet of schooners to parade past him in homage, or, *Who knows*, Bree thought, *maybe to spot an island for sale?* He lifted one hand and pointed south.

"You can see the Boston skyline from here," he said. "It's incredible."

Bree had turned away and looked up at the mansion again, the glory of the ocean sucked out of her by the sight of the house. She walked back to the fan of steps leading to a stone patio that stretched the width of the mansion. Yellow, orange, and rose-colored leaves skittered across the stones. The veranda was wide and empty, save for groupings of chairs and tables covered in canvas—gray ghosts in the fading light.

Bree shivered, wrapping her arms tightly around herself, wondering about the power this house seemed to have over her, blurring the grandeur of the ocean and filling her instead with uncomfortable prickly feelings.

It was just a house. A formidable one, and grand, too. She would give Spencer that. A majestic fortress, But it was still a *house*. Nothing else. She shook her head, only half believing her words. *A house*, she repeated.

"I'm going back around to the front," she called out, her words tossed away by the wind.

Spence was halfway down the flat steps leading to the water.

It was a while later, after taking photos with his phone and walking the stone patio for dimensions and imagining the events he could host on the property, the people he could impress, that Spence walked back to the front of the estate. Bree was sitting on a low stone wall that bordered the property.

"Hey, what's with you?"

"I'm tired and it's freezing out here. It's time to leave. I promised Izzy and Nell I'd stop by the yarn shop to help with a window design. They'll be waiting for me." *And I like them*, she said silently. *I like their friendship and their yarn shop and the warm feeling I have when I sit in the back room and make magical things out of silk and cotton and bamboo.*

She stood and looked once more at the house, as if it might have been a trick of her imagination. But it was still there. She stared at the curtained windows and the foreboding stillness within.

The windows stared back.

Spence forked his fingers through his hair. "You're being weird tonight. Do you have PMS? Get a grip, Bree."

Bree didn't answer her husband. She took a deep breath and tried to shake the feeling that was chilling her bones. Slowly, she released it and braced herself, as if the house itself was about to reach out and grab her. Unconsciously she flexed the muscles in her arms, strong and toned and ready to ward off danger.

Spence looked over at her, then back at the house. "Do you want to look inside? Is that it?"

She looked at him. "Break in? Of course, the perfect way to endear you to Sea Harbor voters."

Spencer laughed. "I'm serious. Not about the breaking in, but I could make it happen."

Bree took a few steps away, then glanced at the house again as if it might follow her.

"Something's going on here," Spence said. "What is it?"

"Nothing. It's nothing." *But it isn't nothing. It's something. Or someone. Sometimes feelings become tangled and complicated, the reasons for them blurred. But whatever is worming its way through me is real, a warning that things aren't always what they seem to be.*

Without waiting for another question or reply or subtle rebuke, she walked through the gate, out to the safety of the sidewalk and the narrow winding road that ran in front of the stately Sea Harbor Cliffside homes.

Spence caught up with her as they reached the car. He started to say something, then thought better of it and clamped his mouth shut, holding in his irritation, and walked around the car, sliding in behind the wheel. Bree stood on the passenger side, her fingers curled tightly on the door handle, her body still and her eyes peering through the towering trees, back to the house that stood at the top of the incline, proud and haughty. Sure of itself.

She stood there for several more minutes, until an irritated tap of the horn pulled her attention away. But the house wasn't done with her and she looked back once more, meeting its glare, returning it with a silent vow:

I will never live in you, house. Never. Bad things will happen there.

Then she opened the door and climbed into the car, the engine already running and Spence's long fingers tapping impatiently on the steering wheel.

"It's perfect," he said to his wife, reaching over and patting her thigh. "Just perfect."

Chapter 2

Rose Chopra stood on the sidewalk, oblivious to the life teeming around her. Her palms were damp, her stomach tight. Behind her, fishing boats were making their way to the docks, ropes were thrown, rough voices shouted, and crates and traps opened and emptied. Scolding and big laughter carried on the wind.

It had taken her by surprise, the sensation that snaked its way through her body. Her shoulders stooped automatically, years of yoga gone in an instant.

And for that one brief moment, Rose Chopra wanted to shrink to nothing.

She was eleven years old, sitting in the stern of a sailboat. Her chin lowered to her chest, her body folding in on itself, disappearing. She prayed for the ocean to open its mouth and swallow her.

And then, as suddenly as the moment came, it passed. Gone. Poof. Disappeared. Pushed away in an instant.

Rose straightened up, shoulders back, and took a deep breath. Her shoulders shifted and fell into a comfortable place; her smile lifted to the sky. *Head over heart. Namaste.*

She took a step back from the curb as a freckled-faced boy flew by on a skateboard, his hair flying wildly and his grin proud and wide. Rose grinned back, feeling confidence fill her bones and her mind. She continued on down Harbor Road.

Parts of downtown Sea Harbor appeared untouched by the years. Sights and sounds were familiar: people heading home from work, fishmongers packaging up the day's catch. And the incessant caw of the gulls and blasts of the lobster boats' horns coming in after a long day. It was comfortable. Easy. Not foreboding.

She slowed as the familiar blend of garlic, olive oil, and tomato sauce assaulted her senses wondrously from Harry Garozzo's deli. She stopped and looked through the window. It was still there, the ratty, slightly sun-bleached sign in the window. SEA HARBOR'S ONLY TRUE MUFFULETTA, it read. *And the only one*, people joked.

But what Rose remembered best was that Harry offered half muffulettas—for delicate appetites, he said—but Rose always got the whole roll, stuffed with briny, garlicky vegetables and every kind of salami and cheese known to man. Fat and thick and dripping with flavor. And she always finished it and it always made her happy, even when she went home with a button on her jeans loosened, her shirt pulled awkwardly over it. She pressed one hand on her abdomen, along with a grimace of shame. Even her dad only ordered the half.

Harry's deli would be here forever, she thought. People like Harry Garozzo didn't die. Without even looking, she could imagine the talkative Italian baker inside, his apron stained, his voice loud and welcoming as if he were standing in front of her, handing her the hefty sandwich.

The idea of coming back to Sea Harbor had rolled around in her mind for a long time, but always back in shadowy corners. Her mother talked about it, wished for it. Their reasons different, but both compelling and real. And necessary.

Rose would twist and turn the idea around until reasons for not returning had been smoothed away, erased completely, and revisiting the seaside town had been a given. Something she had to do.

It was true that she wanted to see the beauty of Sea Harbor through her mother's eyes, to savor it in a way she never had. But the reason she *needed* to come back was to throw away fragments of the past that were no longer a part of Rose Woodley Chopra.

Her old therapist, and then friend, had weighed in heavily. Many times. "Do this," Patti had intoned. "You're one strong lady, Rose Chopra."

Rose knew she was strong. Strong and mighty her dad used to say, his way of complimenting her height, the extra pounds she'd carried then, her strong face. But that same physique, when wrapped around a painfully shy preteen, was described differently by others.

She had stayed quiet and let Patti go on listing reasons why Rose needed some time near the sea, time to remember the places and pockets of the small seaside town that were truly magical. The place her mother loved so much she composed poems about walking by the sea.

The sea and me,
Its healing rush.
Infinity in its caress.

She had tuned back in to her therapist just as Patti finished her list.

You promised your mother you'd take her back to the sea. A promise that carried her through chemo and injections and excruciating days.

And you promised yourself, too. To do it for you, Rose.

Patti's soft voice was caring and loving, even when she asked, *And what happened, Rosie? You waited too long. And she died.*

Rose had felt the air being sucked out of the room.

And that's when she packed her suitcase and headed to Massachusetts.

Rose realized she was now a block past Harry's deli, standing still on the sidewalk again. Like a statue.

"What do you think?"

The voice wasn't Patti's and it was no longer inside her head. It came from near her elbow. Rose looked over.

The woman wasn't looking at her, but at a shop window a yard or two in front of them. Her hands were on her hips, her head cocked to one side.

Rose was about to ask the woman what she was talking about. And then she stopped, her eyes concentrating on the stranger who had just spoken to her. The woman was about her own age, no, younger maybe, but that was where the similarities stopped. She was exquisite, that perfect beauty that stared out at you from the cover of magazines. Unnatural. Unreal. The woman's looks made Rose feel naked—as if every one of her own imperfections was suddenly in bold relief as she stood near the stranger. She had an urge to turn and walk away.

It wasn't until the woman's expression turned to confusion that Rose realized she was staring at her.

"You don't like the window display?" the woman asked.

Then, as the woman brushed a strand of platinum hair over one shoulder, Rose realized her first impression was wrong. This wasn't unnatural beauty. It was the opposite. Pure, natural. Unaffected. Not a spec of makeup. She wasn't tall like a model, but small, delicate looking, but her tight jeans showed muscles beneath. And her Harvard sweatshirt, the sleeves pushed up to her elbows, indicated the woman could probably hold her own. Rose wondered briefly if she even knew she was utterly stunning—or if she cared.

Rose pulled her eyes away and looked at the display window.

Her eyes widened. "Whoo," she said, lifting one hand to her chest. The sound was more a breath than a word, like the sound one made when seeing a famous museum piece for the first time. She stepped closer.

On the other side of the window was a cave, a hollowed-out shape made of something Rose couldn't identify. Papier-mâché, maybe? She had made some with her sister's kids last Christmas. But this wasn't a child's molded rabbit or bird or a tree ornament.

The cavern-like structure was filled with gravity-defying formations—and they were all made from silky strands of fiber: icy gray and blue yarns. Stalagmites and stalactites knit into slender shapes, some that seemed to grow up from the floor, others hanging, shimmering from the ceiling of the cave. Tiny lights hidden in the crevices lit the cavern's beauty.

Rose took off her sunglasses and looked more closely into the scene.

A movement on the floor of the display window pulled her eyes down to a calico cat, unfurling from a nap. It sat up and looked at Rose as if they'd met before.

Rose stared back. The cat tilted its head to one side, its green eyes keen and strangely insightful. *So*, it seemed to be saying, *you're here. Now what?*

Rose shifted from one foot to the other. Finally she pulled away, embarrassed that she had almost answered the animal.

She turned to the woman, who was still standing next to her, waiting. "It's amazing. What is this place? Heaven?"

"Sort of. Yes," she said, a hint of a smile in her voice for the first time.

But her face was still, and Rose wondered if she was one of those models who was told not to smile, to keep the wrinkles away. Rose felt a reserve in the woman, or maybe, she supposed, it could be shyness, although why would someone who looked like she looked be shy?

The woman went on talking. "It's a great yarn shop. I'm surprised there are still people in Sea Harbor who don't know about it." She paused, then looked directly at Rose as if assessing her. Finally she reached out her hand. "Hi. I'm Bree McIntosh."

Rose took the outstretched hand, the woman's friendly gesture a nice surprise, one that lessened the distance Rose had imposed between them. "I'm Rose Chopra. Did you create this window? These absolutely gorgeous pieces of art?"

"It's nice you called it art. Some people might not see it that way. Yes, I helped. It's a group effort," she said. "I'm a disaster at knitting sweaters and mittens. But I love to turn yarn into art, twisting and turning, playing with colors. We're having a fiber art show over in the Canary Cove Art Colony, and the display is partly to advertise that. I'm glad you like it. Be sure you come to the show."

"I love it and I will if I'm still here. It's amazing. And so is the cat. Did you knit it, too?"

Bree laughed. "That's Purl. She's a love. The yarn shop mascot."

"So you work here?" Rose asked.

"I help out when they need me. I'm teaching a class for Izzy and doing some things over in the art colony, too. Art is my therapy. Well, therapy on top of therapy. I've had both."

Rose looked at her, for a minute surprised. But she shouldn't be. Therapy wasn't her private domain. But, even after her own years of therapy, it still surprised her when someone who looked perfect needed therapy, too.

"You should come to a class, Rose. They're fun." Her voice was warmer now, as if somehow Rose had passed a test and they were connected.

"Maybe I will," she said. "Is the shop new?"

"I don't think so—but I've only been in town a few months, so what do I know? Someone said it used to be a bait shack. Kids would sneak cigarettes and smoke behind the garbage cans near the seawall."

A bait shop. Rose remembered it now. An ugly, smelly place with cracked windows and peeling paint. Her mother had warned her never to go inside—the smell would never come out of her school clothes, not to mention the danger that might lurk behind the bins of unsavory wiggly things. And she remembered the boys in the back, too. The cool boys. Smoking and sometimes worse things.

She had heeded her mother's advice about the shack and instead sought the safe and quiet sanctuary of the bookstore next door. Rose glanced over, pleased to see it hadn't changed much at all. A new paint job, maybe, but the gold painted letters on the glass door were the same—Sea Harbor Bookstore— with its creaky hardwood floor and the nice couple who didn't mind Rose curling up in a chair for hours, a stack of books at her side and her shirt smudged from the chocolate-covered peanuts she'd pulled from her backpack.

She had loved that store. And the owner's son, too. Her first silly crush. Danny, the tall, lanky popular kid, lots older and wiser than Rose. One day when he was helping his dad he'd noticed her huddled over a book, and he'd glanced down and read the title out loud. She still remembered it—*Dandelion Wine*. "Hmm," he'd said. And then he said that he liked Ray Bradbury, too. When he walked on, Rose wondered if he had heard the pounding of her heart or knew that his words alone had elevated Ray Bradbury to the status of genius.

Beside her, Bree McIntosh was saying something as cars rushed by, horns honked, and late afternoon shoppers moved in and out of shops. But for a brief moment Rose's memory blocked out all the sounds.

Finally she shook it off and turned back to Bree, but the blonde woman had turned away and was moving off down the street.

A man, leaning against a fence just a short distance from the yarn shop, seemed to be watching her. She probably got that a lot, Rose thought.

She watched as the slender, gangly-looking man pushed off

the fence as Bree drew close. He stood tall, his thick hair pulled back in a ponytail. Everything about the man looked rough and messy to Rose. Even the bright orange bicycle next to him. He lifted up his sunglasses and continued to watch the woman coming toward him, and for a brief moment, Rose wondered if Bree would be all right. Then she scolded herself. She was in Sea Harbor. Of course she'd be all right.

She shook away the thought and turned back to the yarn shop, surveying it more carefully. Fresh paint, a bright blue awning, windows that sparkled. Everything about it was welcoming, including the sign above the door. THE SEASIDE KNITTING STUDIO.

At that moment, the shop door opened and several women walked out, laughing and carrying canvas bags with identical yarn logos printed on the side. One of the women glanced over at Rose and smiled. About Rose's height but slightly broader in girth, the woman wore a bright yellow blouse, tied neatly at the neck with a small bow. She paused, then cocked her head and opened her mouth as if to say something.

Rose shifted uncomfortably beneath the woman's look.

But then the woman closed her mouth and shook her head slightly, as if apologizing for her stare. She turned away, stepping off the curb and following her friends across the street, horns honking to hurry them along. Rose watched their reflections in the yarn shop window as they gathered on the opposite sidewalk, mouthing good-byes before scattering in different directions.

The woman in the yellow blouse pulled open a heavy glass door between McGlucken's Hardware Store and an ice cream shop and walked inside. It was a door Rose knew well. It led to creaky wooden steps, a musty hallway above, and small offices huddled above the shops.

Rose remembered climbing those steps every week, heading up to her orthodontist's office, where her mouth had been filled with wires. Unconsciously she put a finger to her lips. The teeth were straight now, but the procedure never quite pulled her front teeth together. It didn't matter, her mother said. Gladys Woodley could name—and frequently did—every movie star with the tiniest space between her teeth. It was distinctive, her mother told her. And Rose was distinctive and lovely, too.

A scratching on the window pulled her attention back to the calico cat, its mouth shaped into a meow. Waving at her, its small paws moving back and forth on the glass.

Rose leaned down and pressed her fingers to the window, mirroring the cat's paws.

Come in, the cat seemed to be saying.

Rose smiled at the cat. *Okay*, she said, and headed to the door.

Chapter 3

Mae Anderson stood behind the checkout counter, tallying the yarn shop's daily receipts.

The bell above the door jingled, startling her. The shop manager looked up with a frown, ready to scold whoever it was for coming in at closing time. All their customers knew the shop closed early on Thursday night.

"Thursday night, early clos—" she began.

But her sentence fell off as the interloper, as Mae had already named her, tripped on the welcome mat, grabbed the edge of a round display table, and stumbled to the floor along with a basket of cashmere yarn. In seconds, Purl jumped off the raised display window floor and began rubbing against the woman's leg.

"Good grief, girl. Are you all right?" Mae rushed from behind the counter and across the room, a wad of receipts still in her clenched hand and strands of gray hair flying loose from her bun.

But Rose was already getting up and scooping up the scattered skeins of yarn. "I'm so sorry," she said, her cheekbones flushed with embarrassment. "Such a klutz. And such beautiful yarn. I hope it's not—"

"Oh, poo. Don't mind any of that," Mae scolded, peering over her glasses to be sure the woman had no obvious wounds. "What are you doing falling like that? Trying to make an entrance, are you?"

Mae chortled at her own words, and Rose relaxed slightly.

She looked at the receipts in Mae's hand. "You're closing, aren't you? I didn't read the sign. I'll come ba—"

But before Mae could assure her that new customers were never turned away, a commotion near the back of the shop interrupted. A husky voice, too loud for the size of the shop, filled the space.

"Mae, help. I need you." In seconds a long and lean Izzy Perry caught up with her voice. Her cheeks were flushed and strands of damp multicolored hair hung loose to her shoulders.

Mae put her skinny hands on nonexistent hips and stared at the shop owner, the woman beside her momentarily forgotten. "Good grief, Izzy, slow down now. And why is your hair wet?"

"It's a flood, Mae. There's a leak in the ceiling over the library table. It's coming from the apartment."

"Why don't we fix it, then?" Mae suggested calmly, the lift of her thin brows expressing some doubt as to her much younger boss's competence at that moment. She walked over to the computer and began tapping on the keyboard with long bony fingers, searching for the plumber's phone number.

"I could look at it if you want. At least while you're waiting for the plumber?"

Izzy looked over at the stranger standing a few feet away. A nondescript woman cradling Purl in her arms.

Mae's fingers stopped moving. "Are you a plumber?"

Before the woman could answer, Izzy spoke up. "Do you know about broken pipes that leak through the ceiling?" Professional credentials mattered little when a steady stream of water was puddling on the massive old library table, which was far too heavy to move quickly and way too close to baskets of yarn.

"Yes," the woman said, looking up and attempting a smile. She rubbed Purl's soft belly. "I can try anyway."

"Well, all right then," Mae said, peering at the stranger over the top of her rimless glasses.

"Great. Follow me," Izzy said, spinning around and heading toward an archway and a short stairway.

Rose followed the long-legged woman, her eyes on the shop owner's loose blue sweater, traces of a summer tan still visible on her long neck, and thick wavy hair loose on her back. She noticed damp splotches creating a crazy pattern on her white skinny jeans, a cell phone protruding from the back pocket. The woman had no shoes on, but thick green socks with orange polka dots also showed signs of the ceiling leak. Somehow, even with the water damage, the woman looked put together. *Geesh*, Rose thought, *has Sea Harbor turned into some kind of Stepford Wives place with only beautiful people allowed in?*

Izzy led the stranger through the archway and down three steps to a cozy knitting room, and around a long table holding several bowls half-filled with brown water. The ping of additional drops was the only other sound in the room.

Rose noticed several other women on the other side of the room but Izzy ignored them, bringing her attention instead to the widening stain on the ceiling before ushering her out the alley door and up an outdoor staircase to the apartment above.

Once the alley door banged shut, Cass Halloran walked over to a high window near the back door. "Who the heck is that?" She put her elbows on the sill and peered out at a step and the bottom half of two legs. The jeans were slightly frayed at the bottom, the tennis shoes worn.

Birdie Favazza spoke up from an old leather chair near the

fireplace, her small silvery head lifting. "Patience, Catherine. I suspect we'll know soon enough."

No one ever called Catherine Mary Theresa Halloran anything but Cass, no one except Birdie Favazza, who reserved it for gentle chides or admonishing Cass about such things as refusing to rip out a lumpy row on a hat or coming to knitting night smelling a bit too much like lobster.

"She must be a fix-it person," Birdie said, wagging a knitting needle as she talked. "She looks strong, solidly built, and has good arms and hands. Rosie the Riveter, perhaps, come to save us." Birdie's sweet voice trailed across the room.

Cass laughed, amazed at Birdie's eyesight. She had seen a brown-haired blur in jeans. "But you're wrong, Birdie. She didn't have the right hairdo for Rosie. My ma had a poster of that gal in our kitchen for years. I kind of related to her."

Birdie chuckled, her bent fingers deftly casting on a sleeve for the alpaca sweater she was knitting for Nell. She was trying hard to imagine the lobster fisherwoman's thick black hair cut short into bouncy black curls. "The real mystery here is how Izzy found her in the three minutes she was out of this room. A pipe leaks and a ponytailed Rosie the Riveter shows up? Our Izzy has karma."

"Either karma or she's a witch," Cass said. She turned away from the window and walked over to the library table, following the enticing odors of their dinner.

Nell Endicott had been quietly standing on the sidelines, wiping away small puddles of water that had collected on the thick wood and stirring her casserole periodically. She looked up. "I wonder if she's a real plumber or someone like Ben, who *thinks* he's a plumber, until the leak gets worse and he calls a *real* plumber."

Mae appeared in the archway, as if summoned by Nell's wonderings. "Sure she's a plumber. Although I think Iz would have taken a Ben Endicott if one had appeared. But the gal said she's a plumber." She stared at the damp ceiling above Nell's head, her thin face pinched in a frown. "Well, maybe she didn't say that. She said yes to something. I don't know the girl, but Purl likes her and that's worth something."

"Izzy is trying to protect this shipload of yarn that just arrived. I saw her nearly faint when two drops landed on the cardboard box." Nell nodded toward the FedEx boxes, now safely moved to the floor.

"Someone better protect that yarn," Mae said, all but wagging a finger at Izzy's aunt. "I just paid the invoice. Costs a fortune. What're you girls doing, knitting gold like that little Rumpelstiltskin guy?"

"It will be transformed into beautiful art, and art is priceless, my dear Mae," Birdie said, a myriad of tiny wrinkles spreading out from her gray eyes.

"So who is she, Mae?" Nell lifted the lid off the casserole, stirring the seafood concoction once more before replacing the cover.

"I don't rightly know. She's young, younger than you, Cass. And Izzy, too. And I had the feeling she knew what she was talking about, no matter who she is. She had that air, you know?"

They didn't know.

"Well, sure you do. But anyhoo," Mae went on, "now that missy no-name is about to save us from a flood, I'm going to close up shop and skedaddle home to meat loaf and *Grey's Anatomy*. You gals behave yourselves." Mae wiggled her fingers at them and disappeared into the main shop area. In minutes the lights dimmed and the creak of the heavy front door signaled her official good-bye.

Cass carried a bottle of chilled wine over to the coffee table. It would take more than a leaky ceiling to halt their Thursday night ritual: Birdie's wine, Nell's dinner, knitting socks and sweaters and hats and sharing lives and gossip while the moon moved slowly over the ocean—it was sacred, a life-affirming time.

A ritual from which great friendships had been born.

Nell walked over and set a tray of olives and figs and a pot of tangy bar cheese on the low coffee table. "This should keep your stomach from groaning until Izzy comes back."

Cass fiddled with Izzy's iPad to find some music, finally settling on an old Beatles station, but her eyes were on the Crock-Pot.

Nell caught the look on Cass's face.

"It's fine, Cass. It won't be overcooked. And not a drop of the ceiling water got in. Trust me."

Cass walked over and lifted the lid, just to be sure, inhaling the intoxicating aromas of wine and lemon and freshly chopped dill.

"Cod," Nell said, and smiled at Cass, knowing she probably had already identified the other ingredients.

Suddenly the Beatles' guitars were overshadowed by a banging from above. They stared at an old hanging lamp now swinging back and forth above the table. Heavy footsteps and the sounds of metal against metal rattled the tin plates on the ceiling.

"Goodness," Birdie said, "let's hope the good guys win."

And then it stopped, just as the voice of Ringo Starr rang out from the speakers: *"I'd like to be, under the sea . . ."*

They broke out in laughter as Cass snapped her fingers in the air, moved her body across the room, and began singing along.

Once they assumed the plumbing work was coming to an end, Nell began pulling out plates and napkins from the bookcase, relieved they could soon concentrate on things more important than leaky pipes: food, wine, and finishing knitting projects.

Cass joined her, lining up utensils on the library table and inching closer to the casserole. It was only the creaking of the alley door and rush of outside air that kept her from lifting the lid and taking a spoonful.

"Yay for Rose," Izzy said, stepping inside with her arms stretched wide. She moved aside and ushered the ponytailed woman in. "This is Rose. She's a magician. We owe her profound thanks."

Rose? The three women all looked at the woman directly behind Izzy. Was her name really *Rose?* Maybe Izzy *did* have karma.

The woman behind Izzy was leaning over to pry off wet tennis shoes. She struggled to look up at the same time, acknowledging Izzy's rattled-off introductions. A brown limp ponytail fell over one shoulder.

"I hope you didn't finish all the wine," Izzy said, "because we need it for a toast." Then she stopped and glared at Cass, who was hovering over the fish soup.

"Don't get yourself in a state, Izzy. The food is safe. But I'm about to faint, so let's get on with this toast." She offered a half smile at the stranger. "No offense. You definitely deserve a toast."

"And a meal," Izzy said. "I told her it was the least we could do."

Rose looked unsure but followed Izzy across the room.

Nell gave the sauce a quick stir, covered it again, and picked up the second bottle of wine that Birdie had brought. Cass followed with glasses and they gathered near the fireplace, shoving knitting baskets beneath the coffee table and eyeing Rose discreetly—her pleasant, oval-shaped face, the practical ponytail. Her jeans were clean but faded, and she seemed comfortable in her body, neither fat nor thin.

"Sit," Birdie urged, then filled the wineglasses and passed them around. She lifted hers and smiled at the others, her eyes lingering the longest on their guest. "Here's to fixed pipes, dripless ceilings, and to the person who has saved the evening for us—to Rose."

Glasses clicked and Rose's cheeks flushed. "It wasn't anything, honestly. I didn't even finish the job, like I told Izzy—"

"It wasn't anything?" Izzy interrupted, her brows lifting up into scattered bangs. "It was *everything*, Rose."

Birdie patted Rose's slightly damp knee. "Although our Izzy can be a little dramatic, you did appear at just the right moment. Our own deus ex machina."

"There's something to be said for keeping the ceiling from falling on Nell's dinner," Cass added. "That's definitely worth a toast."

That drew a smile from a slightly more relaxed Rose. She looked around at the baskets of yarn, the paintings on the wall, and the shelves lined with books about knitting and fleece, sheep and alpacas. "Izzy said that you have a weekly knitting group here."

"Oh no, dear. It's far more than that," said Birdie, short silvery waves moving with her words. "Some knitting, some gossip, some catching up on one another's lives. We've been known to solve all the world's problems, right here in this very room. We are quite good at it." Birdie took a sip of wine and sat back.

Rose smiled, warming to the small woman who was nearly lost in the wide leather chair.

But what the octogenarian lacked in stature, she made up for in charisma and wisdom and her presence. Sea Harbor's grande dame. And the others in the room could see that Rose was feeling her spell.

"Do you knit?" Nell asked.

"Oh, no," Rose said quickly. She spread her hands apart, palms up, and looked at them. "See? Big fingers. I'd mess up such delicate art."

"That's poppycock," Birdie said. "Everyone can knit."

"I'm proof of that," Cass said. "I came in here one night because I smelled the food. Then I kept coming, pretending I knew what needles were. But now? Now I am practically a master at winter hats for my lobster crews. Dozens. Hundreds. Thousands. My men don't go bareheaded. Not ever."

Izzy laughed. "That's mostly true. If Cass can learn to knit, anyone can."

"And speaking of me—" Cass looked over at the casserole on the table, "I'm going to collapse if we don't eat in the next two and a half minutes."

Laughter followed and in minutes the coffee table was filled with silverware, warm rolls and butter, and deep bowls of fish chowder.

After allowing Rose a few spoonfuls of soup, Birdie asked, "Have we met before, Rose? There's something about you that's familiar to me."

Rose paused, her spoonful of chowder held in midair. She looked closely at Birdie. "I don't think so. I would remember you, Birdie. I know I would."

"So where are you from?" Cass asked.

"Nebraska." She took a drink of wine and concentrated on Purl, now purring comfortably in her lap.

"You're on vacation?" Cass prodded. "A leaf peeper?"

"Sort of."

And then Rose mumbled something about bringing her mother to see the ocean, and how her mother had died before they could make the trip. The words hung out there awkwardly.

"Sometimes life is like that. Things happen," Izzy said softly.

"Yes, they certainly do," Birdie said, looking at Rose. "But you've brought your mother back to the sea in your heart and that's a loving thing to do."

Rose was silent and for a few minutes, the only sound in the room was that of soup being slurped. Finally Nell asked, "Where are you staying, Rose? Do you need suggestions?"

"A boarding house on Bell Street. It's very reasonable."

Nell's eyes widened. Mrs. Bridge's Victorian Bell Street house was on the verge of being condemned. An assortment of bugs, broken locks, and suspicious odors were a few of the most recent citations recorded in the *Sea Harbor Gazette*. "Oh, Rose, that might not be wise."

"She should be paying you to stay there," Cass said. "It's a dump. I hope you've been vaccinated."

"She *was* staying there," Izzy said. She looked sternly at Rose not to object. "That's the other reason for our toast. The apartment's been lonely. It's probably why the pipe burst. Rose is my new tenant."

Nell and Birdie exchanged looks.

The apartment above the yarn shop was cozy and clean and warm. And presently empty, except for Purl, who had found a secret way of getting to it through the yarn shop rafters. But the three women were acutely aware that Izzy had a dismal track record picking appropriate tenants. Especially when the decision was the spur-of-the-moment kind.

Nell brushed a strand of salt-and-pepper hair behind her ear and then looked over at her niece, her expression questioning.

Izzy ignored her aunt's look. "Like Rose said, the leak is fixed but the job isn't finished. It'll be easier for her to do the work if she's right there."

Birdie broke the awkward silence. "Well, that's a nice solution, then. A collaboration of sorts. And you'll be comfortable there, Rose. Purl will love the company."

Izzy looked over at Cass, silently warning her not to pursue the tenant decision.

Cass complied and changed the subject completely, asking, "How did you learn how to fix pipes?"

They could read Cass's thoughts. It was an easier question than asking Izzy if she had lost her mind, inviting a perfect stranger to stay in the empty apartment simply because she was handy with a wrench.

People killed people with wrenches.

"My dad was a fix-it guy. He taught me," Rose said. "So those are my credentials. Or lack of them. If you need someone with real ones, I totally get that."

"Absolutely not," Izzy said. "You're fixing it. That's all I care about. We don't need college degrees."

"Well, I have that, too, if it helps."

"Oh?" Birdie said.

"Children's literature."

Izzy was impressed. "The older my amazing Abby gets, the more appreciative I am of children's books. Do you have a favorite author?"

"Only about two hundred. But I've been in love with A. A. Milne's *Winnie-the-Pooh* books since I was two."

"Ah," Birdie said, her voice singsong. "'*You are braver than you believe, stronger than you seem, smarter than you think, and loved more than you know.*'" She smiled and sat back in the chair. "I don't think Milne actually wrote it, but Christopher Robin said it somewhere—in a film perhaps? I'm fond of it. And many other wise words from Pooh and Christopher Robin."

Rose looked startled, as if someone had crawled inside her head. "Yes," she said, her eyes meeting Birdie's. "Children's literature taught me a lot about myself."

"Do you want to be a librarian?"

Rose hesitated, then said, "No. Although my mother thought I should be that, or maybe a teacher."

"Tell me about it," Izzy said. "My dad has never gotten over all those years of helping his only daughter through law school, only to have her land in a yarn shop in a tiny little town."

"But I can see you love this shop," Rose said, glancing around the room. "I fixed up a lot of student housing places I lived in and I loved doing that." She looked embarrassed for a minute, as if she'd been too personal.

Then she looked at Cass. "But about the apartment, I know you don't know me from Adam, and suddenly I'm invited to stay above a shop you love because I fixed a pipe. I'm a stranger."

Izzy started to stop Rose, but she went on. "I wouldn't have accepted Izzy's offer, except"—she nibbled on her bottom lip—"well, except that I'd like to hang around Sea Harbor a little longer, and having a place to stay would make that possible. I'm a good tenant, I'm neat, I don't throw wild parties—not ever." She managed a half smile and looked down at her hands, as if she'd said her piece and now it was up to the jury to decide.

Rose looked like she had used up every bit of vim and vigor she possessed.

Birdie eased the awkward moment. "I'm sure you'll be a good tenant, Rose."

"See? I told you," Izzy said to Rose. "Birdie's wise. I'm happy to have someone staying up there. It's been empty too long."

"It's beautiful. This whole place is. It feels safe."

Nell watched the array of expressions flitting across Rose's face. She prided herself on reading people, honing her skills on Boston's wealthy donors when she was a nonprofit director for all those years. But Rose eluded her. She was vague when talking about herself. And the gaps seemed unusually ominous. There was more to Rose's visit to Sea Harbor than a sweet girl visiting the sea to honor her mother.

As if anticipating more questions, Rose put her napkin on the table, a half-finished bowl of soup in front of her, and stood up quickly. She glanced at her watch and quickly explained that she had to leave.

Izzy dropped her spoon. "You don't have to go yet. Finish your soup at least."

But Rose was already stepping away from the table. She

thanked Izzy and then the others, murmuring something about being tired, of needing to get back to the boarding house.

"But you'll move in tomorrow," Izzy said. "And we've no house rules, except to pet Purl hourly and make sure the pipes don't burst."

Rose gave Izzy a thumbs-up and disappeared out the back alley door and into the night.

They watched her go—and wondered if they would ever see her again. And if they did, was that a good thing . . . or not?

Chapter 4

Izzy had declared the subject of Rose Chopra off-limits while they were clearing the dishes, and soon the four women had settled into their Thursday night routine, opening knitting bags and pulling out yarn and needles and partially finished projects. The coffee table was soon littered with soft skeins of alpaca, stray bits of yarn, and one of Izzy's half-completed neon green socks that she was knitting for her husband. "It'll go perfectly with Sam's orange high-tops. Perfect, right?" And her husband would love it because Izzy made it—his fashion sense totally dictated by Izzy's remarkable sense of color and finding beauty in odd matches.

But later, after they'd locked the doors and were standing on the front steps of the shop, a full moon creating puddles of light at their feet, Cass decided she was no longer muzzled.

"So. Do we even know her last name?" she asked, including Nell and Birdie in the question but her deep, dark eyes settling on Izzy.

Izzy finished locking the shop door and pulled a piece of paper from her jeans pocket.

"Chopra. Rose Chopra." She handed it to Cass, then dropped the key ring into her bag.

"Chopra. Chopra. I don't know any Chopras," Birdie said.

"I'm curious why she came to Cape Ann. She could have found an ocean view that was easier to get to. We're not exactly on the beaten path." Cass held the card under a streetlight, repeating the name scribbled on the paper scrap.

Izzy snatched the card back. "Rose Chopra. That's who she is. You're too suspicious, Cass. Danny's mysteries are rubbing off on you."

Izzy looked at the silent faces around her and shook her head. "Okay, here's what I think. It's better to judge a prospective renter face-to-face. It's like looking at jury members. I could read things on their faces that I'd never discover on a piece of paper. Besides, Purl likes her. And she probably won't be staying long, anyway. Enough said."

No one asked *How long?* They knew Izzy was finished answering questions.

"It was nice meeting Rose, and I made great progress on my sweater sleeves," Birdie said, clearly ready to bring the evening to a close. "But this body is tired." She slipped one arm through Nell's, wiggled her fingers at Izzy and Cass, and began walking toward Nell's car, her thoughts already moving on to a long, lavender-scented bath and a soft bed.

Izzy watched the two older women walk away, thoughts of Rose Chopra and bursting pipes fading as a flood of affection washed through her—an unexpected reminder of goodness in her life. Birdie and Aunt Nell walked slowly beneath the lamplight near the Brandleys' bookstore, two shadowy figures weaving together, then apart, as if in some age-old dance. The twenty-year age difference between them wasn't visible—nor significant.

Nell slowed, then leaned in, her head lowered to catch

Birdie's words, a softness between them. Birdie's small chin tipped up into some quiet secret they shared. Then Nell straightened and began walking again, her long steps slow to accommodate Birdie's, their bodies again moving in the rhythm that mirrored a friendship they sometimes claimed began in another life.

"Gifts," Izzy murmured, her brown eyes filling. She blinked the moisture away, then felt Cass beside her, following her look.

Cass nodded. "I know," she said.

The blare of a horn from a passing car broke into the moment and Izzy and Cass turned their attention back to why they were standing together on the curb. Waiting.

Cass pulled out her phone and checked the time. "The Sox game should be over by now. Where do you suppose our knights in shining armor are?"

Thursday night Sox games at the Gull Tavern were nearly as regular for Danny and Sam as their wives' knitting night.

Izzy looked down the street. Coming toward them on the opposite side of the street, in no obvious hurry, were the men in question, heads buried in conversation.

"I see four bodies over there," Izzy said. "Only two are ours. Who are the other guys?" She squinted through the darkness.

Cass looked across the street just as the men walked beneath the lights in front of Scoopers Ice Cream shop. Danny and Sam were both six feet plus, but the dark-haired man with them was an inch or so taller. The fourth man was average size—short compared to the others—with a mop of black hair covering his eyes and round glasses filling a good part of his face. "The short one looks like Harry Potter. The tall guy is Spencer Paxton. Geesh, he seems to be everywhere these days."

"Oh," Izzy said. But the *oh* wasn't a happy one.

"I agree. He always seemed too big for this town, even when he was a kid. I'm surprised he moved back."

Izzy looked over again. She hadn't grown up in Sea Harbor like Cass, but she agreed that Spencer Paxton sometimes seemed too big for things. What was it Birdie always said, *Too big for his britches*? "He was in my Boston law firm for a while. Charmed plenty of our staff."

"Not a surprise."

"He might have made a decent lawyer—he was smart enough, anyway. But he figured he could make more money in the family development business. Or politics or whatever. Power seemed to be important to him, even as a newbie, just out of law school."

The truth was, Izzy hadn't liked him at all. Maybe it was the stark ambition that had turned her off back then. She remembered feeling guilty, that maybe she was jealous of the younger law school grad who came in and seemed to take over the Elliot & Pagett firm. He knew everyone, or pretended to, anyway. She wondered if he had sensed her feelings back then. Probably not. She had an irritating tendency to go overboard with niceness in covering up ill feelings. He probably thought she had a crush on him.

When she ran into him now in Sea Harbor, he acted like they were old friends. And she liked his wife, Bree. So that was one thing in his favor.

Cass was watching the men across the street, their bodies shaking in laughter. "Do you think they're going to stay over there telling bad jokes, or take us to the Artist's Palate deck for a beer like they promised?"

"I wonder if Spence is coming," Izzy said. "He might not be all that welcome over on Canary Cove."

Cass agreed. "If Paxton Development thinks they can improve Canary Cove, they're daft." She dismissed the thought as ludicrous.

Izzy shrugged off the concern. She watched Danny and Sam, laughing and talking. And Spencer Paxton, his tall body leaning in, listening. Just two nice guys being friendly.

Cass put two fingers in her mouth and let out a whistle that sliced through the air like a well-thrown javelin.

Heads jerked around their way.

"So who won the game?" Izzy called out.

Sam broke out in a bad rendition of "Sweet Caroline" and a victory sign. He led the trio across the street and stepped onto the curb, wrapping his wife in a hug.

Danny stepped up beside Cass. "Not only did the Sox win, but we are rolling in the dough." He pushed his glasses up with one finger and forked back a handful of hair, pulling some bills out of his jeans pocket and flapping them in the air. "You and I are riding high, m'love."

He nodded toward Spencer Paxton, standing slightly behind him. "Hey, Spence, you know these two gorgeous women, right?"

"Absolutely," Spencer said with a courtly bow.

"Who's the guy you left behind?" Cass asked, pointing across the street to the younger, shorter man. He was trundling off toward Gus McGlucken's hardware store. As he passed beneath the streetlight, his round glasses lit up as if touched by a wizard's magic.

Danny followed her look. "You know him, Cass. Robbie McGlucken, Gus's son."

"Of course I do. I just didn't expect him to be with you guys." Robbie was a kid, twentysomething, not to mention that anyone she used to babysit for would always be a kid to her.

"Robbie works for me," Spence explained. "He and I were having a beer and ran into these two guys."

"Robbie knew every Sox stat," Sam said. "Put us all to shame."

Spence laughed. "Fantasy sports. All that sort of thing. He's a computer genius. Amazing kid. He's great."

This time it was Izzy who looked surprised. Robbie lived in an apartment above his dad's hardware store and she saw him nearly every day, sometimes in his dad's store, mostly just coming and going on his motorcycle. But Robbie didn't talk much, and he always seemed happier if Izzy pretended she didn't see him. He was a loner, and the image of him bonding with guys over a baseball game was incongruous. But sort of nice, she thought. He probably could use the company.

Cass was watching Robbie, too. He was fumbling with a key, then shoved open the glass-fronted door that led to the offices and apartments above the shops. "Well, that's good," she said. "I'm sure his dad is happy he has a job. Robbie needs a break or two. Now what's all this about a pot of money in our possession?" She looked at Danny, her thick dark brows lifting.

Danny held up the fistful of bills again and Cass plucked them from his hand and glared at Spence. "So what's this? Are you bringing sin to River City? Have you lured these once respectable men into gambling?"

Spence laughed. His dark hair, about the same length as Danny's mussed-up mop, didn't seem to move, the swept-up wave held in place. "It was I, I confess. But they did well."

"Since we took all his money, we invited him for a beer," Sam said.

Izzy smiled brightly and tossed her car keys to Sam. "That's fine. Let's go then."

The drive to the Canary Cove Art Colony, a narrow spit of land that housed dozens of galleries and cottages and several restaurants, was a short one and soon they were walking up the deck steps to the Artist's Palate bistro, a haven not only for the dozens of artists who called Canary Cove home and averaged at least one meal a day at the place, but anyone who loved good burgers and beer. Hundreds of tiny white lights outlined the deck, waiters maneuvered their way around picnic tables, and people jostled for seats. Tom Petty's mellow voice filled the air from well-placed speakers. It'd been over a year since the music artist's death, but the restaurant's owner still began and ended every evening on her deck with one of his songs, and then tossed some in between.

When Danny Brandley teased her about it one night, wondering when she'd be adding vigil lights, the owner did the next best thing, adding battery-powered lights above the bar that flashed whenever a Tom Petty song was played.

Tonight Merry Jackson stood beside the outdoor bar, standing on tiptoe and directing traffic. The owner spotted the newcomers and greeted them with a flying wave, then elbowed a tall, skinny man standing next to her, sending him to take her friends to an empty table near the back of the deck.

The waiter grinned and waved the group across the deck to the table, meeting them with a pitcher of beer and basket of fried clams.

Danny laughed when he recognized who it was. "Hey, man, what are you doing here? Merry has you working now? Are you paying for your breakfasts or did you do something bad?"

Josh Babson laughed and put the tray down on the picnic table, a rivulet of beer sliding down the side of the pitcher. He wiped his damp hands on his apron and gave Izzy and Cass high fives, then reached across the table and greeted Sam. "Nah, well, maybe. The little boss lady was busy tonight, so I grabbed an apron from someone—probably that crazy cook she has back there—and pitched in. She'll owe me big." He counted the beer steins, then the group sitting down, and then forked his fingers through a messy flop of long blond hair and hooked it behind one ear.

Izzy shook her head and handed him a scrunchie. "Here. You're going to scare people away."

Josh laughed and wound it around a fistful of hair. "It's good to see you guys. I've been seeing Izzy here now and then with this fiber art show coming up. Love your shop, Iz. Love this whole idea. The artists around here are all psyched. Yarn art. Who'd have thought?"

"So when are we going to teach you to knit?" Izzy asked, her brows lifting. "Then you'll get the whole experience."

"Hah, that'll be the day. But I'm loving all that soft squishy yarn, and some of the designs I've seen are great. It's really sensual, you know? Bree McIntosh's work is amazing. And have you seen her paintings? It's going to be quite a show. You fiber artists rock."

"Of course we do. And we knitters do, too. And your help is much appreciated. I have it on the Brewsters' authority that you are at our beck and call."

Josh laughed. "Yeah Count on it. It pays to have the art colony founders on your side, right?"

Izzy knew Josh meant more than that the Brewsters were good bosses. Jane and Ham not only founded the art colony, they practically saved Josh Babson, drawing him into the art community when he was unjustly fired from a teaching job at a private school a few years back.

Sam looked over toward the railing, almost forgetting the extra man in the group.

Spence was standing with his back to them, looking down the incline to the water, ten feet below.

"Hey, Spence, you still with us?"

Spencer turned back to the table. He spotted the newcomer and nodded a hello.

"Bad manners," Sam said. "Spence, have you met Josh Babson? Beneath that dirty apron and all that hair is a pretty talented artist."

"*Very* talented," Izzy said, looking up into Josh's face.

"He's a good guy, too, even though he sometimes looks like he needs a good meal," Danny said.

"I usually do need a good meal," Josh said. "Hey, sorry, I didn't get your name. Sam mumbles." He held out his hand.

"Spencer. Spencer Paxton."

Josh dropped his hand.

"Bree's husband," Izzy prompted, seeing confusion on Josh's face. She poked him playfully. "Say hello, Josh."

Instead, Josh took a step back and shook his head as if he'd been thinking of something else and was trying to clear his mind. He looked away from Spence and then at the others around the table. "Hey, are you guys okay here for the moment? There's a pitcher—" Then he took a quick breath and looked across the room, pointing toward Merry. "Looks like my boss is calling me. Gotta go. Later." The artist turned abruptly and walked away.

Izzy watched him disappear. *How odd.* She wondered if things were okay with the art exhibit. They'd been asking a lot of Josh. She excused herself, then quickly followed him across the crowded deck.

"Hey, Josh, what's up?"

He turned around and looked at her, his face unreadable.

"You seem upset, Josh. I wanted to be sure we hadn't done anything that caused it." She forced a smile. "We were heading to give you a great tip. Hope you'll be back."

Josh didn't smile. He looked down at his paint-spattered sneakers for a minute as if exploring his options. Then he looked at Izzy again. "Just so you know, Iz, that Paxton dude at your table isn't a good guy. I like all you guys a lot. And I don't want you taken in by him. He's bad. A bad, bad guy."

Before Izzy could hide her surprise or ask him what he was talking about, he turned and hurried over to the restaurant owner. Izzy watched him lean down to whisper in her ear. Then he ripped off the apron, handed it to her, and went down the deck steps two at a time.

Chapter 5

The weather had turned dreary and damp, as sometimes happens in Sea Harbor as one season tries to decide whether to stick around or to let the other one in.

Birdie and Nell walked quickly up the entrance steps to the Sea Harbor Yacht Club, jackets zippered against the wind. A quiet and strangely subdued Rose Chopra walked between them.

Rose's demeanor gave Nell the fleeting sensation that they were leading a reluctant student to the principal's office for some kind of punishment, rather than to a lovely lunch at the yacht club's restaurant. The dining room had a spectacular view of the sea, one that they were sure Rose's mother would have appreciated. Which made them think it was the perfect place to take Rose and officially welcome her to Sea Harbor.

Rose didn't seem to think so. She had resisted the invitation with a vehemence that surprised them. "It's not necessary" was repeated multiple times, followed by several other excuses. But for two women who didn't operate on what was necessary but rather on what was kind or good or enjoyable or simply a nice thing to do, Rose's protestations didn't make sense, nor did they listen to them.

"When someone moves into a new place, one brings freshly baked bread to welcome them," Birdie explained. "Nell and I don't bake bread. We do lunch instead."

"But you've spent the past two hours helping me move into this amazing apartment," she had said, a final excuse.

And that they had done, keeping their promise to Izzy to make Rose's move easy and pleasant—fresh cotton sheets on the bed, a refrigerator stocked with essentials, and a vase of sweet alyssum and honeysuckle warming the room with its scent.

When they had finished, Rose had stood at the apartment door surveying the slipcovered sofa, the fireplace with a painting of the sea above it, and a bookshelf stocked with books. Her face flushed with happiness. "It's absolutely beautiful. The flowers, the smells of the sea—everything."

Her emptied, battered suitcase and a backpack leaned against the wall next to a chair.

"I travel light," Rose had said, catching their looks. "I don't have much more than this back home. A clean slate."

"Are there things you need, dear?" Birdie had asked.

"No. My sister took a few of my mother's things and the rest we gave away. I'm looking forward to starting fresh."

"I can relate to that," Nell said. "Ben and I did much the same thing when we moved up here to retire. We brought little and took our time, gradually filling his parents' long-time vacation home with art we loved, colors that warmed us, furniture that fit our bodies just right. A new chapter."

Birdie had nodded absently, a slight smile on her face, and Nell knew why: Her dear friend's philosophy was the opposite of her own. The Favazza seven-bedroom estate on Ravenswood Road had been built by Sonny Favazza for his young bride— and Birdie would be living in it until they had to carry her body out in a box, as she often said. Sonny was the love of her life, and his memory was as alive in the house as her housekeeper Ella's daily soup and sandwiches. The sweet cherry scent of Sonny's pipe tobacco still warmed the den. His telescope and old English desk, his Winslow Homer seascapes and hand-carved ship collection were all in exactly the same spots as they were the day he died. That was exactly how Birdie wanted it. And that is how it would always be.

"So," she said now, smiling up at Rose, "Let's stop the chatter. Your excuses to have lunch are falling on deaf ears, and I shall faint dead away if we don't eat soon. And I don't believe Izzy has the time today to scoop up an old lady from her building's steps."

Liz Santos, manager of the Sea Harbor Yacht Club, greeted Nell and Birdie as she always did, with hugs and a kiss on each cheek, a welcome that was nearly as comforting as the clam chowder she'd soon have delivered to their table.

A few steps behind them, Rose managed to smile through the introductions.

"Chopra," the elegant manager repeated, smiling into Rose's deep green eyes. "I don't believe I know any Chopras. But I'm happy to meet one. Come. I saved a nice table for you. The clouds are gathering out there, but sometimes that's the most majestic view of all." She waved her menus toward the ocean side of the room, a peek of blue-green water and churning waves visible from where they stood.

They followed her across the cozy dining room, weaving between tables and carefully arranged plants. Paintings of the sea and sailboats added color to the walls, but as Liz had promised, the view took center stage.

Halfway across the room, a wild wave brought a smile to Birdie's small face. She stopped walking and waved back at Stella Palazola. The young Realtor was sitting at a corner table, an iPad in one hand and a young couple sitting directly across from her. Stella grinned again, then focused back on the couple, her iPad, and a scattering of papers and photographs in front of them.

The club manager had seen the wave, too. "Stella brings clients in here to talk them into signing with Palazola Realty," Liz explained. "It's a smart move. Our clam chowder gets them every time."

Nell chuckled. "Your sister is born to this job. I see her FOR SALE signs everywhere. You must be proud of her."

"I absolutely am. Who would have ever guessed our Stella would become this real estate guru? She's expanding the firm, adding services, like fixing up old places before she puts them on the market so houses get turned over fast. Who knew she would save crazy Uncle Mario from bankruptcy—or maybe prison? Mom was never sure which would come first. We're all really proud of her, even though Stell was Mom's last chance at having a nun in the family."

Birdie laughed. "I could have told Annabelle a long time ago that her youngest would do something like this, running a business. Stella's a lot like your mom, Liz. Only putting her business sense into houses instead of a restaurant."

"With Ben Endicott's help." Liz looked at Nell. "Stell says he helps her understand all the contract mumbo jumbo and has tackled some of Uncle Mario's messes, of which there are many."

Nell smiled. "He loves it. Stella keeps him on his toes. And in spite of Mario's shenanigans, Ben likes the old guy, too."

Liz stopped at a table near the windows and pulled back three chairs. "Don't leave without stopping by my office," she said to Rose. She would give her the cook's tour of the club, she promised.

Birdie insisted Rose sit facing the view, then smiled a thank-you to the waitress as she set a small platter of tequila shrimp and crisp toast points in the center of the table.

Before any of them had a chance to sing the shrimp's praises, a click of stilettos drew attention away from the food.

"Thank heavens you're here." Beatrice Scaglia looked from Birdie to Nell, her greeting landing on the table with a thud.

Nell and Birdie looked up and smiled, ignoring the confusing tone in the mayor's voice. Beatrice was dressed in her uniform—an impeccably tailored suit—today a bright pink outfit with an orange scarf looped twice around her neck. Colorful and memorable, trademarks of the Sea Harbor mayor whom few had ever seen in jeans or with windblown hair.

She air-kissed Birdie and Nell, then stopped short when she saw Rose.

"Who are you, young lady? Why don't I know you?" Her words were punctuated and distinct, sounding like a fifth-grade teacher being tricked by a student. She looked more closely. "Or do I?"

Rose shifted beneath the scrutiny. One hand fiddled with a napkin near her water glass.

The mayor tilted her head, examining every inch of Rose and trying to place her among her constituents. No matter what else people said about Beatrice Scaglia, she cared about her flock, as she called Sea Harbor residents. And she especially cared about their votes. On the chance that Rose might be one of them, she continued to hold her with a steady gaze.

Nell finally broke Beatrice's inspection with introductions. "Rose is new to Sea Harbor."

Beatrice shook Rose's hand, holding on and once again scanning Rose's face for something, although none of them were sure what. "You're the young woman living above Izzy Perry's shop," she said finally.

"The Harbor Road gossip mill is in fine working order," Birdie said with a smile at Rose.

"Yes." Beatrice's frown deepening. "It can be an evil thing, a gossip mill."

"Evil?" Nell asked.

Beatrice seemed not to hear. Her gaze was still on Rose, now on her brown, nondescript hair, her painfully tight ponytail.

"Beatrice?" Birdie said gently, hoping to avert Beatrice's habit of offering unsolicited fashion advice.

But the mayor seemed to have other things on her mind and she turned her small body away from Rose, shifting her attention to Nell and Birdie. Her expression was grave.

"There is a meeting scheduled early next week at city hall. I hope you will come." She looked at them, glanced at Rose as if she wished she'd go away, then turned her back to her and said to Birdie and Nell, "No. I *need* you to come. Both of you. And Ben, too. The Perrys. I need all of you to be there." She looked at them both, her forehead distressingly tight. "I need this desperately."

Then, without a good-bye or explanation, Beatrice turned, straight and stiff as a pencil, and headed toward another table, this one occupied by several businessmen whose conversation was about to be interrupted by whatever Mayor Scaglia wanted them to hear. And whatever it was, it was very important to her.

"She's interesting," Rose said.

Birdie and Nell both laughed.

"She has a good heart," Nell said. "She grows on you."

"And she's passionate about being mayor of Sea Harbor," Birdie said, passing around the platter of shrimp. "It's her whole life, and for the most part, she's been a good one. She sincerely cares about this town and the people in it. And she won't forget meeting you or your name—"

"—especially around election time."

The conversation changed to lighter topics, and the appetizer quickly disappeared over talk of Izzy's apartment, the softness

of the bed, the windows that opened to the sea, and the loveli-
est yarn shop east of the Mississippi. Or maybe anywhere.

By the time the table had been cleared to make room for
three steaming bowls of clam chowder and a basket of sourdough rolls, Birdie had run out of chatter.

She looked at Rose as garlicky steam rose up between them.
"Now that you have a decent place to stay and a bed without
bugs, what do you plan to do while you're here? And do you
know how long that will be?" To keep her manners intact, she
added, "I hope it will be a long, leisurely stay and we will have
plenty of time to teach you to knit and to show off our bit of
paradise."

There. They'd asked one of the unknowns that had lingered
after Rose had finished with fixing the pipe. It was puzzling all
of them. As was Rose herself. A conundrum, Nell said. One
with a degree in children's literature, a love for Winnie-the-
Pooh, and an aptitude for fixing pipes.

Rose looked up from her soup. She shifted in her chair. "I
planned on coming for a couple days, that's all. But . . . well, I'd
like to stay a little longer. I'm in between things right now, figuring out my next chapter. My mom's illness and all."

"Of course," Nell said. "Losing someone has a way of
putting plans on hold for a while and letting life take its time."

"That's it, exactly. A friend practically packed my car and
pushed me out of town. I'm not used to thinking about myself,
but I've been told that's who I should be taking care of now."

"Such good advice," Birdie said. "It may seem selfish, but it's
not. It's where you live, after all. Yourself."

"You sound like my therapist." Rose wiped a dollop of
cream from the corner of her mouth. "My older sister wants me
to move to Seattle, where she lives."

"It's a lovely town," Birdie said.

"Somehow it seems so far away."

Nell looked at her quizzically. Sea Harbor, if her geography was correct, was nearly the same distance from Omaha as Seattle. But she tucked the thought away. Sometimes emotions factored into how distances were perceived, and what was near or far.

"Sea Harbor can be a perfect interlude for you," Birdie said. "Time to clear your head and to think about your life."

"Maybe. If only I could live on air—" She offered a half-hearted smile. "I'm grateful to Izzy for putting me up, but I've never been a freeloader. I always pay my way, no matter—"

Rose's thought dropped off as a sweep of yellow enveloped Birdie from behind, two arms wrapping around her and hugging her close.

"Sold another house, Birdie. That's two this week."

Birdie swiveled out of the hug to beam up at Stella Palazola. "Of course you did, dear. Who could say no to you?"

Stella gave Nell a quick hug, too, and then focused on Rose. "Hi. Hey, sorry to barge in like this, but Birdie is my guardian angel and I had to share my news. I'm Stella Palazola." Then she stopped, her eyes widening. "I think I know you. We met the other day, right?"

Rose looked at her, then the blouse. It was the same bright yellow blouse she'd seen walking out of the yarn shop.

Stella adjusted her glasses. "Well, we didn't really meet, but I saw you outside Izzy's shop, right? Sorry about staring at you. It's a bad habit I have. I was trying to figure out if we knew each other."

"Stella, dear," Birdie said, interrupting the flow of words, "this is Rose Chopra."

"Rose Chopra," Stella repeated, then looked at Rose again. "Nope, I guess I don't know you. That happens all the time. What do they say, there're seven people in the world who look just like you?" Stella laughed, a full laugh that made them all smile. "I think I have a hundred of those. People always think they've met me before, too. But anyway, Rose Chopra, it's nice to meet you."

"Rose fixed Izzy's broken pipe and saved us from building an ark," Birdie said.

Stella looked puzzled. "Ark?"

"As in Noah. It was raining in Izzy's shop." Birdie patted the empty chair next to her, her eyes lighting up with a thought. "Can you sit for a minute, Stella?"

Nell watched Birdie's mind working from across the table. She was putting the law of attraction to work. Or maybe the law of need, if there was such a law. She sat back, smiled, and watched it unfold.

"You fix pipes?" Stella plopped down in the chair, dropping her briefcase on the floor with a thud.

"Yes, she does," said Birdie. "Rose has fixed up many old houses, made them new again." She smiled brightly at a waitress placing four slices of lemon bars on the table. Flakes of powdered sugar decorated the plates.

"So you're a plumber, then?" Stella glanced over at Birdie and laughed. "Or maybe I should be asking you, Birdie? Are you Rose's manager?"

Birdie chuckled, a forkful of lemon bar on its way to her mouth.

"I do a little bit of everything," Rose said.

Stella put her elbows on the table and leaned in toward Rose. "Everything?" she said. "Are you in the market for a job? Part time? Long time? Anytime? I need you, Rose." Her deep eyes held Rose's amused gaze.

Birdie was right. Few could refuse Stella Palazola, and there was something about the way Rose Chopra was listening to Stella that suggested she was happily being taken in by the friendly Realtor. For friendship or a paycheck, Birdie wasn't sure. But before the last lemony crumbs had disappeared from their plates, Stella had dug into her briefcase, handed Rose business cards, addresses, a company ad, and extracted from her a promise to meet at eight o'clock the next morning for coffee.

Birdie might be Stella's guardian angel, she said as she stood up, slinging the strap of her briefcase over one shoulder, but Rose just might be her savior. And then she left, her smile as wide as her face.

"Well, look at that," Birdie said. "You have a job, Rose Chopra. Now isn't Sea Harbor a very nice place to be?"

Nell chuckled. "Did you want a job?" In spite of Stella Palazola's charming ways, it seemed a sudden decision for something that usually required a little planning.

But Rose looked pleased. Happy, even excited beneath the quiet demeanor.

"Stella's office is right across the street from Izzy's," Birdie said. "You can roll out of bed and be there in three minutes, depending on traffic."

Rose knew exactly where the office was. Across the street and up those familiar wooden stairs. A small smile softened her face as one of her mother's familiar refrains slipped out, one meant to make the regular trips up those steps happy ones for her daughter. *Up, up, up and away . . . Dr. Dentist will make our day . . .* And the trip was always made sweeter by a hot fudge sundae on their way back home.

"What, dear?" Birdie said, her brows lifting. She'd been complaining of late that her hearing was dimming like a worn-out lightbulb. But also wondering why the younger generations seemed to mumble their words.

Rose smiled. "Oh, nothing. I was just saying that it was a wonderful lunch. Absolutely the best clam chowder I've ever had. You were right, Birdie. Thank you both."

While Birdie signed for the meal and Nell chatted with the waitress, Rose wandered over to the French doors opening onto the club patio. The stone expanse fanned out in a crescent shape, leading down to the manicured beach below, empty today because of the ominous heavy clouds above. She stood still, mesmerized by the endless motion of waves leaping high and crashing with abandon against granite boulders, then folding in upon themselves and sliding back. Dramatic and powerful. She could see her mother in the motion of the water—her sweet, generous smile. Her soft eyes that saw only goodness and goodwill and beauty. A fairylike world, gossamery and delicate and light. And *fragile*. *Gladys Woodley saw no evil.*

She finally pulled her eyes away from the tide and forced herself to look in the other direction—up the too familiar beach, past a grove of pine trees and waving sea grass, beyond the boathouses and vacant picnic tables. Her mind's view stopped when it reached the neat rows of elegant sailboats in their slips, lined up like soldiers, swaying in the heavy wind. And finally the last group, the dinghies, tucked into their slips, ready for the gangly youth racing down the hill for sailing classes. Tanned, good-looking college instructors waiting with clipboards, whistles hanging from lanyards.

Block. Jibe. Boom. Bow. Keel. The words came in a rush, like the crack of bullets from a gun.

She placed a palm against the cold, damp window, drizzles of rain catching the patio lights, and steadied herself against the memories.

"Rose, are you all right?" Nell's gentle voice came from behind her. She touched Rose's arm lightly.

Rose took a breath, released it, and turned away from the window. She looked into Nell's concerned and caring face and her mind and body came together. She felt a lessening of whatever was caged inside her. A *loosening*. She hadn't thought she could come back to this spot, to see that beach. The sails. The memories. But she had.

And she was fine.

She smiled at Nell and silently rejoiced in the feeling of control and resolution that slowly passed through her. She felt her mother beside her. Within her.

Yes, I am going to be fine.

And Rose believed it.

She picked up her bag and followed Nell and Birdie across the dining room to the hostess desk, where Liz Santos stood waiting to take them on a tour. She was eager to hear about Rose's first taste of the yacht club's famous New England clam chowder.

Amazing, Rose would tell her with a smile.

And, thank you, yes—she'd love a tour of the yacht club.

Chapter 6

It was a cosmic explosion, one that might never have happened if the sun and moon and stars had not been aligned perfectly that cloudy, drizzly day.

Or, in this case, if Beatrice Scaglia had not chosen to walk out of the Sea Harbor Yacht Club at the precise moment a tall, casually dressed man had chosen to walk up those same steps. He was coming from the circle drive, his head thrown back in laughter at something that a man near him had said, seemingly oblivious to the weather.

Beatrice Scaglia had donned a plastic rain cap to protect her hair from the drizzle and tied it beneath her chin, then lowered her head to protect her makeup, her eyes focused on her already damp Christian Louboutin heels.

It wasn't until she heard a voice calling out to her that she looked up, a smile beginning as she readied herself to greet a friend or potential voter or businessman.

But the smile fell away before it had completely formed when she saw the self-assured, handsome man in front of her. Face-to-face.

Her face drained of color, the rain cap slipped back off her head and gathered around her neck.

Then, seemingly without thought or planning, she dropped her purse to the steps and took a huge lungful of air, puffing up her chest and raising her body to her Louboutin-assisted height.

In the next second Mayor Beatrice Scaglia did something that mayors seldom do. She lifted her slender arm, flattened her hand, and smacked the man across his face, the sound echoing in the wet air.

Finding that the higher step gave her surprising leverage, Beatrice followed the first slap with another. Harder this time. And then the pummeling began, her hands turning into small, balled fists that landed one after another on the man's well-muscled chest.

As the man attempted to collect himself, a torrent of words began to spew forth from the small woman. Rough, audacious words that seemed to be coming from someone other than the petite mayor.

In that moment, Beatrice Scaglia was the eponymous Carrie White at her most ferocious, determined to best her foe at the high school dance.

"Hey," Spencer Paxton III said, his arms outstretched and palms flat out, prepared for another possible blow. "Mayor Scaglia, stop, what's going on?"

"What's going on is that you are a lying, lowlife, heinous person who needs to be wiped off the face of the earth before your germs spread. And if there are no volunteers, I will do it myself."

Ben Endicott heard the onslaught of words as he walked across the circle drive, hurrying to keep his luncheon appointment. He rushed toward the entrance, then stopped suddenly, looking from one person to the other, a space now opening between the two as Spence took a step backward to safety, massaging his cheek with one hand.

He turned toward Ben, one hand lifted in greeting and a perplexed look on his face.

Ben looked beyond him to the mayor. "Beatrice? Are you all right?"

"Ben, thank the Lord you're here. Am I all right? Of course I am not. I am in distress. This man—" She raised a hand and pointed wildly, then dropped it and continued. "This man is a despicable excuse for a human being."

Although her arms had finally fallen to her sides, her clenched hands quiet, Beatrice's face was pinched tight with anger, her cheeks flushed and raindrops dotting her forehead.

Ben's voice was calm. "I'm worried you're going to have a heart attack," he said, reaching out to take her arm. "I'll walk you to your car and get you out of this rain. We can talk there." He glanced at his lunch companion for understanding.

Spence managed a half smile.

But Beatrice refused to move and ignored the raindrops running down her cheeks, taking traces of mascara with them. She spoke to Ben as if he were the only one there on the steps, as if she'd already beaten the other man into oblivion. "He's a lying fake, Ben. Don't you forget it. And he's trying to steal what's rightfully mine with lies and innuendoes. That isn't what we do in Sea Harbor. That isn't who we are."

Her voice became quieter, her body loosening as Ben encouraged her to breathe.

Footsteps from the club's open doorway drew attention to a small group of women gathering just outside the wide doors. A bright blue canopy shielded them from the rain.

Nell's eyes met Ben's, confusion on both their faces. She remembered now why he was there. A luncheon invitation from Spencer Paxton. They'd both been surprised by it. But the drama going on in front of them diminished that surprise to nothing.

A few steps behind Nell, Birdie and Liz Santos stood still,

their conversation stopped midstream by the ruckus below. Liz took a step forward, clutching her cell phone, ready to call for help. "Is everyone all right?"

But Beatrice had calmed down, and when Ben snapped open his umbrella, she took it graciously and, having pulled a clean handkerchief from her pocket, proceeded to wipe the mascara from her face with one hand, balancing the umbrella with the other. She nodded to Ben, then waved to Liz, and continued down the steps as if she'd just had a lovely meal and it was time to get back to work.

Which may have ended the rainy afternoon drama, except for a cry and a thud directly behind the women standing at the entrance to the club.

The cry was from Birdie herself. She had felt Rose's return from the ladies' room, felt her standing close behind her, looking over her shoulder at the commotion on the steps.

The next thing Birdie felt was a shudder, followed by a rush of air. When she turned around, Rose Chopra was falling to the ground, as graceful as a ballerina, her long face pale and her eyes fluttering, until they finally closed completely and she lay still on the floor of the yacht club entryway.

Chapter 7

It was a smaller group than usual that gathered at the Endicotts' home for a Friday night dinner on the deck, and although Nell loved having Friday nights alive with music and laughter and drop-in friends and neighbors, the quieter, close-knit group seemed to suit the mood of the day.

Birdie stood at the kitchen island unwrapping several loaves of *pane casareccia*, still warm from Harry Garozzo's deli oven. "Harry said it's 'crusty on the outside, spongy within,' in a way that seemed important to him. So please tell him you enjoyed it."

"That sounds like a fine description of the old baker himself," Nell said, inhaling the comforting fragrance of freshly baked bread. "The food of life. A good thing for tonight. I thought for a moment today we were going to lose one."

"Whose life, exactly?" Birdie asked. "Spencer's or Rose's?"

Nell nodded with a slight smile. But the earlier commotion at the club hadn't been taken lightly. It had left them all slightly unnerved.

She and Birdie had made sure Rose was safely in her apartment, then asked Izzy to run up from the shop and check on her before coming to dinner that night.

Izzy had found Rose sitting cross-legged on the floor with a piece of sandpaper in her hand, examining a section of pine floor that had been damaged when the pipe was repaired. Soft Indian flute music was playing in the background. To Izzy, Rose looked more like a yogi than a plumber.

Rose barely turned around when Izzy walked in, but she said that she was fine. And then she went back to sanding, moving the paper slowly back and forth, as if the rhythm itself was soothing to her.

"So how is she?" Cass asked. "Rose, I mean." She smeared a cracker with spicy fig jam and took a bite.

"She seemed fine," Izzy said. "She was embarrassed, but she said she faints easily. My roommate in law school had the same reflex. Things like trauma or sudden pain or seeing blood can trigger a sudden lowering in blood pressure. Law school exams used to trigger it in my friend Jenny."

"We had a hard time convincing the manager that it wasn't the food," Nell said. "Liz was beside herself, but Rose was adamant that she was fine. And the mayor was fine when she walked away, too. Spencer Paxton seemed to be the only one left with scars. Ben said he may have a black eye tomorrow."

"Our delicate mayor, punching him out like that? I wish I had been there," Cass said.

"I know, right?" Izzy said. "She's such a lady and always perfect. Sometimes I want to muss up her hair. But you can't help but like her."

"Ben was helpful calming things down," Birdie said. "Do you suppose Spencer invited him to lunch to be a bodyguard?"

"I don't think Spencer had the slightest idea he was going to be attacked by the mayor," Nell said, and set out a stack of napkins.

Just then Ben walked through the deck doors, wearing a heavy sailing sweatshirt and smelling of mesquite. Sam and Danny followed a few steps behind, empty beer bottles in hand and deep into debating the merits of some football coach.

Ben walked over to the sink and began washing his hands. "If you think I'm a match for Beatrice Scaglia, Birdie, you missed some of the action. That woman has a crazy uppercut. Spence invited Robbie McGlucken to join us, too. Maybe that was supposed to be his role. If so, he failed. Paxton was completely taken off guard. Not to mention the fact that he thought he and the mayor were friends. He donated to that city arts fund she started, they've dined together. He's been hanging around city hall for weeks, learning things, making friends, and the mayor was one of them."

"I've seen them together at a few events," Birdie said. "Beatrice seemed to be enjoying introducing Spence to people in the know. Her behavior today was definitely odd."

"I wasn't sure why Spencer invited me to lunch today," Ben said, "but I think it's what you described, Birdie. Goodwill. Learning more about how the town is run. Making connections. Who knows, maybe he was impressed by these silvery strands that keep appearing on my head."

Nell smiled and touched a finger to his temple. "I know I'm impressed."

"I certainly hope so." Ben chuckled. "Apparently I was on Spence's list of people to connect with. Not a bad thing—I got an amazing bowl of the club's clam chowder out of it."

"It sounds reasonable. And not at all what we thought when rumors of his company developing big box stores in our sweet little town began circulating," Birdie said.

"Exactly," Ben agreed. "His interests seem less about his development company and more about civic involvement. That's why he came back to live here. He thinks he has a lot to offer Sea Harbor and that the town would benefit from his ideas and his leadership. Since he grew up here, he sees it as giving back."

"He wants to be a leader?" Cass asked. "That's weird."

"Maybe not. He sees himself that way. He actually had some good ideas for social programs, said he'd been successful other places. He asked if I'd use my connections to help him with his efforts. He isn't a shrinking violet, that's for sure. In fact, at times, he was a little . . ."

Ben took the martini Sam handed him. "I don't know, too much, maybe? The line between being egoistic and being self-assured can be thin. But he speaks a good line. He left the waitress a wad of bills. The ideal citizen."

But the sound of Ben's last words was tinged with something Ben wasn't very good at—sarcasm.

"He sounds calculating," Cass said. "I had an accountant like that, though I guess accountants have to be calculating."

Ben laughed. "Calculating. Maybe. But hey, if he means what he says, does what he intends, who cares if he's puffed up a bit."

Nell opened the refrigerator and removed a tray of scallops, setting it on the counter. "So why was Robbie McGlucken there?" There was something incongruous about the image of Robbie McGlucken in his leather jacket, dining with the young, well-dressed businessman and her Ben.

"Spence hired him to help with some Internet things. Spence is a Luddite in that department, he says. Robbie was fine, he even cleaned up a bit for lunch. Seemed engaged. Took some notes on his iPad. And he devoured three bowls of clam chowder."

"He was with Spence at the Gull the other night, too," Sam said. He stood next to Izzy, his strong fingers rubbing her neck and filled them in on their beers at the Artist's Palate.

"Hey, you two," Cass said. "No PDAs for old marrieds."

Sam grinned at Cass and reached over, kneading her shoulder, too. "Robbie and Spence get along great. Robbie even told a joke or two. Sort of. Something I don't think he does much. Gus says his son mostly communicates with computers."

"Dear Robbie," Birdie said, shaking her small head in that way she did when regretting someone's hard life or misfortune. "Good for him."

"I agree," Cass said. "Robbie needs focus. I used to babysit him. The only things he was interested in back then were Dungeons and Dragons and arm wrestling."

"You arm wrestled with Robbie McGlucken?" Danny asked his wife in mock surprise.

Cass took a drink of Danny's beer and wrinkled her nose at her husband, her dark eyes on him. "Not now, you goof. Not with all those tattoos on his arm."

Danny stepped close and made a show of straightening his glasses, lifting a brow—a small smile teasing his wife.

But Cass silenced him immediately with one wicked look.

Danny would be sleeping on the couch if he dared reveal that his wife had several secret tattoos of her own.

"My mother was a friend of Robbie's mom," Danny said, suspecting it would be wise to change the subject. "After she died, Mom used to look out for Gus's kids. She thought the older one was a saint, the way she cared for Robbie. Mom always kept cookies in the back of the store for them."

Birdie smiled. "That is a very Harriet Brandley thing to do."

"Speaking of cookies," Ben said, picking up the platter of scallops. "It's time to eat. Grab your fleeces, a martini, a blanket if need be, and join me at the fire pit. Rain is gone and I need fresh air."

The group rallied, loading trays with mint-roasted vegetables and a spicy slaw salad and parading to the deck.

Cass plugged her phone into the Bose speaker, and soon the deck was humming with the soul-stirring voice of Aretha Franklin. The old maple tree, growing right through the deck, was still wound with hundreds of tiny white lights from Danny and Cass's wedding a year before. Tonight they cast a warm glow across the relaxing friends.

In minutes, plates were filled and bodies were settled comfortably on the plush cushions of the deck chairs and lounges around the fire pit, warmed by the dancing flames that cut right through the evening chill.

Without more talk of Spencer Paxton or angry mayors, the small group settled in for an early evening and easy talk of simpler things.

"The fiber show is the talk of the art colony, Jane Brewster tells me," Birdie said. "And Bree McIntosh is leading the charge. A lovely young woman."

"Not to mention that she does things with yarn that no sheep could have dreamed up. I love that woman." Izzy took a bite of a sweet scallop.

Nell settled back in a chair. She felt present and not present, listening and watching as the evening played out in front of her—Bree McIntosh and her husband were absent players on a stage. She liked Bree and had spotted her talent early on. It was curious that Spencer Paxton and Bree seemed almost as separate as their different surnames, barely mentioned in the same breath. Some marriages, she supposed, thrived on that kind of separateness. But the thought left her wondering, and whether it was because of the ire that Spencer Paxton had elicited in their town's mayor that day—or the fact that she liked Bree McIntosh—she couldn't be sure.

She set her plate on the wide stone ledge of the fire pit, then settled back again, her head resting against the back of the Adirondack chair, her eyelids heavy. She hadn't realized how tense the episode at the club had made her until her body slowly began to relax. Friends and a fire—the perfect combo. She stayed put in her chair, letting others pass around seconds and refill wine and water glasses, their voices soft and comforting around her.

As the fire and the music filled the chilly night air, Nell closed her eyes and played with the many strands of conversations, trying to knit them together in some meaningful way. There were no Friday night bombshells, no emergency phone calls or sirens in the night or knocking at the door—all things that had sometimes happened at the comfortable home on Sandswept Lane.

But even a second glass of wine couldn't completely erase the niggling feeling inside her. A tiff at the yacht club couldn't be contributing to it. Nor a young stranger settling in above Izzy's shop.

All should be well . . .

"Nell. Nell—" Ben leaned over her, one hand resting on each arm of her chair. He leaned low, his voice so close she could feel his breath before she saw his smile.

She tugged her eyes open and looked up. She was wrapped snugly in a blanket, the fire pit now an ant hill of glowing embers.

"You fell asleep," he said. "I think it was the Super Bowl argument that had Cass, Danny, and Sam in a tither. Izzy and Birdie showed their distaste by going inside to watch *Casablanca*. Cass and Danny finally took Birdie home."

"The dishes?"

"Done. Everyone is gone. So come inside, m'love. It's time for bed."

Ben helped her up and took her in his arms, holding her close for a minute.

Nell stayed still, breathing in the comforting smell of him— the clean soapy smell of his aftershave, mixed with the scent of fall and burning embers and fallen leaves. Ben. Her rock.

And then they headed up the back stairs, turning out the lights as they climbed. Soon they were settled beneath the thick down comforter, the windows opened a crack. Ben turned out the lights and reached over, pulling her close, filling her with gentle desire. Not crazy and wild like in their college days, but deep and satisfying and loving—and warming her to the very marrow of her bones.

A short while later Ben's breathing slowed and his body loosened, one arm still looped across Nell's chest.

She lay still, their bodies pressed together as she watched him sink into sleep. Finally she unwound herself and lay, hips touching, and closed her eyes.

But sleep escaped her and she thought back to the moments on the deck earlier, the quiet evening, the easy talk. And her mind going fuzzy as she drifted off to some other place.

She tried to remember what she was thinking about as dessert plates were being collected and Ben was pouring coffee.

The sound of Aretha Franklin's powerful voice came back to her. And with it the emotion that had floated up as she tried to make sense out of her week.

Nothing truly bad had happened, nothing to keep her awake. But when her eyes finally closed again, she began to sort through what it was that was bothering her. What had floated around the evening's talk, the togetherness.

A quiet Friday night, with the warmth of friends and the fire dispelling the chilly air. But there was something else, perhaps something brought about by the change of seasons. The air had been laced with something tonight, a feeling that filled her with an odd unease. An unnerving feeling about the weekend. A feeling that, just like the weather, what comes in like a lamb . . . may go out like a lion.

A fragile peace, she thought as her lids finally closed and she drifted off to sleep.

Chapter 8

Rose was right on time to meet Stella at Coffee's, the crowded coffee bistro in the middle of the Harbor Road shops.

The weather was sunny but with a brisk wind, leaving the patio nearly empty of people and full of leaves from the maples lining the back alley. Rose walked through them, feeling the crunch beneath her boots and inhaling the pleasing smell of fall.

She spotted Stella in the back of the coffee shop, sitting in a booth and talking to a tall man. As she walked closer, she realized that she knew the man. No, she didn't know him, but she'd seen him before. The man who was leaning against a fence near Izzy's shop that day. He had seemed out of place, that's why she remembered him.

Today he was leaning, too, his hands shoved in his pockets and his angular form bent to talk over the noise of the espresso machine and chatter of the crowd. He reminded her of a gentle giraffe. With a ponytail. Less off-putting as he had been when she'd seen him before.

Stella spotted her then, and waved wildly in the air. Rose hurried over.

"Rosie, meet my buddy Josh," Stella said. "Josh is an incredible artist. A great painter."

Josh straightened up and turned toward her, and she saw what she hadn't seen before—hooded and searching eyes—the color of the sea before a storm.

She blushed slightly, wondering how readable her thoughts were. "Hi," she said, sliding into the booth across from Stella. She looked up at the man. "I'm Rose. I think I saw you down the street the other day. Near the yarn shop?"

"Could be," he said. He nodded.

"An orange bike?"

"Musta been me."

"I was hypnotized by the shop's window display so could have gotten my colors mixed up." She laughed.

"That fiber art display," he said, nodding. "Great window display, I agree."

A small, smiling woman walked up behind Josh. "Hi, again," she said, looking at Rose.

Rose grinned. It was like seeing an old friend. "We're talking about your window art in the yarn shop."

Bree smiled, flattered, then greeted Josh, and looked at Stella. "I'm not sure we've met."

Rose felt a surprising pleasure that she knew someone whom Stella didn't. As if she belonged, in some odd way.

Josh shook his head. "Hey, sorry. I thought Stell knew everyone in town. Stell, meet Bree McIntosh. She hangs out around Canary Cove. An art groupie," he joked.

Bree laughed and poked him in the side.

Josh ignored the jab and said to Stella, "Actually, she's an artist. A talented one. You should get one of her paintings or hangings before everyone realizes it."

"He means they're cheap," Bree said.

Stella laughed.

Bree glanced down at the photos littering the table. "What do you do, Stella?"

"Real estate," Stella said. "My uncle Mario is officially the owner, but I figure if I don't remind him, he'll forget." She rummaged around for a business card.

Josh groaned.

"Josh groans, but that's what we Realtors do—we push ourselves on people. So if you're in the market for a house . . ." Stella lifted her brows, handing a glossy card to Bree.

Bree looked at the card, her face blank. Then, with a slight slap, she set the card back on the booth top. "No," she said, "I'm definitely not in the market for a house."

She turned toward Josh, murmuring that Izzy needed him to move some displays over at the yarn shop. And the staff over there needed coffee, too. Now.

Rose watched them walk quickly away, Josh's head high above the crowd, and Bree's disappearing in the swarm of bodies.

Stella looked at Rose, slightly embarrassed at the quick departure. "I get that. Not everyone wants to buy a house. I was probably a tad too pushy. Now where were we? Is our coffee cold?" She slid one mug across the table to Rose. "It's crazy in here. Way too noisy. But I thought it'd be better to meet here first. If this isn't a gig you want to get yourself into, it'd be easier to walk out on me in a coffee shop than in my office."

She grinned, then turned to a plate of éclairs. "I hope you like éclairs. They're my personal favorites, but Coffee's owner makes great cinnamon rolls, too. In the meantime, here are some things for you to look at." She began shuffling more papers while simultaneously greeting people who walked by the booth to say hello.

Rose watched with interest as Stella juggled talking to her and greeting friends and neighbors and clients without missing a single beat. She had learned everything she needed to know about Stella Palazola in the last few minutes. She made people feel good about themselves, just like she'd done with her.

In between interruptions, Stella opened a notebook as thick

as a dictionary and began paging through it, turning it sideways so Rose could see.

"This is my bible," she said. "Houses on the market or ones we've sold. Lots of these houses are good to go or will be torn down. Those we don't need to worry about." Stella grinned and pushed her glasses up her nose. "Darn these glasses," she said, and then explained that when she was in high school, Birdie had bought her contacts but they never worked quite right, so she was stuck with her horn-rims and was actually okay with them most of the time. "They make me look intelligent, right?"

"Absolutely intelligent." Rose picked up an éclair and took a bite. "Birdie bought you contacts?"

"She's my unofficial godmother. My soul mother, I call her. I love Birdie Favazza with my whole heart and soul." She tapped her chest, then took hold of a yellow tab and flipped the pages over to another section in the notebook. "These are the houses that we need to pay attention to. The ones right here." A blunt finger left the plastic page with a creamy smudge.

The page was filled with a half dozen photos of beautiful houses.

"I've promised the owners that I'd do a little fixing up on a couple of these—" She looked up at Rose again and smiled. "What I mean to say is that *you*—not me—would do a little fixing up on these. Some owners become irritated when a home inspection reveals things that should be repaired. They just want the house sold. Then and there. So I'm going to eliminate some of those stumbling blocks right off the bat. And then, boom! We'll have a fast sale. Our job is to make that happen, right?"

Stella finally stopped talking and looked directly at Rose, who had only spoken single words here and there. "I talk a lot, don't I? I'm so sorry, Rosie, but meeting you the other day was serendipity. Even before I knew how accomplished you were, I knew it was meant to be. I'm not putting you off, am I?"

Rose smiled. "Of course not." She wondered briefly if Stella was right and their paths had crossed somewhere, sometime. It was possible. Stella was older by a few years, not important now, but in childhood it can be huge.

Stella Palazola. The name rippled across her memory. What was it Ray Bradbury said about memory?

"Memory is an illusion, nothing more. It is a fire that needs constant tending."

She looked at Stella again, watching that nice face. Pleasant but not showy. Dimples showing every time she smiled, which was often. Rose was liking everything she saw in that face, but she was unsure if she'd seen it before.

Maybe later she'd stoke the flames of her memory. Right now she needed to be looking at pictures, thinking of fixing things, and listening to Stella Palazola in a crowded coffee shop.

She wrapped her fingers around her mug and took a drink of the coffee, concentrating on a map Stella was showing her, names of sellers she was working with, and photos lying on the table. Her head began to spin with Stella's words.

Stella looked over at her. "I hope I haven't scared you off with all my talk."

"Of course you haven't." And that was the truth. She liked being able to sit quietly, listening to Stella's enthusiastic plans as if she was already a part of them.

And she very much liked the warm, friendly cocoon Stella was spinning around her.

"So speak," Stella said with a grin.

Rose laughed. She looked down at the heavy notebook, the map, the lists, and finally at Stella. And then she said with an openness that surprised herself, "All right then, let's get to this office of yours. Looks like we have lots of work to do."

*   *   *

Nell was the first one to see the email attachment that day. She was cleaning out her computer, approaching it like a neglected closet, tossing and deleting notices and posts and emails with a vengeance. But for some reason, she opened this one.

And then she called Ben away from a book he was reading.

"Come look at this," she said, pushing her coffee cup to one side and staring at the screen as Ben walked across the family room toward the kitchen island.

He looked over her shoulder, his cheek brushing against her hair. "Nice," he said.

"What's nice?" she said.

"You. You smell good." He pulled his glasses from the top of his graying hair and put them on, reading aloud from her screen.

Sea Harbor Scoop . . . "Hm," he said, then read the tag line below: *2day, Yesterday, and 2morrow.*

"Kind of corny," he said.

"Below that." Nell pointed at the digital photo, front and center beneath the headline.

It was a photo of Beatrice Scaglia slapping Spencer Paxton on the steps of the Sea Harbor Yacht Club.

Behind her she heard Ben's sharp intake of breath, its expulsion moving her hair. And followed by a mumble of words Ben Endicott didn't often use.

None of them had seen anyone with a cell phone out, but clearly someone had had one. And snapped a photo at the worst possible time.

"What is this thing?" Ben finally asked.

"It looks like an online newsletter. Some local thing." She began to scroll down, looking for names. "I don't know how I got on this list."

"You'll probably never find out how you got on it. I'm probably on it, too. Maybe the whole town. He walked over to the sink, staring out the window and trying to remember who was around that day. But he and Nell both knew that it was futile to try to figure it out. People holding cell phones was about as normal and natural now as people wearing clothes. He turned back to Nell. "What do you think the newsletter—if that's what it is—is for?"

"I don't know. A mishmash, I think. A bit of local news. Opinion pages and lots of requests for comments."

She clicked on a link titled "Local History" and scanned the screen. Under the heading of decades—thirty years ago, twenty, etc.—were old newspaper pictures: dedication of the library, the opening of a restaurant. The items randomly chosen, it seemed.

She smiled as a familiar face looked out from the screen. *Danny Brandley.* Only it wasn't Danny, but his father years before, youthful and proud and jubilant, his arm around his wife, Margaret, and standing in front of a brand-new bookstore: SEA HARBOR BOOKSTORE, the gold letters read. *Okay*, Nell conceded: one good point for whoever put this together.

She continued scanning, noticing years were skipped over as if the editor was hurrying to get to more contemporary history. Headlines were misspelled, captions sloppy. She thought of all the painstaking hours and care she had put into making sure her grants were always written impeccably.

"It's slapped together," Nell said. "And apparently it's not the first issue. I must have already put some in the trash." Then her finger stopped moving as a more recent newspaper photo, larger this time, filled the screen. It was from a few years ago, as the heading indicated. A year Nell remembered well. Her eyes grew large and she lifted a palm to her face. "No," she murmured to the screen, chastising it.

The photo and brief text chronicled an event that had taken place a while after she and Ben had become permanent residents of Sea Harbor. They'd already become an integral part of the tightly knit community. The event, and what led up to it, were hard to forget; they had thrown the entire town into turmoil.

Nell knew the photo well.

And she knew the man in the photo.

And the woman in the background.

"Ben, this is awful," she said. She enlarged the photo, and Ben leaned in close. He stared, a frown filling his face, his strong jaw rigid. It was worse than the first. Worse for Beatrice. And it would cause more pain.

Beatrice Scaglia, then a councilwoman, stood solemn-faced in the back of the Sea Harbor Court House. Chief Jerry Thompson stood next to her, as if providing support. Toward the edge of the photo was a judge, and standing in front of her bench, front and center and shackled, his head lowered and his face filled with fear, stood Beatrice's then-husband, Sal Scaglia, being indicted for the murder of his mistress.

Ben gripped the edge of the island with one hand. "It's reprehensible. Scurrilous. Why bring pain to a woman who has already suffered her fair share?"

There wasn't much text, just the photo and some links directed to articles with titles like "What Did the Wife Know?"—rumors that had long been debunked along with a scandalmonger who had since left town.

"Poor Beatrice," Nell said, the words sounding hollow.

Finally she shut off her computer, as if the black screen would make both the photo, the memory, and the pain her friend would suffer all over again go away. "There's no reason to rehash all this. Sal Scaglia was guilty. He was punished. Justice was served."

And by his own hand, Sal Scaglia had lost his life in prison, just as those who knew him well had feared would happen. The affair was meaningless to him, but losing Beatrice meant losing his anchor, his life.

Ben pushed his mug and the laptop aside and wrapped Nell in his arms, holding her close, breathing in the smell of her.

Nell nestled into his chest, finding inordinate comfort in the brush of his sweater against her cheek and the smell of his after-shave on her own skin.

It was only later, after Ben went off to a meeting and she had talked to Izzy, Cass, and Birdie, that Nell finally picked up her cell and called Beatrice Scaglia.

The Palazola Realty office was exactly what Rose had expected it would be: old and musty-smelling, with a slanted hardwood floor that made you tip slightly as you walked, with tall, heavy windows that opened with difficulty and did little to ward off ocean gusts just a block away. She loved it.

The main room was slightly bigger than a reception area, neat and airy with a round shiny table and four comfortable chairs for client meetings, a bookcase next to it, and two old wooden desks, one located under each window. Stella plopped her purse down on one, scattering papers and yellow sticky notes that were stuck down in haphazard rows. She pointed to the other desk, empty and wiped clean with Murphy Oil Soap. She grinned. "That one's yours."

"Do I need a desk?" Rose asked.

"Sure. It gives you a place to drop your backpack or purse or whatever. And it's a place for us to gab and eat donuts." She pointed out two rooms off the main office, one with a closed door.

"The room with the open door is storage. Gus McGlucken—he owns the hardware store next door—gave me a deal on saws and toolboxes and plumber's tape and some things I didn't rec-ognize. Oh, and bandages, too. We have another storeroom above Gus's shop. It's connected to Robbie's place—that's his son. Robbie and I share it, but there's plenty of extra room. Gus knows everything about tools and equipment, anything you might need. We have an account at his store. Just sign for anything you need."

Rose laughed. It was a small-town thing. She remembered

her mother doing the same thing in the Brandleys' bookstore, then trying it once in Omaha and being surprised when the Barnes & Noble clerk nixed the idea and asked for a credit card.

Stella pointed to a closed door near a bookcase. "That's Uncle Mario's office. It has a window onto the fire escape, a quick escape when my aunt Sophia comes looking for him. It's his private space. Lord only knows what goes on in it."

A loud noise from inside the room alerted them that they weren't alone. "I guess he's here," Stella said. "I never know. Uncle Mario comes in occasionally for a nip of bourbon and a nap. Late morning. Middle of the night. Sunday morning. One never knows."

At that moment the door opened and a short man with a large flat nose and thinning hair lumbered out of the room. He was shorter than Rose and Stella, nearly round in diameter. His cardigan sweater had leather patches, professor style, and beneath it a striped shirt stretched tight over his belly. A thick gold chain was nearly hidden in the folds of his chin.

"About time you got here, Stella, m'girl," Mario said, but with undisguised affection in his voice for his niece. He followed his comment with a robust chuckle. "Now tell me who we have here." He lifted his furry eyebrows and smiled at Rose with rheumy eyes, wiping one of them with a large white handkerchief.

Rose guessed he had more hair in his eyebrows than on his head. Caterpillar brows. The thought made her smile. As did Uncle Mario. While Stella did the introductions, Rose moved mentally from thinking about his eyebrows to replaying several scenes from *The Godfather*, sure that she had seen Uncle Mario in one of them.

Mario held out his square hand, two giant diamond rings blinking in the sunlight. He started to welcome Rose with a handshake, but midway through changed his mind and wrapped her in a hug instead, then a kiss on each cheek that required him to tip up his chin since Rose was taller than he by an inch or two.

"Thatsa how we do it in Sicily." He grinned, pulling away. "My Stell says you're gonna be working for us, making us millions, she says." He winked and gave her a wide smile.

Rose suspected the nip of bourbon had been underestimated. But she liked Uncle Mario and grinned back.

And then without a good-bye, the owner of the firm was gone, lumbering through the front office door and making his way down the narrow flight of stairs. His footsteps echoed loudly.

Stella walked out after him, watching from the top of the stairwell to make sure he made it safely down. "He's probably going down to Harry Garozzo's deli or to chew the fat with Gus next door," she said, walking back inside and closing the door. "They watch out for each other. My mother watches out for him, too, but the rest of the family has pretty much disowned the old guy. He's harmless, though, and has a heart as big as that huge belly of his. Besides, he lets me do anything I want, including taking over the books. I insisted on it and I don't think he even notices that some of the huge chunks of money that used to pass through here from suspicious sources aren't coming in anymore. The family's hope is that I can keep him out of jail. Uncle Mario hasn't always kept the most accurate books, if you know what I mean."

Rose listened with half an ear. Stella was kind. And caring. And she liked Uncle Mario. That's all she really needed to know.

Stella's cell phone rang—or rather the mellow refrain from "Take Me Home" rang out, sending Stella rummaging through a large purse on her desktop. She nodded into the phone, as if the caller could feel her enthusiasm, and promised that she was "on it."

A muffled noise from the other side of the office wall muted the end of the call and Stella hung up.

"Geesh, what was that?"

Several thumps and rising voices began to pour through the wall from the other side.

"That's Robbie's apartment." Stella frowned.

The voices grew louder and louder, until Stella considered knocking on the wall, quieting them down. Though the words weren't clear, she recognized Gus's voice, calm at first, then Robbie's—rising higher and higher until he was screaming at his father. Loud, awful words that brought both women back to their desks, as if distance would keep them from hearing the anguished, angry deluge of words passing between father and son. Most of it was said with such fury they could barely decipher the words, only the anger that carried them. *Liar* rose up above the others, then settled back down.

And then it stopped. A door slammed, loud enough to rattle the books on Stella's shelf. And a pounding of footsteps on the back outdoor staircase indicated someone was leaving.

Stella and Rose stared at each other.

"I'm sorry you heard that," Stella said.

"I hope they're all right."

"Gus is a nice man. He's a long-time friend of Uncle Mario's. And Robbie is usually quiet. In fact he rarely talks. I hardly ever see him. I doubt if we'll hear anything like that again."

"Maybe it's one of those parent-son things," Rose said, although she couldn't imagine in a million years talking to either of her parents like that when they were alive.

"Well, they're gone now," Stella said, grabbing her purse from the back of the chair. "Let us be gone, too."

In minutes the two partners, as Stella was already calling them, were heading down Harbor Road in Stella's SUV, the back filled with FOR SALE signs, moving out of the commercial areas and into neighborhoods marked by treed yards, large homes, and the sound of the sea. Between the gates and narrow paths between properties, Rose caught bright blue glimpses of the ocean and the magnificent sky above it.

"I have one listing out this way and if I could sell it, we'd be set for the rest of the year," Stella said. "Our lives, maybe. It's where we're headed."

"These are incredible homes," Rose said. "Mansions. I can't imagine living in them, though."

"Me either," Stella said. She slowed down and clicked a gate opener on her visor, then turned into a wide cobblestone drive. "My criterion for a house has always been that I wouldn't be afraid to babysit in it. None of these fit the bill, but they sure are beautiful." She turned off the engine and they sat for a minute, looking through the car windows at the house.

Dozens of trees protected the property from neighbors on either side. "I got this listing because Uncle Mario's good buddy Anthony died and he had it written in his will that his kids had to live in the house themselves or give it to Uncle Mario to sell.

"He and his buddies were like that—loyal to the end. Or maybe there was a favor owed, who knows? But the family is anxious to sell it and fast. *Who wants a house with seven bathrooms?* they said. Who does, right?"

Rose nodded. "It would be hard to fill a home like this. It's beautiful, but, well, maybe if you had a big family."

"I have a guy interested in the place. Really interested. It's someone I knew as a kid who has come back to town and somehow fallen in love with this humongous place. I guess his dad tried to buy it once but the deal fell through. So maybe it's a childhood dream. Or maybe he wants to pull off something his dad couldn't do. Or prestige maybe? This guy is kind of like that. The bigger the better, you know the type."

"Does he have a large family?" Rose thought about her mom and tried to imagine her in a house that was so close to the sea.

Three rooms would have been plenty, even one if it had looked out onto the water.

"Just a wife."

"Does she like the house?" Rose strained her neck to see all the way to the top of the house.

"That's a good question. He's the only one I've talked to. In fact he's been over here a lot. He even brought Mario a bottle of his favorite bourbon the other day and spent most of the morning in with him, schmoozing. Talking about what, I don't have a clue. I left to do more productive things.

"But anyway, these are just more reasons why I am so grateful you came into my life, Rosie. The house isn't on the market yet. I promised this guy I'd show it to him but only after we had time to take care of a few things. You'll understand why when we go over. The kids want it sold ASAP. But believe me, the problem we're about to fix—well, it could have turned the most reasonable buyer away." Stella rolled her eyes, then opened the car door. "Come on. I'll show you."

The house had been closed up for several months except for Stella going in a few times to check on things. Inside it was clammy and gathering the stale, unwelcoming smell of unused spaces. Heavily draped windows blocked out sunlight and Stella clicked on lights as they walked through the massive entryway. Then she pulled out a key.

"There's an elevator but it needs a key. Here's yours." She handed Rose a brass ring with a several house keys and one smaller key hanging from it. "I have one, too, and Uncle Mario has one in the office. I guess the Bianchis had little grandkids running around and were always afraid they might get stuck on the elevator. Anyway, it's a good thing for us that they have it, because the repairs are on the top floor. It was where old Anthony Bianchi used to spend his days. He and Uncle Mario were great pals along with a couple of others, and according to folklore, they spent many happy hours in their 'tree house,' as my uncle called it."

Stella inserted the key in the lock and the walnut-paneled elevator door opened, then whisked them up to the third floor. The doors slid open and they stepped off, finding themselves in an open room with windows on two sides, bookcases and paneling and a giant television screen on the other.

There were no drapes on the windows, and sunlight flooded the cherrywood floors, the fine Persian rugs, leather couches and chairs comfortably worn and cracked and showing the shape of bodies. A wooden stand still held an assortment of Rinaldo pipes, and a brass telescope at one of the windows looked ready for use. And at the street-side end of the room, a massive mahogany pool table took center stage.

It was an amazing place. Except for a fetid odor that caused Rose to take a sudden step backwards. Her hand shot up to cover her nose and mouth. It felt like a deadly gas attack. She gagged.

"I'm so sorry, Rosie." Stella pulled a small white cloth from her bag and handed it to Rose, using another to cover her own nose. "You're probably thinking Uncle Mario's dead friend is still up here somewhere, right? It's awful, I know. But you can see why I need help before I show it to anyone. Even my eager-beaver client would be turned off."

Rose covered her nose with the cloth and looked in the direction of the odor, noticing a rug that was pulled back near the wall, a chair moved.

"It was a squirrel," Stella explained. "I guess the little missus knew this would be a great family house. Except she got trapped, along with a baby or two, inside that wall."

Stella followed Rose over to the scene of the damage.

"The good news is that they'd done some renovations up here and it's drywall, not plaster. Gus McGlucken knew someone from animal control who came out and removed the recently deceased family a couple days ago, but he had to cut through the wall and left a mess. Finding someone to do the rest of the work on such short notice and for such a small job was nearly impossible—even for Gus, who knows everyone. He even had his son come up and give it a look, but he declined the job. Robbie is more into computer video games than this kind of work. Oh, but look at what Robbie showed me while he was here."

She walked over to a wall of paneled bookshelves, moved one book, pressed something, and stepped back. The panel began to move, turning like a revolving door, until it clicked into place and the shelves holding the World Book Encyclopedia were replaced by a tidy, mirrored bar, still equipped with fine brandies and Scotch.

She gave Rose a *Can you believe it?* kind of smile, as if they were both in on some private joke, and then returned it to its more literary façade.

"Things like this happen more than you think. House secrets, I call them. Secret bars, squirrels. One never knows. Yet another reason I need you, Rosie. Is that the thirtieth or fortieth now?"

Rose warmed inside. She didn't even mind the nickname, one she had worn for more years than not. She looked more closely at the wall, the damage. "It will be easy, Stella. Fun."

"How long will it take?" Stella checked her phone. "I promised the interested buyer an update. And Uncle Mario says there are other people calling him about the house, too."

"A few days?"

"Perfect."

"Fixing this kind of thing reminds me of the work I did in the college rentals we lived in. Landlords loved me—their houses were in much better shape when we moved out than when we moved in. But I must admit, I never found a hidden bar."

"Ah, college days. I loved college. Many memories. I went to

Salem State, near here, and lived with six girls. We had great fun, but none of us were much into fixing anything, even meals. Four years of pizza and ramen noodles."

"I didn't have that problem. My roomie and I were, well, nerds I guess you'd stay. We had a good time together talking and sharing ideas. We were both quiet, and helped each other study, usually at the house. Maybe that's why I fixed up the places we lived—we spent so much time in them. Prem made amazing Indian meals, did sweet things for me, and told funny stories. I was a great rehabber and a good listener and helped him through English lit and math while he helped me through science classes. We were best friends. We even had the same therapist for a while, but we both knew we were best friends and didn't need therapy."

"Oh?" Stella waited.

"And then when we graduated, we got divorced."

Chapter 9

Rose turned her key and rode the elevator up to the third floor in the seaside mansion as if she'd been doing it all her life. She'd been over several times the day before. Then earlier today. And one final time, before calling it a night. It gave her a thrill each time the elevator started to move and she felt the lightness of her body, the lift and the pleasant flip of her stomach. And then the slight lurch as the cables locked in place and the doors slid open.

At first she had thought she would be afraid, being in the enormous house alone—especially toward the end of the day. But the dark emptiness of the mansion below disappeared quickly, her world restricted to the elevator and the cozy room at the top. She opened the windows wide each time, ushering out the fetid odor, paint and plaster smells refreshingly taking its place.

She imagined that Mr. Bianchi—she had learned the owner's name from the framed awards still hanging on the walls—was somehow pleased with her efforts.

Anthony Bianchi. The name rolled off her tongue dramatically as she had worked on the gaping hole. She imagined his life in

this room with his friends, and she smiled, even laughed sometimes as she let her imagination take her into an imaginary
world of pool, tobacco smoke, and good whiskey. And great
friends. She'd sashay back and forth, her brush in her hand as
she adhered a mesh patch to the wall, feathering the edges.

The room was hers, Anthony's, and his good buddies', and
she smiled at the pleasure of it all.

She had told Stella earlier that day that she'd be finished in
one or two more days. A sober Uncle Mario happened to be in
the office, and he'd congratulated her with a vigorous slap on
the back that made her cough. Then he told her what she already knew, that Anthony Bianchi was his *paisano*, his great
lifelong friend. And he proceeded to regale her with wild stories of the great times they'd had in the third-floor room. "Old
Gus McGlucken would join us, too. Harry from the deli. It was
our private little place," he said, his eyes bright with memories
and merriment. "Did you feel the secrets packed into those little nooks and crannies? There're plenty of them, Rosie my
girl."

And then he kiddingly asked her if she'd found the hidden
bar and explained that Anthony's wife, Mirabella, didn't believe
in evil spirits—which is what they henceforth called their stash
of whiskey. *Evil spirits!* Mario had shouted, his belly shaking
and his raucous laughter echoing in the small office.

Stella had calmed him down, and then congratulated Rose on
how fast she was getting the work done. "Hurrah, Rosie," she'd
said. "So how about dinner tonight? We'll celebrate our first major
success together."

Rose had happily accepted. She gathered up her things and
headed over to the house, plans unfolding in her head. She'd
apply a coat now and leave it to dry overnight. Shower away
the paint and odors. And off to dinner at the Ocean's Edge.

A great celebratory spot, Stella had said.

Rose rested her brush on the edge of the paint can and

looked up at a ship's clock on the bookcase. It was later than she thought. Shadows fell across her canvas tarp and onto her bag. She sat back on her legs and looked once more at the freshly painted sheetrock. Time to finish up. She'd be a little late, but Stell would understand.

Stella seemed to understand everything about Rose in that accepting way of hers. But Stell didn't know everything, and it was bothering her. It hadn't mattered at all when Rose first came into the town, when she was planning to stay just long enough to make things right in herself, *for* herself. But it mattered now. *Stella* mattered. She would talk to her. Soon.

The thought made her feel better, cleaner somehow. She'd head back to the apartment, clean up, and meet her at the restaurant. She was looking forward to sharing her day—and hearing Stella's full-throated laugh when they talked about Uncle Mario's stories and life and the houses waiting to be fixed.

And maybe tonight was the night to bare her soul to someone who had come into her life unexpectedly, and someone whom Rose hoped would stay. No matter what she had to tell her.

She peeled off her work gloves and walked over to close the windows, breathing in the bracing air. Below, waves crashed against the shore, white curls of froth exploding.

Power and glory. Truth and redemption. The last poem her mother had written about the sea. Rose could almost see her, sitting by a window in the sterile hospital room, a smile lighting her sweet face, her spirits rising even as her tiny body was disappearing, reciting her poem out loud. She was somewhere else that day. Her special place. Power and glory. The majesty of the sea.

Suddenly Rose's head jerked. A movement below pulled her close to the window, her palms on the sill, and her eyes peering into the near darkness, searching the grounds below. At first the shadows near the steps appeared to be from the bending branches of the massive old oak trees surrounding the stone patio.

But the shadows began to move across the yard, away from the trees, coming together then moving apart. And finally, as they moved closer, two figures emerged. They moved apart, a wide space between them. One stood stiff and rigid, the other moving, arms lifting and falling.

Rose squinted, trying to see what was happening. The Bianchi family had asked Stella to hire a man to come by each night to make sure things were secure, but it was too early for that. And this was clearly a man and a woman. She frowned, wondering where they had come from and why they were trespassing in such a bold way, as if they owned the place. And then it came to her. Of course. They *did* own the place. They were probably Mr. Bianchi's adult children.

But from the looks of their bodies, the waving arms and loud voices tossed around by the wind, they weren't happy. They were arguing angrily, the man towering over the woman. She couldn't hear words, only angry, hateful voices.

For a minute she thought the man was going to attack the woman, but as Rose watched, she spun around suddenly and walked away, fiercely, as if daring anyone to stop her or come after her. And then she disappeared into the heavily treed property along the side of the house.

The man didn't move.

Rose hadn't explored the property enough to be sure where the woman was headed. But she supposed she was going around to the front of the house. *Is she coming into the house?* The door was locked, but the family might have a key. It was still *their* house. Of course they would have a key.

Her heart began to pound, but she took a deep breath and tried to dispel the anxiety, realizing the foolishness of her thoughts. The family had pressed Stella to have the repairs made. They had every right to be there, but so did she. Maybe they had come to see the progress—or simply to check on the house.

But the thought of being caught in a family argument wasn't

appealing, no matter how proud she was of her work. She reached out to pull the casement window closed, and then she stopped, her fingers frozen around the brass window knob. Her heart pounding wildly in her chest.

The automatic patio lights had gone on, lighting the steps like a stage. And standing in the center of it was a tall man. His hands were in his pockets, his legs apart, as if the earlier anger hadn't happened, or if it had, he had come out the victor. He was looking around the property, his eyes lingering on a guest cottage near a copse of white pines, and then the winding path down to the boathouse.

Suddenly, the man's head swiveled, as if hearing someone near the trees. Then he relaxed again, settling back, his shoulders down as he continued to survey the grounds. Finally he turned around toward the house. His eyes moved across the lighted patio. Then the first story with its curtained mullioned windows, its heavy French doors. Then up to the balconies ringing the second floor.

And finally, resting directly on Rose Chopra's face.

Rose spun away from the window, a small cry escaping her lips.

She looked frantically around the room as if Anthony Bianchi himself might show up, might help her through this. Help her to think clearly. To get away.

But her fear was foolish, ridiculous. Why would he be here, at this house? Tonight? Her memory was playing games with her, her imagination blowing up like a balloon.

She took her phone from the table and stared at it, begging it to tell her whom to call. But she had no reason to call anyone. This wasn't her house; she wasn't the person to report someone on the property. She took a deep breath, then released it slowly as she'd practiced over the years. Then another, and the calm slowly came back into her, moving through her body, finding its way into her limbs and her mind and the shadowy corners of her memory.

What would Patti say? Her friend and therapist had once compared her to a butterfly, slowly emerging from that shy, folded-in person into a glorious spirit.

Don't go back into the cocoon, she'd say. *Your fear—that's your enemy, Rosie. Not people. Face it, cast it out, and don't ever let it back in.*

And she didn't. She wouldn't. Each time it tried to gain entry, she'd push it away. Again and again, whenever fear reared its ugly head.

Logically she knew there was no reason to be afraid. Practically, the house was locked, the elevator was operated with a key. And emotionally, she was finally in charge of herself. She was no longer the child who let others define her.

But deep down Rosie knew the elevator would start. And she knew without question whom she had seen out the back window. And she knew it would finally be okay.

You are Rose, as Patti would say. *And Rose is wonderful, a lovable person. Love her.*

Another breath. She dropped the phone into her backpack and walked quietly across the room to the elevator. Her eyes stayed on the door, knowing that the elevator would soon be ascending.

And then it was, and her ears were ringing as the steady grind of the cables brought the walnut paneled car higher and higher.

Chapter 10

The glow of candlelight turned the Ocean's Edge dining room into an inviting magical place.

The large dining room was crowded tonight, but made intimate with well-placed ficus trees, wood-carved mermaids that lured diners to the high-backed booths, and a sea of white clothed tables. A small piano trio played soft jazz in the lounge. Although it was too chilly to sit outside, the back deck was lit with tiny lights framing the harbor, and a canopy of stars shone down on sailboats and fishing boats, bobbing side by side.

"It truly is magical," Izzy said, as Sam pulled out her chair. "And my favorite season. Well, along with spring. And I love summer. But the smell of burning leaves, the hint of snow in the air—it makes me feel alive."

"Well, you are very alive, my dear," Birdie said, leaning over and kissing her cheek before sitting down. "This weather also gives you reason to wear that amazing coat." Birdie held the edge of Izzy's long cashmere cardigan between her fingers. Izzy had worked on it for months. It was simple and beautiful, with muted navy and gray blocks, and an occasional orange circle placed across the coat willy-nilly. "Bree suggested I add the ping of color—a treat for the eyes, she said."

"She was right. I'd ask you to knit one for me if it wouldn't make me look like a ball of yarn that hadn't yet been worked into a sweater. Purl would have a grand old time trying to unravel me."

They chuckled but no one denied it. The coat needed Izzy's tall, willowy figure to pull it off. Nell looked at the two empty places at the table. "Where are Cass and Danny?" She moved aside as the waitress poured champagne into the flutes.

"Right here," Cass said. She gave Nell a hug. "You know Danny. Had to get that last chapter written."

"So she says," Danny said, taking Cass's coat. "Crazy woman. She insisted we stop by the pier to check on some new lobster traps."

The evening had been planned for several weeks. Although dinners together didn't require reasons, this one was Ben and Nell's idea: a thank-you for no reason. Their treat, they had said. A thank-you for . . . *Just fill in the blanks*, Nell had said. *Gratitude feeds the soul.*

The fact that it had been exactly ten years since Ben Endicott's life-altering heart attack—ten years since the couple upended their too-stressful life on Beacon Hill, retired, and moved to Sea Harbor—hadn't been mentioned anywhere in the invitation. But the fact that the six people gathered around the table had been integral to building their new lives in Sea Harbor—as close and as loving as family could be—rested silently in their hearts. Something to celebrate. Certainly something to be thankful for.

A shadow fell across the table and they looked up into the eyes of Chief Jerry Thompson, dressed in a suit and tie. People did a double take when running into Jerry out of his police chief's uniform, the shiny brass badge catching light. It was like seeing a teacher out of school, buying cabbage in the grocery store. It didn't always compute.

"Just on my way out but wanted to say hello to my good friends," Jerry said. "Also to let you know, Ben, that we're making progress on figuring out where that online piece of crap about the mayor came from."

Ben nodded. He and Jerry had met with Beatrice earlier that day, and in spite of Beatrice's strong and loud assertion that Spencer Paxton III was behind it and that he was trying ruin her life and take her job, there didn't seem to be any proof. But no one denied that someone had it in for her.

"Is there a chance he really does want her job?" Danny asked.

Jerry shrugged. "Rumors. We've all heard them. But as far as I know, there's been nothing official."

"This is so difficult for Beatrice," Nell said. "I guess I'd be upset, too, if someone were digging up the most painful moments of my life and reminding people of them. I wonder if that's what this meeting is that she practically demanded we all attend tomorrow night."

"I'm sure it is," Jerry said. "She insisted I be there, too, probably wanting me to arrest some hidden blogger who maybe lives in India."

They laughed.

"Maybe she just wants our support," Birdie said. "And I for one am happy to give it to her."

They all agreed.

Ben suggested that most of the newsletters probably went into people's spam folders anyway.

"Maybe" Jerry said. "But some folks at the station were saying that once the rumors started, people went back and dug them out of the trash to see what all the fuss was about. Social media can be a nefarious, pretty awful thing if you don't use it right."

"True. People forward things like that," said Sam. "It's the innuendoes that hurt. Why would anyone want to hurt Beatrice? It makes you wonder what's next."

They all resisted the term *fake news*, though that's what many of the links below the photo were. Misconstrued comments the mayor had made, twisted facts that made her look bad.

"Beatrice seems so certain that Spence is involved. She probably overheard something around city hall," Ben said.

"She said as much to me," Jerry said. "And she's usually right about things. Beatrice doesn't lie; she doesn't make up things and not much gets past her. She could be absolutely right, but so far there's nothing that corroborates it."

"If she's right, it explains the way she acted the other day at the club," Nell said.

"But Spence seemed sincere that day, surprised, all those things, right?" Izzy said.

The story had been spun around and around during the weekend, but in every version, Spencer Paxton had come out of it as an unsuspecting innocent.

Izzy went on. "I mentioned the online posts to Bree yesterday and she was genuinely surprised. She hadn't seen any of them. She doesn't do social media, she said. She did mention that Spence isn't savvy with things like that, either. Paxton Development had people who did that sort of thing. Spencer mostly just used his phone for texting."

"What did she say about the confrontation between Spencer and Beatrice?" Danny asked.

Izzy shook her head, her smiling brown eyes reflecting the candlelight. "She didn't know. Can you believe that?" She tilted her head toward Sam. "I don't know what I'd do without you to listen to every thought in my head, but Spence hadn't said a word to Bree about it. Nothing."

"What did she say when you told her?" Nell asked.

"Not much. Well, she said one thing. She said sometimes Spencer had that effect on people."

"That's a little strange," Cass said. "I'm surprised, though, that she didn't know about it."

"Bree doesn't seem to be in the mainstream," Nell said,

"which is probably much nicer for her. Away from rumors. A safer place for sure, especially if your husband happens to be in the middle of the gossip."

"She's an interesting person," Izzy said. "She knows what makes her happy—art and people who just let her be and don't impose on her. Money and looks are definitely not important to her. She's a genuinely nice person. And I think she'd be miserable if she thought her husband was involved in hurting someone like Beatrice."

The police chief stood quietly near Ben's chair, taking in the conversation, looking as if he were trying to sort out some thoughts of his own.

"I'm glad she's escaping the rumors. We should all be so lucky. Unfortunately rumors feed on rumors," Ben said. "People here are good folks, but no one wants to be left out if there's something spinning around at Coffee's or in Jake's bar. But people also want to protect Beatrice. If Paxton is behind this effort to make Beatrice look bad because he wants her job, I think he's already lost."

That sobered everyone, not because this was the end of the world, but because someone they had known for a long time was hurting. And jumping to conclusions either way wasn't going to help.

"It's a muddle, but it will be sorted out," Birdie said. Her eyes, however, looked worried.

Jerry smiled at Birdie with a nod and an understanding smile. "We'll figure it out, Birdie. You're right. We take care of our friends."

When Jerry's cell phone rang, conversation stopped.

He took a step back and pulled it from his pocket, glancing down at the screen. A police chief's bane, they all knew. Never really off duty. Not even when your dinner companion was waiting across the room, chatting with a group of friends but looking forward to a quiet after-dinner evening with her date.

Jerry finished reading the text, then looked around the table, not with a smile or frown, not good news or bad. But with a look of slight surprise. "That was Esther Gibson, who has absolutely convinced me that police dispatchers—at least this one—know everything first. I swear, Esther has a magical power. Here's proof: She has it on reliable sources, she said, that Spencer Paxton III filled out papers to run for mayor of Sea Harbor. They'll be filed tomorrow."

He shook his head and allowed a small smile. "Do you think I should fire Esther? Paxton got the papers on Friday afternoon and our ever-vigilant police dispatcher didn't find out until today—a forty-eight-hour lapse. She's clearly losing her investigative edge."

Then Jerry was gone, shaking his graying head at the strange turn of events as he wove his way through the dining crowd, waving here and there to those who recognized the imposing chief no matter what he was wearing.

Ben looked around the table, his brows arched. "Well," he said.

"Well, indeed," Birdie said.

"Sometimes competition can be energizing," Nell said in an attempt to disguise her surprise. "But it doesn't really matter, it's a small-town election, a job. It's not the end of the world."

But it was the end of Beatrice's world if she lost, or so she had insinuated on the steps of the Sea Harbor Yacht Club.

Chapter 11

It seemed to Rose that the elevator was moving in slow motion, its cables resisting the man inside the box.

Rose stood still, listening to the sounds, her eyes held fast on the elevator doors. She practiced her breathing, and then she begged her mother, wherever she was, to stand steadfast by her side.

And Christopher Robin, too.

She needed them to be with her. To send good vibes. *You are braver than you believe, stronger than you seem, smarter than you think . . .*

The mantra hummed in her head, once, twice, and again, even as the elevator sounds grew louder.

Stand firm and tall, Rosie Woodley, she murmured to herself. No fainting. No second thoughts. It was why she had come, after all. Finally.

A sense of relief swept through her, as bracing as a shower—and every bit as cleansing.

The cables lurched as the locks engaged. A shudder. Then silence.

And then the doors slid open.

The man was startled at first when he stepped off the elevator and stared directly into the eyes of a woman just a few yards away, facing him. A stranger in jeans and a messy T-shirt, a tight ponytail and a calm oval face. Neither beautiful nor ugly. Plain. Forgettable.

Immediately the muscles in his face tightened. He flicked a spec of elevator dust off his jacket and stared at her. "Who are you and what do you think you're doing here?" His voice was demanding. Harsh. "This is private property. I'll call the police." His hand went to his pocket, then stopped.

Rose said nothing, waiting. For what, she wasn't sure. For him to say something to her? To recognize her? To apologize?

Finally, she looked directly into his eyes, locking him to her. Forcing him to look at her. And look and look.

"Do you remember me?" she finally asked.

He leaned his head to one side, then back. Looking. He took a step closer, stopping a foot or two away from her, his eyes hard. He scanned every inch of her with cold eyes, up and down and up again, finally settling soundly on her unremarkable face. There was no flicker of recognition as he continued to stare.

Rose felt assaulted, but she held firm.

Finally, after the silence was almost more than Rose could bear, the man broke into it with a harsh laugh. "Okay, lady. I give. Tell me why I would ever remember someone like you."

His tone spoke to all the reasons why he wouldn't remember someone like her. Rose breathed in, then out. And then she told him why he *should* remember her.

When her voice reached her ears, she was amazed at how remarkably steady and calm it was, as if she were telling a story to a class of youngsters, an interesting tale with a beginning, a middle, and an end. And with each chapter in her story, Rose grew more distant from it, released from its power.

She told Spencer Paxton III that he *should* remember her because, after all, she had provided him with days of fun and laughter when she was a shy and chubby kid in Sea Harbor. When her well-intentioned mother, anxious for her beloved daughter to have friends, had signed her up for swimming and sailing classes at the yacht club each summer, the last place on earth Rose wanted to be. Those years when girls like her were quiet and hesitant— and unnoticed if they were lucky. When she was fragile, unsure of herself and where she fit into life.

And then she carefully explained to Spencer what his role was in that life, a role he played out magnificently.

"You stepped in and took it upon yourself to help me out, to mold that image I was forming of myself." He—the tall, handsome, entitled kid who captained the sailing team, threw a football like Tom Brady, who managed to manipulate a win in every class election.

Spencer started to say something, then stood back, his arms crossed, his stance relaxed, as if enjoying some kind of play.

"You were the one who teased and taunted me in order to entertain your friends, to make them laugh and to puff yourself up, the coward's way to feeling important.

"You were that young, privileged boy who thought bullying was your birthright and a solid part of that privilege." Rose paused, her look unwavering.

And then she said, "You were wrong."

Spencer stood still as she talked, a slight frown creasing his tan forehead, as if curious what would come next—and with another part of his brain, trying to place this deranged woman in his life.

Rose went on, reminding him of how he had noticed her in his summer sailing class, the girl who disguised her chubby-sized suit with a towel, the towel he had pulled off her like a magician would do and joked about her stomach rolling like the waves during a nor'easter.

About how he had directed her to the starboard side of the boat while moving the rest of the sailing class to port, insisting it was the only way to balance it. And how he had waited far too long to let someone throw a tube to her when she fell over the side one day. But those were only the tip of the iceberg, Rose said.

And she reminded him how he had gathered his friends outside the school to poke fun at the tall, overweight girl who was out of breath from doing calisthenics with the other girls, who couldn't climb the rope ladder and had trouble manipulating the climbing wall.

Suddenly, when Rose paused briefly, an odd look came into his eyes. He held up one hand, as if he'd finally finished a difficult puzzle, the last piece falling into place with a clunk that startled him.

The first words out of his mouth were loud and profane, and the next ones a surprise to Rose.

"*Math Olympiad,*" he said, nearly spitting the words out. His eyes narrowed with scorn, and then turned to anger as his memory cleared.

Rose stared back, startled and confused. And then a light turned on in her own eyes and she remembered, too. *Math Olympiad.*

She forced calmness into her voice, a new understanding washing over her. "Good grief. Yes. I remember now. Math Olympiad. I. Won. Two of us won. Another girl and I won. We beat you," she said, her voice lifting. "You lost that day, Spencer Paxton—in front of the entire school."

"You're a liar, you stupid broad. You both lied. Everyone knew it. Everyone talked about it. The medal was mine."

Rose had almost forgotten about the math program, about winning the competition. How easy it was to remember with such precision the damage that had been done to her by this man. But the awards—the happy times in her life back then—were so easily pushed to the shadowy part of her mind.

But now, with Spencer as the catalyst, it all came back to her. It was May, the end of the school year.

Everyone—students, faculty, and family members—had gathered in the school auditorium that day to support the Math Olympiad contestants and cheer the winners. High school students, and one student from the middle school, from the gifted math class. Rose Woodley.

The whole crowd had watched with interest as three students made it to the final grueling round: two quiet, plain girls—one the youngest in the competition—and another, a tall, self-assured boy who grinned at his friends as he walked out on the stage, waved to his parents, and gave the entire audience a thumbs-up sign.

And that's when it all went down. In less time than Rose could remember, the two girls soundly and convincingly defeated Spencer Paxton III—becoming the contest's first dual champions. First female champions. Rose remembered it all now, a blush coloring her cheeks.

And then it had happened. Spencer's classmates in the audience had giggled, the sound rippling through the audience. And then others joined in and it got louder and louder until finally Mr. Pritchard, the moderator, stood up and waved the air down with his palms, quieting the noise, his face beet red as he proclaimed the day a success, and weren't the kids all wonderful? All thirty of them. Champions for sure.

Every single one.

Rose's mouth dropped open, putting it all together in her head.

That's when it had all begun in earnest, she realized now. She hadn't been the only one Spencer and his friends picked on when they would see her around town and at the beach, and on the middle- and high school campuses. But with her victory that day, it had accelerated into a thunderstorm of shaming and embarrassment that went on that whole summer. And that awful, terrible freshman year when the bullying got worse. The year she wanted to hurt herself, to erase the image that others saw. The image she came to hate, and the one that had taken years and heartache and hard work, meditation and yoga and therapy, to repair and wash it all away.

But now, on this day, it was finally over.

No sooner had the police chief left Ben and Nell's table at the Ocean's Edge, than a pleasant waitress approached with an hors d'oeuvre tray filled with the Ocean Edge's specialties, including roasted figs with prosciutto, salmon and crème fraîche blini, arancini with almond pesto. Danny and Sam raised crooked brows at the fancy fare, claiming they never ate food whose names they couldn't pronounce. Instead they greedily scooped up several deviled eggs with salmon, and the basket of calamari.

"We're simple men," Danny explained and offered Cass a bite of his egg. "I grew up on pigs in a blanket. Amazing."

Soon the delicate flavors of the appetizers had shuffled the talk of politics to the side, and the dining group turned to more pleasant things, laughing and toasting and reveling in the news that Izzy and Sam's little Abby was learning her letters, and Birdie's granddaughter was earning more ice-skating medals than she could fit on her backpack, that next week would be perfect for apple picking, and that the Fractured Fish were playing for a party on the Harriet Webster Pier at the Maritime Gloucester museum.

And all the while leaving the world's problems—and even tiny Sea Harbor's—temporarily out to sea.

Appetizers were followed by plates of tender pork tenderloin with fresh apple chutney, warm chunks of sourdough and corn bread—and toasts to Nell and Ben's ten-year anniversary in Sea Harbor, which hadn't been forgotten by any of them, no matter what their hosts had thought and how cagey they had tried to be.

As Danny pushed his chair back to take a breather, he spotted Stella Palazola, sitting alone at a table for two, staring at her phone with a studious look on her face. "Hey, there's Stella," he said. "She looks very spiffy tonight. But it looks like she's all alone. We can't let that happen." He started to push back his chair.

"Maybe she's waiting for someone. A date?" Izzy said. She checked her watch. "But it's kinda late."

"Geesh, I hope no one stood her up."

As if sensing their looks, Stella looked up from her phone and spotted them looking her way. She quickly abandoned her table, walking over with her phone still in her hand.

"Hey. Hi, everyone. I didn't see you sitting over here." She tried for a smile that quickly failed, and replaced it with a worried expression, aiming it at Izzy. "Iz, have you seen Rose today?"

"Sure. I saw her this morning. She said she had a full day of work ahead of her. And she described it as if she were going on a cruise to Hawaii instead of fixing up an old house. She's loving this work, Stella. And she thinks you're pretty great. You must pay well."

Stella didn't seem to hear the compliment or the tease. "But you haven't seen her since then?"

Izzy shook her head.

"Is something wrong, dear?" Birdie asked.

"It's probably a miscommunication. We were supposed to meet here about an hour ago for dinner." She checked her watch. "More than that, really. We were going to celebrate her new job, my new employee. Good things. But she hasn't shown up."

"You called her?"

Stella nodded. "Maybe she didn't see my texts or she forgot to take her ph—" The sudden sound of a phone message stopped her words and the worry lifted for a brief second as she studied the screen. But when she looked up again, her face was pale, her expression unreadable. She held up her phone.

"This is about a house listing I have. I . . . I really need to go," she said, and without explanation or her usual bright smile, she grabbed her purse and hurried through the maze of tables until she had disappeared from their sight.

Chapter 12

It wasn't until Rose had stepped off the elevator and rushed out of the house and through the gate that she realized she had left her backpack inside. Her car keys. Her wallet.

She stood for a minute, staring back at the house and the front door that had swung closed and locked behind her. Her eyes moving up to the third-floor room.

The shuffle of leaves on the side of the house startled her. An innocent squirrel, she thought. Or a neighborhood cat.

Fear, be gone, she commanded. *There's no room for you here.* And her body obeyed.

No, she couldn't go back in, not now. With a farewell glance at the house, she turned and began walking down the winding street, finding herself smiling into the crisp fall night. *Smiling*.

She looked across the street at the sound of bicycle wheels crunching leaves. A nice, normal sound. She wondered briefly if the woman she had seen earlier had left on a bicycle and was coming back. But the hunched-over figure was too long, the bike a collection of aluminum angles in the dark night. Then the biker rode beneath an old lamplight and she saw a flash of bright orange handlebars.

Rose squinted, wishing she had her old glasses on instead of the contacts that sometimes failed her. The man on the bike looked familiar. Or at least the hair was familiar—light colored and flying beneath the helmet. Thinking she'd seen the man before, she started to raise her hand in the air, to wave.

Then she realized she couldn't really see much at all. The colors of the bike and the hair. Not to mention that it was dark out, the rider had a helmet on, and in the dark night she could barely spot the color of the cars on the other side of the street.

It was wishful thinking. She wanted it to be someone she knew. Someone friendly who would say *Hi, need help?* Perhaps he'd have a phone and she could use it to call Stell.

It was a moot point anyway; at that moment the man lowered his head and sped up, crossing over to the other side of the street. Heading in the direction of the house she'd just left. Then disappearing in the dark shadows of the night.

Rose watched for a minute more, then turned and walked quickly away, past the elaborate homes and the wrought iron fences, the low granite walls, until the street sloped down to the sea and she came to a rocky stretch of shore.

Above the water a white moon was taking its place among a blanket of stars. She continued walking along the gravelly shore until the rocks grew bigger, huge granite boulders flung from some giant's hand and trailing out to sea. She walked out toward a smaller boulder, balancing one foot on an outcropping and pulling herself up to the top, then walking farther out as the boulders grew larger, reaching up to the moon. She continued on, one boulder after another, oblivious to the cold spray of the sea, the salty drops clinging to her ponytail. Small tide pools formed in the crevices along her way and she dipped the toe of her sneaker in one, then stepped across and moved on until she couldn't go any farther. A smooth spot on the last boulder provided a comfortable seat, and she sat down, nearly surrounded now by the sea.

In the distance the lights of the harbor were visible. She

pulled up the hood of her sweatshirt and wrapped her arms around her knees. Strands of damp hair crossed her forehead, and her eyes were bright from the sting of the sea.

She looked out over the water for as far as she could see, tiny lights appearing here and there, the black sky and sea becoming one.

Power. Majesty. The mystery of the sea. This was it, what her mother had loved her whole life long. What fed her spirit and lifted her soul.

Rose smiled out into the dark, lovely night. "For you, Mom," she murmured. And then she picked up a handful of loose rocks and tossed them, one by one by one, into the black water below, sending them to the bottom of the sea.

Hours later, Rose finally made it back to the yarn shop, thoughts of the cozy apartment and Purl's soft purr—and Stella— quickening her step.

At one point, after climbing off the boulders and back onto land, she had taken a wrong turn and ended up walking along a stretch of smooth beach where a late-night group of partiers had built a bonfire and sat around it in warm fleeces and blankets, singing old songs, their bodies close and intimate.

She stood at a distance, invisible in the dark night, and soaked in their ease and friendship, dancing figures lit by the fire.

Far away a siren had blared, its piercing sound nearly overpowered by the comforting, happy sounds so close to her that she felt a part of them.

Finally she began walking again, toward the faint lights of Harbor Road.

Downtown was quiet at this late hour, with just a few stray revelers making their way home. She stood for a minute in front of Izzy's yarn shop, then walked around to the gravel alley, lit at the end by two spotlights and large chunky boulders that warned drivers to stop. Beyond the rocky barrier the land dropped away to the sea. The waves were gentle now, lapping against the rocks as the tide went out. A peaceful sound that seemed to rise up inside of her.

She yearned for her mother, to tell her that at last she understood her mother's love affair with the sea.

She walked over to the steps and slowly made her way to the top. To the cozy apartment and Purl, who would be waiting on the windowsill just inside the door, ready to scold her for coming home so late.

She wished she had her phone so she could have called Stella earlier, to tell her not to worry. To let her know that her prospective home buyer had decided to take himself on an early tour of the house. But the house was fine. It would finally all be fine.

And could we reschedule the dinner? My treat this time.

As she neared the top, she stopped. Her fingers tightened on the rail and her breath froze. She stared into the shadows.

A huddled form sat motionless on the platform beside the door. Rose stared into the darkness as the figure began to pull itself up.

A moan filled the air as strong, quivering arms reached out and pulled Rose close.

"Oh Rosie, Rosie, you're safe." Stella Palazola clung tightly to her friend, sobbing uncontrollably into the fabric of Rose's sodden hoodie.

Chapter 13

It was Birdie who couldn't let go of the look on Stella's face and her sudden departure from the restaurant the night before.

And it was Birdie who showed up at the Endicotts' the next morning, bringing her concern with her.

Nell was sitting at the kitchen island reading the paper, the coffee gurgling in the background and the smell of scones in the oven. Ben was standing at the window, gauging the direction of the wind for a sail and checking his cell phone messages.

Birdie slipped off her jacket and hung it across the back of a stool.

"Have you heard anything from anyone?" she asked.

"Stella?" Nell asked. She'd been expecting a morning call from Birdie, telling her everything was fine. Some kids crawled through a window in an empty house Stella was listing, or someone decided not to sell their house after all. People selling their homes often exaggerated emergencies.

At first, they had all been relieved when Stella had muttered her brief explanation the night before. Problems with a house listing could surely be easily resolved. It was problems with people that caused true concern.

But when Nell and Ben dropped Birdie off later that night, she had shared her feeling that Stella's behavior indicated something else, and reminded them of an incident when Stella first joined her uncle's company. It was one of her first listings, and the house had burned down the day she'd received an offer on it. Stella had handled the whole thing with a calmness that was extraordinary—and even a trace of pride in herself, knowing how well she handled emergencies. It had impressed them all.

"Stella doesn't frazzle easily," Birdie said. "I called her before I went to bed last night, but she didn't pick up." She wrapped her cold fingers around the cup of coffee Ben handed her. "I know something's wrong. I know it right here." She pressed a palm over her heart and looked up at Ben. "What do you know, Ben?"

Ben was checking the scones in the oven. He closed the door and chucked the oven mitts onto the counter. "Birdie, you give me way too much credit. Any earthshaking news I hear is from you and Nell or Izzy and Cass."

But Nell sided with Birdie. Ben *did* know a lot, especially when it involved areas they might not have access to. Like the police chief's cell phone. "You've been checking your phone more than usual for this hour of the morning," she said to him.

"Just getting my day in order," he said, looking down as another message came in. He read it and shook his head. "See? That's why I check it. My whole morning just opened up."

"Aren't you and the chief going sailing?" Nell asked.

"*Were*," he said. "This is a group text from the secretary down at the station. She's clearing his schedule for the whole day. He must have some kind of bug. I hope he's not sick from something he ate last night."

"Of course he isn't," Birdie said, straightening her back. "Police chiefs don't get sick, and especially not from eating at the Ocean's Edge."

Nell agreed, at least about the food poisoning. She reached for the newspaper again and began to scan headlines and the local hospital and police reports to find an event that might cause Jerry to cancel a morning sail. But the most she could come up with was a mother and her twins being locked in a toy store all night—the children's dream come true—and a side story about a fisherman being pecked by an angry gull.

But something wasn't right, and Birdie's mood had somehow made its way into her.

Ben watched Birdie and Nell communicate the way they often did, without the need for words. They both had an uncanny sense of when the universe was tilting in the wrong direction. He knew never to disregard their feelings.

He walked away from the kitchen island and across the family room, then put in a call to Jerry Thompson. *Maybe he'd want to reschedule the sail?* Or maybe Birdie and Nell were right.

"I couldn't sleep last night," Birdie said to Nell, pulling herself up on a stool, her feet just reaching the rung. She poured another stream of half-and-half into her mug and stirred it slowly. "Stella Palazola is one of the sweetest, most unflappable young women I know. You know that, too, Nell. I don't want to make mountains out of molehills, but I'll feel better when she answers her phone."

"She did seem concerned last night, but her house listings are probably like kids to her. She needs to take care of them, especially if the sellers have already moved out. Empty houses can be prey to all sorts of things. But even so, at least an empty house is exactly that, empty. And people aren't in danger. Besides, I think we'd have heard if she needed us or if something had happened." Nell realized she was rambling, so she stopped and looked out the window at a parade of clouds skittering across a blue sky. Her words sounded vacant, even to her. Made-up words to ease worry.

The evening at the Ocean's Edge had been a lovely one, and yet she had had trouble sleeping, too. She'd heard noises in the night, branches slapping against the side of the house and shutters rattling. And farther away, floating up from the beach, were more noises, not ominous, not portending danger, but intruding on sleep. She had smelled smoke from a bonfire when she'd closed the bedroom window, and suspected a final beach party was in full swing. Fireworks sizzling up into the sky, and a fire on the beach keeping everyone warm. The beach gatherings were a weekend staple until the weather finally said *no more*. As she crawled into bed, something had cut through the partying sounds. A shrill, piercing sound. But she'd told herself it was probably an illegal bottle rocket that was whistling its way over the water. Shrill and piercing.

Like a siren.

She looked up and saw Birdie's mind sorting through things, too, calming her mind.

And at the other end of the airy living space, Ben stood still, one elbow leaning on the fireplace mantel and a phone pressed to his ear. He wasn't saying much, but his face was serious and attentive to whatever he was hearing.

Finally he walked back across the room, shaking his head once, as if to himself. Clearing his thoughts. He put his palms flat on the island and looked across to a quiet Birdie, who waited for him to speak.

"Birdie, never, ever will I doubt your intuition. Nor Nell's."

Birdie refrained from saying *Of course you won't*. Instead she nodded as if to give him permission, as if to say, *It's all right, dear Ben. You can tell us.*

Nell put her coffee down and twisted her wedding ring around her finger, waiting.

Ben sighed, then said, "The good news is that Jerry Thompson didn't get food poisoning at the Ocean's Edge last night."

"Of course he didn't," Birdie said softly. "Go on, Ben."

"And Stella is fine."

Birdie's small chest rose and fell in relief.

Nell looked at the sadness in Ben's deep brown eyes. She walked around the island and touched his arm. "But there's more," she said softly, and he nodded.

"The sad news is that a security guard Stella had hired found a body on the top floor of one of her new listings, one of those big houses out on Cliffside Drive."

For a few minutes, the only sound was the coffeepot gurgling and the steady swing of the pendulum in a grandfather clock.

A body. So impersonal. Nell said a silent prayer it would stay that way. *Impersonal, removed, someone I don't know and would never know. Someone completely removed from everyone I love.* A selfish wish, but a very fervent one.

"That's why the security guard called Stella at the restaurant." Birdie spoke into the silence, ignoring the obvious question and connecting two dots instead.

"Yes. He saw lights, so he went in to check. The door was locked, but Stella had given him a set of keys. He found the body on the third floor of the house."

"Did he know who it was?"

"Not the security guard, no. But the police knew immediately. It was Spencer Paxton. He's dead."

Chapter 14

Ben waited for the news of a death to land with a crashing thud, then soften into an emotional reality when words would once again have meaning. Nell's wish lay empty. It wasn't a stranger or someone far removed from their lives. That would be sad, but easier to absorb.

The fact that Spencer hadn't died of a heart attack or a fall hadn't been spoken out loud, but even before Ben spelled it out, they knew it wasn't a natural death. Ben's face said as much. They knew that Spencer Paxton had been murdered.

The police were holding the details tight, Ben told them. They hadn't been able to get in touch with Spencer's wife last night. And although the usual police-chasing reporters had shown up at the Cliffside house, they were kept at a distance.

"No statement will be released until they talk to next of kin," Ben said. "That's why there was nothing in the news today. Most likely there will be a statement later today or first thing tomorrow."

"Stella went out to the house right away, as we know. She didn't know until she got there that someone had been killed.

The police got the necessary information from her—her connection to the house, phone numbers of the owners, things like that—and then Tommy Porter sent her home and told her to get some sleep. There was a lot of work to do around the crime scene and he or Jerry would talk to her more today."

"Did she see him?" Nell asked, praying the answer was no.

"No," said Ben.

Birdie looked up. "How did he die, Ben?"

"He was hit with a pipe wrench. Several times."

Ben didn't go into detail, but he didn't need to. Spencer Paxton was beaten badly enough for the police to want to protect his wife. *Bludgeoned* was the word that came to mind.

"Father Northcutt went over. I don't know if Spencer was religious but it doesn't matter to Father Larry. Sometimes I think he goes to help the policemen who have to deal with grisly scenes, to give some prayer or blessing that will help erase the horror they see."

"But Stella was saved from that," Birdie said, reassuring herself. Stella was a strong woman, but she was also young.

"Yes, Stella is doing okay," Ben assured Birdie again. "You'll be able to see for yourself shortly."

"She's coming over here?" Nell asked.

"She was at the station when I talked to Jerry. Stella insisted that the police not worry her mother, but as you'd expect, she was pretty shaken by it all. Jerry knew I'd been helping her with the business, so he suggested she come over here. In addition to the shock of it, she's concerned about her responsibility as the Realtor. It was her listing, she had a contract with the owner. She's probably worried about some of the legalities." He looked at Birdie. "She'd called your house first, Birdie. She was glad to know you are here."

Nell walked over to the sink and poured glasses of water. Birdie had said Stella was unflappable, but would that be enough to get her through something like this? Stella had a million friends, but no one special in her life as far as Nell knew. She suspected her confidants were few.

"Why was Spence in the house?" Nell asked, passing around the water. "Which house was it?"

"It's the old Bianchi house over on Cliffside Drive. He wanted to buy it."

"To buy it? That's an extraordinary place," Nell said. She and Izzy often jogged by, pushing Abby's stroller up the hilly road. They were both taken by its grandeur, but agreed that it wasn't the kind of house they'd be comfortable in alone. Maybe not even with a whole roomful of people.

Birdie's estate was nearly as large, but her home was filled with cozy corners, open windows, soft lighting, and low-slung, slipcovered furniture—the kind that welcomed you to sit and stay awhile. The Favazza place had a sense of home that she suspected the Bianchi house would have trouble achieving.

"The listing is a feather in Stella's cap," Ben said. "She was rightfully proud when she got it. The Bianchi kids live in California, so they're depending on her to handle everything. Palazola Realty was looking to profit nicely from the sale."

Nell leaned against the counter as she listened, fitting Spencer's death into the last couple days. "Poor Bree," she said. "I wonder if Izzy or Jane Brewster know. I think they know Bree better than most of us."

"They couldn't locate Bree last night. But Jerry said someone was going out today to that Canary Cove home they're renting."

"This will be so awful for her." Nell tried to picture Bree and Spencer and realized that she had rarely seen the couple together. Fancy events mostly, where they'd be noticed immediately, a couple so handsome and youthful it was difficult not to stare. Bree brightened up the room with her beauty, but she often seemed to disappear as soon as she politely could. She'd told them at the shop one day that she didn't like to dress up, a surprising admission from someone so lovely.

Birdie watched Nell as her thoughts were mirrored in her face. The worry for everyone involved in Spencer Paxton's death.

Ben watched, too, knowing that Birdie and Nell only knew half of it, not the whole complicated story that would soon weave its uncomfortable tentacles around them.

A minute later the doorbell rang, a foreign sound in Nell and Ben's home, where close friends didn't know they had a bell at the door.

"That's Stella," Ben said. He headed across the room, calling back to ask Nell to put more coffee on and take the scones out of the oven. Fortunately he'd doubled the recipe.

He reappeared with a hollow-eyed Stella at his side.

And a surprise.

A step behind her was Rose Chopra. Neither looked like they had had a minute of sleep.

When Stella spotted Birdie, her face lifted and she was around the island in a second, wrapping her arms around her until Birdie disappeared, except for a small tuft of silvery hair sticking up against Stella's shirt.

Rose stood off to the side, uncomfortable and looking as if her world was spinning out from beneath her. She looked at Nell with an expression that begged for understanding—and maybe something more.

Nell frowned, unsure of the message. But she was relieved to see her. Stella had been worried about her last night at the restaurant, but wherever she had been, she was here now, safe, and except for the look on her face, seemingly fine.

Then it dawned on Nell. Rose had been repairing something in the Bianchi house. *Of course.* Both Rose and Stella were having to deal with the tragic event.

"Well," Ben said, rubbing his hands in front of him. "First

things first, ladies. Coffee, and these scones are probably the best I've ever made."

Nell noticed that Ben's smile went to Rose, as if she needed comfort more than anyone in the room, including Stella Palazola.

The large kitchen island had room and stools for all of them, with Nell standing on one side because she found that she couldn't sit. Not yet. Not with all the emotions and questions silently flying around them.

Stella found it difficult to wait and she started talking, her scone and coffee cooling in front of her. She was sitting next to Rose and her look often went in her direction.

"When I got that message at the restaurant, the only thing I could think of was Rosie. The text and the fact that she hadn't shown up were connected. Sometimes you just know those things. I knew it—and I was frantic, crazy, that something had happened to her."

She looked at Rose, the worry still there in her eyes. "I knew she'd been working at the Bianchi place yesterday—"

Nell looked up. So Rose had been at the house. How frightening. Did she see anyone around the property? Did she see Spencer himself? But she kept silent, sensing it was important to Stella to get her story out as it happened, in her own words.

"The Bianchi kids who inherited the house wanted me to fix something that had happened up on the top floor of the house. It was awful. Dead squirrels," she said, raising eyebrows around the kitchen, but she continued without explanation. "It had to be fixed before we could show the house. The smell was awful and the family agreed, and that was about the time you all dropped wonderful Rosie in my lap. She agreed to help fix the problem for me, and quickly." Stella looked down at her hands, twisting a ring around her finger, then looked up again and said apologetically, "Uncle Mario's firm is doing fine, really, but the commission on this house would help us tremendously in paying off some debts. And Rosie was doing her best to help us get it sold."

She looked again at Rose, biting down on her bottom lip, her face filled with emotion.

Nell looked at Ben. She could read his mind. He, too, wanted to help Stella unravel the story more quickly. But Stella needed to do this herself. There was healing in sharing it, and however long it might take, they had the time.

"It was all working, all going according to plan. We even had a couple other queries about the house, though I had told Spencer he was first in line. The thought of other interested parties upset him, I guess. He asked for a key a few days ago. I wasn't going to do it, sure. But he didn't like people saying no to him and he raised a fuss, and Uncle Mario told me to give him the blankety-blank keys. Whatever he wanted. So I did. Uncle Mario was sure it was the right thing to do, but now . . . now I'm so sorry I did that." She looked at Rose again, and her eyes were damp.

Rose hadn't said a word. She picked at her scone, and drank the glass of water Nell handed to her.

Stella's story was unraveling in ways that were difficult to follow. She was speaking more to Rose than to the whole group. Apology after apology for getting her into this mess.

Finally, to pull them back on track, Birdie spoke to Rose, her voice comfortable and easy, the voice that made people feel they were all alone with Birdie in some protective, safe place. Stella called it Birdie's church confessional voice.

"Rose," she said, "were you at the house last night?" The question wasn't specific, but Birdie knew Rose understood what was being asked. Was she there when Spencer Paxton came into the house? Was he alone? Why did he come up to the top floor?

Rose nodded. "I was just finishing up. I went to close the window and that's when I saw them. They were out on the back patio. I was surprised to see anyone out there. I thought they were trespassing, but I didn't think too much about it. The house was on the market and people knew it was empty. People snoop."

"Them?" Birdie asked.

"There was a man and a woman. But she left."

"And he came upstairs?"

"Yes." Rose looked down at the floor. "I heard the front door open."

"He came up to the third floor?"

She nodded. "He came up on the elevator. I heard it moving, and I was frightened. He was upset when he saw me. He said it was *his* house. He owned it. But I knew, well, I didn't think he owned it, not yet, anyway. Stella and I were getting it ready to sell." She looked down at her coffee cup.

Nell watched Rose closely. Her voice was careful, as if she were reading from a book but skipping some paragraphs.

"Can you imagine how frightened she must have been?" Stella asked. "A man comes into that huge house and she was there all alone? He . . . he threatened her. Said he'd call the police. Oh, Rose, I am so sorry you had to go through that." Her large, sorrowful eyes went to Rose again. Then back to the others. "I'm so grateful she got out before . . . before anything happened. But she left in such a hurry—wouldn't you?—that she forgot her backpack. Her car keys, her phone, everything. It was dark by then, and she had to walk all the way back to Izzy's shop apartment, all alone."

"It's okay, Stell. I didn't mind walking," Rose said quickly. "I . . . I liked it. I like walking. It gave me time to calm down. It was all fine. But you . . . you needed this sale, Stell—and now . . ."

And now the buyer is dead.

Looks passed back and forth between Rose and Stella, each one blaming herself for complicating the other's life. Each one sorry the other was upset or scared, or losing a commission.

Nell looked at Birdie and read her thoughts. It was nice they were caring for each other, but Nell and Birdie both suspected that it was Rose Chopra's life that would be impacted more. And in ways not easily repaired.

"Do you think the woman who had been with him was still around when you left?" Ben asked. "Did you notice her outside?"

Rose considered the question, then shook her head. "I thought I heard a car drive away, but I suppose it could have been a car driving by. But, no. I didn't see her when I walked away. I didn't see anyone." She stopped and thought again. "Well, one person. It was dark, but I saw a guy ride by on a bike as I was walking off in the other direction. That was it."

Stella looked at Ben. "Ben—is there any way you can help Rosie? She needs to get her things back, but Tommy Porter told me today that they needed to keep them. Why?" There was a note of desperation in her voice, as if getting her car keys or wallet back would solve all Rose's problems.

Even though they all knew it wouldn't.

"I'll be okay," Rose said.

Nell looked over at Ben. Stella was right. Practically speaking, Rose would need identification and keys. And without a cell phone? It might be a relief sometimes, but still difficult.

Before answering the question, Ben asked another. "Rose, have you talked to the police yet?"

Jerry hadn't mentioned interviewing Rose when they'd talked on the phone. The thought was troublesome. He didn't want to overstep anything that was the purview of the police department.

Stella answered before Rose had a chance. "She did. They did. They talked. After I told Rose what had happened, Rose said she'd better go with me today, to fill in her part of the night's events. She wanted Chief Thompson to know that she was there and what she saw. And, I guess, what she didn't see. Like who did this to him."

Stella's eyes got bigger as she spoke, her glasses clouding.

Ben smiled at Stella, who looked like she needed to curl up in their guest room and get some sleep. And then he said to Rose, "Let's see what we can do about your things, Rose. The problem is that the room—the whole property—is a crime scene right now. It may take a while, but I'll check to see if we can at least get your keys and wallet back. The police's first priority is finding out who did this but they're not unreasonable."

Rose nodded. "I'll be okay, Ben. But thanks. You're very kind."

"Did you recognize the woman Spencer was talking to outside?"

"I didn't know who it was. I was looking from the third-floor window and they were way out at the edge of the patio. At first I thought it was the Bianchis. You know, the family members who were selling the house. It looked like they were arguing about something. Then the woman left."

"Do you know where she went?"

"I wasn't sure. I haven't walked around the property so I don't really know what's there. All I know is that it's a large estate, so she could have walked off near the guest house. But a few minutes later I thought I heard a car start up. I think she left."

"So then Spencer came upstairs alone," Birdie said, confirming the sequence. Then she frowned. "Why do you suppose he went up to the third floor?"

"He looked up toward the third-floor window—probably because it was lit up and the rest of the house was dark. He saw me standing there. I think he came up because he wanted to know why someone was in the house."

"So the person who killed him must have come upstairs after you left," Nell said.

Rose nodded. And then she frowned. "But you need a key to work the elevator. The person who came up would have needed it. And the front door, too. I heard it lock as I left."

They all listened, wondering how easily elevator keys were to come by.

"That will be helpful to the police," Ben said. "You are able to give them a framework—a time line."

But it was the other information that Rose had given the police that was worrisome: the fact that she was the last person who had seen him alive. At least the last one anyone knew of.

Birdie looked over at Stella and saw the gravity of the situation sinking in. Her face was filled with sadness and regret, and then with affection for this woman whose life was going to be complicated for a while. Rose had been in absolutely the wrong place at the wrong time. And it was because Stella had asked her to be there.

"You've both already helped the police out," Ben said, sensing the emotion building. "It takes a lot to put the pieces together when something like this happens. But Jerry's team will figure it out and you two shouldn't worry. They'll find out who killed Spencer Paxton, and hopefully we'll put this behind us soon."

Stella finally ate one of the pieces of scone she'd been playing with on her plate. She looked at Ben. "I was so worried about Rose that I didn't even give much thought to the fact that someone actually killed someone else. And in that very room where Rosie had been working. It's terrifying. It's hard to grasp when it's someone you recently talked to—and then . . . and then that someone is dead."

Stella seemed to be absorbing the facts as she spoke them, her voice rising and falling with her words. "I didn't know the guy very well, but I can't imagine anyone wanting him dead."

No one said anything. Ben refilled coffee mugs and passed the cream around.

But Stella's comment echoed in the room. It hovered heavily in the scone-scented kitchen air.

And they knew that given pen and paper, they could put together a list of people who had reasons to want Spencer dead in less time than it'd take for their coffee to cool.

And it was possible they might even be missing one or two.

Chapter 15

Nell looked around at the small houses on the hill above Canary Cove. It was peaceful. Postcard pretty. Golden and ruby-red leaves fell in slow motion to patches of still-green grass. Above, a blue sapphire sky spread out forever, a giant comforter, and up and down the hilly street shutters and house doors were painted in joyful, living colors that spoke to life.

It was a disturbing contrast to why they were there.

The power of death, Nell thought as they walked up to the bright green door. It strips the day of color and sounds that bring joy—the songs of birds, the bright laughter of children. It mutes the life it leaves behind and turns it gray.

Beside her, Birdie pressed the doorbell and they both gave a small jolt. The sound was shrill and deafening, scattering three gulls patrolling a garbage can next door.

Nell nearly dropped the basket of comfort food she'd hastily put together, the jar of jam clattering against a container of noodle soup.

"I hope there's no one sleeping within a block or so," Birdie said apologetically, glaring accusingly at the round button. She held back a comment about it waking the dead.

But Izzy didn't. She opened the door instantly from the inside and said, "I know—it's loud enough to wake the dead." She ushered them into the entryway and closed the door. "I'm so glad it's you two. I keep thinking some reporter is going to show up and I'll say bad things to him."

"Ben says the news is still under wraps," Nell said. "People know there was an accident at the Bianchi house, but that's about it. How's Bree doing?"

"She's painting."

"Oh?" Birdie said, at first surprised. Then walking it back. Of course she was painting. She was a painter. That was exactly what she should be doing.

"I'm like that, too," Izzy said. "Well, not painting. But when I'm worried or upset or think Abby's stomachache needs a trip to the Mayo Clinic, I knit."

"We all need a safe place to go to when times are rough," Nell said. "Today definitely qualifies."

"It's such a sudden, unexpected death," Birdie said. "And then to pile the tragedy of murder on top of that—a tragedy *and* a crime. It makes it almost unmanageable."

The sound of padded footsteps turned their attention down a short hallway where Bree appeared, smiling warmly. She wore a pair of paint-spattered jeans, her platinum hair pulled back into a messy ponytail, and a plaid shirt tucked half in and half out of the waistband. Thick knit socks muffled her steps.

Bree looked beautiful. And calm.

Before they had a chance to offer condolences, Bree tucked her arm through Birdie's and led them all through a small kitchen and into an open, airy space at the very back of the house.

"This is my refuge," she said, spreading her arms wide as they stepped into pools of sunlight. "It used to be an old sunporch, but it's been winterized and turned into a studio. It's where I go . . ."

That it was Bree's special place was never in doubt. An easel and small supply cart filled with brushes and tubes of paint stood near one window, a worktable crowded with yarn and sketches in front of one another. The cherrywood floor had throw rugs scattered around with a few paint spatters in between.

And beyond the back wall of windows was a small yard and then the ocean for as far as anyone could see.

Bree saw them looking around. "I know, it's kind of a mess. The lady we rent from is an artist, too, and she told me anything goes. I took her at her word."

They hadn't noticed anyone else in the room until a familiar voice called over from the far end of the room. "Isn't this the best? A bit of artist's heaven." Jane Brewster rose from a slip-covered divan, her floppy skirt covering all but the tips of her Birkenstocks. She smiled as she walked across the room.

"Jane," Nell greeted her close friend. "You blended right in with that sofa."

Jane laughed and hugged her as she talked. "Our Bree here is the Rock of Gibraltar, I swear she is." She pointed to one of Bree's paintings, still wet on an easel. "Izzy and I came over bearing hugs and offers to help, our sad faces down to the floor, and Bree ends up making tea and holding our hands, consoling *us*, and telling us she will be fine."

"And I will be, Jane." Her smile was sad, but her eyes warm toward the woman who'd welcomed her into the family of Canary Cove artists.

Bree *looked* fine, too, but they all knew the erratic pattern of grief, and wondered how long it would take for the facts to settle in and become a reality. Bree would be caught up in an awful frenzy for a few days—with police and reporters and gossip. But then it would be over. And then the pain would have time to emerge and take over her whole being.

"Thank you for coming over," Bree said. "I probably should have had you over a long time ago—I practically live in your shop, Iz. But, well, when Spence was here, well, anyway. I'm glad you're here. I'm kind of a loner except for my family, but I'm learning that sometimes it's nice not to be alone. Especially with people like you." A flush colored her cheeks as if talking about emotions wasn't something she did easily. Nor was she used to people coming into her house.

"Okay," she said, looking around the room. "Let's just sit— let's just be together. You are . . . well, you are like my family." She motioned to the divan and a rocking chair on either side of it, each one painted in wild colors.

"Just shove things aside," she said, waving at a heap of art magazines on a chair.

Jane, Nell, and Birdie sat while Izzy and Bree folded their bodies like accordions onto the floor, straight-backed and comfortable.

"I remember when," Nell said, looking at the gymnast-like bodies.

"I don't," Birdie and Jane said in unison.

Izzy smiled, enjoying being put in the same category as a woman almost ten years younger. "This is a wonderful room," she said.

Bree looked around her studio. "Yes, it is. And it's definitely me. Messes and all. Spencer never came back here. He didn't like much about this house. Too small. Too plain. Too messy."

Her voice wasn't critical, her comment matter-of-fact, and it didn't surprise any of them that someone who coveted the Bianchi house on Cliffside Drive didn't like this small cottage in Canary Cove.

Bree smiled sadly. "But to each his own," she said, more to herself than the others. Her face was young and clear, without a trace of makeup, calm, and lovely—but it was clear she wasn't immune to what was happening. Her eyes reflected the jolt of the news that had started her day. "He hated this house, in fact."

"The thought of leaving it and moving up to that huge place

must have made you sad," Izzy said, looking around at the room that fit Bree to a T. This was Izzy's kind of house, too. Although the house she, Sam, and Abby lived in was a little larger, it had the same warm, cozy and unpretentious vibe.

"I wasn't going to leave here. Spencer knew how I felt about the Bianchi house. I told him I would never live there. Not ever. There was bad mojo around that house. I knew something bad was going to happen there."

She glanced over at her computer and a shiny brass key ring next to it. She pointed to it. "I guess he thought a shiny key ring would change my mind. He left those there the other day. There was even an elevator in the house, he told me. An elevator?" Bree looked up. "Would you want to live in a house that needed an elevator? What if there was a fire?"

Jane looked around for tissues, found a box on the floor and held it on her lap, but Bree didn't reach for it.

"But this isn't about me. And even though I didn't like that house, it's awful what happened to Spencer in it." Her voice quivered.

"It's difficult to get your arms around something like this," Birdie said softly. "It takes time. A lot of time."

"Impossible, maybe," Bree said, looking at Birdie. "I can't grasp it. I can't make sense of it. Nor how I fit into it all. I don't know what I should do. Or not do. Or say. I've never been . . . well, I mean . . ." She shook her head. "I haven't been in a situation like this before. Not ever."

"Well that's a good thing," Birdie said. "And let's hope you never are again." Then Birdie's eyes grew thoughtful, her voice serious. "Bree, dear, is there any chance you might be in danger here? Have the police mentioned that possibility? You're welcome to stay with me for a while until this gets sorted out. My housekeeper is a fortress in her own right."

The others echoed the same invitation, although Birdie was right about her housekeeper and her house being the most impenetrable, if that was an issue.

Bree looked surprised at the invitation. "Oh, Birdie, how thoughtful of you. All of you. But no, I'm sure I'm not in danger. Spencer and I, well, he had his world. And I had mine. It worked for us, you know? Our names aren't even the same, so someone looking for a Paxton would walk right by a McIntosh. Spencer's family was upset when I kept my own name, but . . ." She looked like she might say more, but instead, she pointed to the teapot and extra cups on a shelf next to Nell's elbow, then at the basket Nell and Birdie had brought. "You are kind to bring this."

"I don't suppose you know more about what happened than we do," Nell said, turning to lift the still warm teapot behind her and filling cups. "Nor how anything so tragic could happen."

Bree was silent for a few minutes while Birdie spotted a pot of sugar and some small spoons on a shelf and set them on the end table.

"No. I know Spencer is dead, that's all I know. They want me to come in to the station later today. I think the policeman wanted to give me some time, you know, to absorb it all. I know they will have questions, though I probably won't have any answers. Spencer knows a lot of people in Sea Harbor, everyone probably. He's been getting involved in town things. But I haven't. I don't even know his friends. I only know you all. And the artists here. Canary Cove, your shop, Izzy. That's my world." She looked around, her smile slightly embarrassed, but only at the way it might sound.

"The police will understand all that," Birdie said. "They will probably want you to tell them about Spencer himself. What he was like."

Bree looked up. "Sure. I'm sure you're right. So far the only person I've talked to is the young guy who came by today—the one who told me what happened. He was kind and understanding. It must be awful to have to tell people things like this, that someone has been killed. Murdered." She took a deep breath, then released it and pulled a rumpled card from her shirt pocket. "Tom Porter, that's his name."

"Tommy is a friend and a good man," Birdie said. "He's a detective now—as fair and honest and kind as they come."

The title seemed to have little effect on Bree, but she listened and nodded politely.

"What a horribly long night for you," Izzy said. "To get that news anytime is awful, but in the middle of the night would be shattering. Someone should have been with you—"

"I was okay, really. I am used to . . . well, no, not used to this, sure. But it's okay. And actually, I didn't find out what happened until this morning."

"It was considerate of the police to wait," Jane said. "What could you have done in the middle of the night? Nothing. But I'm relieved a reporter didn't show up at dawn before you'd heard the news, asking you one of those awful questions, like *How do you feel?*"

Bree looked out the window, her face unreadable. Finally she looked back, her words measured. "Actually they did try to reach me, he said. My phone must have been off." She looked over at a cell phone lying on a table, as if it had somehow betrayed her.

Bree's telling of the story was the same as what Ben had told them the night before. But one thing was slightly off. The police hadn't been able to find her. It wasn't difficult to find people in Sea Harbor. Surely they'd have come by the house.

Bree went on. "The policeman said they came by here, but I'm a sound sleeper." She forced a smile.

Jane leaned forward on the divan, her elbows on her knees. A look of concern clouded her face. "Well, no matter," she said. "They found you."

An ear-piercing screech interrupted Jane's calm voice and drew their attention out the windows. A welcome diversion, from the look on Bree's face.

Just outside the cottage, a raucous colony of seagulls had gathered and were fiercely and noisily battling for a mound of food near an Adirondack chair.

Bree watched them for a minute. "Sophie, a sweet little neighbor girl who has become my buddy, came over yesterday with a bag of trail mix to share with me," she said. "We sat out there on the chair, tossing some to the gulls, and when Sophie saw how happy it made the birds, she gleefully emptied the whole thing on the ground and promised to bring more for them today. That must be today's lunch."

When she finally looked away from the birds, her face was dreamy, as if she had gone off to another place in that moment and was having trouble coming back.

Nell used the moment to refill cups. "Lovely," she said, admiring one of the delicate porcelain cups.

"They belonged to my nana." Bree rubbed her finger along the rim. "I'm sentimental. My sister and I used to have tea parties with them."

Izzy stirred her tea with the tiny silver spoon and then shifted the conversation back to something that had been bothering her, something that played into her own crazy fears. "When Spencer didn't come home last night, it must have made you crazy," she said. Izzy knew she was bringing her own hypochondria to the thought. Her middle-of-the-night worry became even worse after Abby was born. She'd once called the state police when Sam hadn't come home from a late-night meeting in Boston. He had been fine, but she wasn't.

Bree looked slightly confused at the comment. And then she tried to brush it off completely. "Oh, you know," she said, her voice clipped and matter-of-fact, "I'm a sound sleeper. Spencer is a night owl. He often goes to bed late. So I didn't think about it."

Izzy hadn't meant her comment to be personal, but somehow Bree's answer left her wondering if she had hurt her feelings or intruded in a way she shouldn't have.

"The police asked me to contact Spencer's sister and brother," Bree said, changing the subject.

"Will they be coming to Sea Harbor?"

"They're both out of the country right now. But no, even if they were in New York, they probably wouldn't come. This could be harmful to the company, and I think they'll try to keep it as quiet as they can, at least that was the impression I got. That's sad, isn't it? The company comes first. And yet their brother was murdered." She looked down, twisting her wedding ring. "When you have as much money as the Paxtons do, you can do whatever you want, I guess. And they want to keep it quiet."

No one was quite sure how to respond to the odd family dynamic, so instead they asked if there were any calls they could make for her or what her own plans were.

Leaving Sea Harbor as soon as she could, they suspected, would be at the top of her list.

But they were wrong.

"Right now what I want to do most is to concentrate on the art show that all of us are planning. I want to work with you and work with yarn, design more pieces—" Her voice picked up strength as she talked until finally, as if running out of energy, she slowed down and looked around the group. "The truth is, I don't have anywhere to go. My mom's in a nursing home. My siblings all moved away. I've never had many friends. You guys have become that to me. I feel at home in Canary Cove, and in your shop, Izzy. And I love being out on that strip of lawn behind my little cottage with my three-year-old friend Sophie, feeding seagulls." Her eyes filled. She took a deep breath and then she continued to talk, as if revitalized by some kind of resolve. Her voice was strong.

"I am so sad this happened to Spencer Paxton. And no matter what he's done, this . . . this act is awful and brutal, and beyond anything I could ever imagine. In my world, in my head, people don't kill each other. Strangers or neighbors or lovers or friends. Even enemies. Nobody deserves to be killed, to suffer like that. And nobody has the right to do that. Not ever. Spencer didn't deserve to die like that. He simply didn't." She looked up at them, her eyes moist, and continued.

"But it's not because he was my husband, or I came here with him, or I lived with him that I feel that way. It's not because of that."

Jane handed Bree the box of tissues, and this time she took it and pulled one from the top. They waited, knowing Bree wasn't finished yet.

In between wiping the tears running down her cheeks, she looked at all of them. And she said, "I . . . I didn't love Spencer Paxton. In fact, well, the truth is—I didn't even like him very much."

Chapter 16

In the space of a day, Sea Harbor had changed. Talk of apple picking and October fests had given way to grim talk about a house on Cliffside Drive, a man who some thought should never have come back to Sea Harbor, and a strong message from the town's mayor that people should lock their doors at night.

By Tuesday morning the *Sea Harbor Gazette* had a front-page story, the three-inch headline screaming at people as they drank their coffee and ate their oatmeal.

WEALTHY DEVELOPER MURDERED IN BIANCHI MANSION

And to further the sale of newspapers and the number of clicks on the paper's website, the subhead, in smaller print but not to be missed, read:

Potential homeowner bludgeoned to death with common household tool

Uncle Mario read the headline bleary-eyed, shortly after waking from an early morning snooze in his office lounge chair. Had he been there all night? He couldn't be sure. He remembered cold air, being out, but maybe not. He heard Stella in the outer office, quiet as a mouse, letting him sleep.

He squinted to make out the words.

And then, when the words cleared, he pounded a boot on the floor and followed it with colorful Italian words of the sort that brought Stella hurrying into his office.

She placed a mug of thick black coffee next to him and ordered him to drink it. Her eyes moved to the crumpled newspaper now on the floor beside his boots.

"It's going to be okay, Uncle Mario. But you need to watch your mouth."

"Oh, *cara mia*. Sometimes cuss words are good ones, happy ones. You needa to learn the difference. It is good." He squeezed his fingers together, kissed them, and punched the air.

Stella looked at him sternly, and then wondered if she should call a doctor. His face was ruddy and the blood vessels in his neck seemed to be pulsating. "Yes, all's good. It will be okay. And once this is all over, we'll have buyers lining up to buy that house. I promise you."

She didn't know that at all. What she knew was that people shied away from buying houses in which someone had died, even from natural causes—they got the heebie-jeebies. Houses in which someone was murdered? The bad juju could be insurmountable.

Uncle Mario seemed on the verge of some kind of attack and it wasn't a good time to talk about bad juju, so Stella stayed positive. "Some other people were interested, you know. A retired head guy from Microsoft who loves it here. He called twice about the house."

Mario's bushy eyebrow lifted and a strange look passed across his flushed face. He took a long drink of coffee and told Stella to sit down, he had a confession to make.

The blood drained from Stella's face. She sat down.

"It *is* okay, my sweet little Stella. You don't a-worry. Everything is okay."

And then he confessed. It was the reason he'd been drinking more than usual. The ugly beast, he called it—something he had learned at St. Frances Xavier Cabrini grade school in Italy. The ugly beast.

Guilt.

"I sold the Bianchi house before the poor guy died up there, Stell."

She stared at him. Then she calmed down, realizing it must be the hangover talking. But when he shuffled some papers on his desk and handed them to her, she realized it was Uncle Mario talking. And telling the truth.

It was the day Spencer Paxton had walked in with a bottle of whiskey and engaged Uncle Mario in an endless conversation. Stella had left the office that day. What she didn't know when she left Uncle Mario alone with him was that Spencer had come in holding a blank check in his hand.

"A blank check, *cara mia!*"

Spencer had heard talk of parties interested in the house, other buyers. He wanted to be sure he didn't lose the house.

"Yes, but—" Stella started to say. But Mario shushed her.

"So I said sure. I knew you were going by the book, my Stell, getting rid of the squirrels, doing it all right, but the guy was getting antsy and becoming a pest—and he didn't even care about seeing the place. Something about besting his old man, he said. Didn't want to take a chance. Just wanted the house. And that was that."

The two men had decided to keep it between them—their secret—let the house get repaired while they waited for the title to be filed and all the t's crossed, and then he'd surprise Stella with the good news.

"The guy paid *cash*, *cara mia*," Mario said again. "Who does that sort of thing these days?"

And then he bowed his head and made the sign of the cross.

"May he rest in peace," he murmured softly in an effort to temper his enthusiasm with a nod of respect for the dead. "House or no house, it was an awful thing that happened there in my friend Anthony's house. That poor guy. Awful awful. He one-ups his old man, gets his dream house, and then, *poof*. Just like that, he's knocked off." He looked at his niece sadly and shook his head again. "*Santi in cielo*. Who does that sort of thing these days?"

Beatrice Scaglia showered and dried herself quickly in the chilly air, then wrapped a thick terry robe around her well-exercised body and sat at the vanity table, a mirror reflecting the dampness in her hair. Makeup was a ritual, one she liked and matched to the day's activities. A slightly smoky mascara, a peach blush that highlighted her skin tone, and a swipe of creamy peach lipstick to her lips. She observed the result, deemed it perfect, and smiled, running her fingers through loose dark hair. She noticed a lightening at the roots and made a mental note to have her secretary make an appointment for color and highlights. But for today, a bun, she decided, and carefully sleeked back her hair, wrapping and binding it expertly with a thick band.

She walked to the closet and moved quickly through an array of color-arranged outfits, pulling out a sea-blue pencil-skirt suit, and slipped it on, smoothing down the sides and checking herself in the long mirror. It would work nicely for her morning interview on cable television when she would talk at length about her vision for Sea Harbor. An exciting vision, the interviewer would agree. Then on to meet with several council committee members and a talk to the museum volunteers. Spreading goodwill. And in between times, perhaps she would drop in at the yarn shop. It was always helpful to take the pulse of Izzy's customers—to tune in to conversations that swirled around the room when needles were clicking and the outside world seemed far away.

The whistle on the teakettle called her to the kitchen, where she poured herself a cup, then sat alone at the table with her tea, a bowl of yogurt and granola, and the *Sea Harbor Gazette.*

She pressed the paper flat on the table, scanned the headline, and then put on her reading glasses and read the rest of the article, one manicured finger running beneath each word, each line, pulling her eye from word to word to word.

Finally, finished with the article and her breakfast, she carefully wiped a few drops of yogurt from the corner of her mouth. Then she checked in a mirror one more time, put on her pressed wool gray coat, and moved into her day.

Another rich, full day in the life of a mayor, a life she loved as much as life itself.

Josh Babson and Merry Jackson sat together on the picnic bench, close to one of the outdoor heaters Merry had installed on the deck of the Artist's Palate. It gave her at least another two or three months of keeping the deck open. With some creative thinking, she might figure out how to keep her restaurant's deck open all year, she said.

And if she did, they'd come—the revelers and friends and neighbors, those wanting a friendly place, a good beer, and Merry's amazing burgers. And in the morning the artists would climb the deck steps, lured by the smell of her Colombian roast, homemade granola, and juices of unknown origin that Merry made fresh each day, an effort to keep *her artists*, as she called them, healthy and fit.

She'd given up on Josh, though, which she told him frequently. He was so skinny she couldn't see him when he turned sideways. Not healthy, was Merry's assessment.

Josh lived a block away, down one of the narrow Canary Cove alleyways and above a glassblower's shop. He was putting together a studio of his own off the back.

That morning he had grabbed a neighbor's paper and brought it with him to the deck, although Merry had one of her own, already spread out on the table. They were an odd pair of friends—the pretty and energetic young owner of the popular hangout and the tall, skinny artist with the shaggy blond hair. An artist with an attitude, some said, though those who knew him thought differently. It was all a cover for a guy who didn't like crowds, wasn't crazy about attention, and sure, had opinions, but along with a laugh the length of the Sea Harbor shoreline. He had kind, soulful eyes, and Merry trusted him beyond question.

He liked her, too. They had forged a firm friendship, which was what brought them together that morning, staring at the *Sea Harbor Gazette*, and then at each other.

"Well, that's a fine kettle of fish, which is what Ham Brewster said to me this morning when he grabbed a cup of granola," Merry said.

Josh nodded and took a long drink of Merry's coffee, feeling its strength as it wound its way through him. "Geesh, what did you put in this?"

"A splash of Michter's," she said. "I figured you might need it."

"Ha."

"I heard the sirens," Merry said.

"You were here?"

"No. We're closed Sunday nights. You know that. Where were you? You look like you haven't slept all night."

Josh thrummed his paint-stained fingers on the table, looking around the deck vacantly. He didn't answer. "Yeah," he finally said, apropos of nothing. Beneath the table, one knee jiggled.

Merry pushed a bowl of yogurt in front of him. "Eat or you'll die."

Josh smiled. He took a large scoop of it and swallowed it down, his prominent Adam's apple bobbing. He looked at the bistro owner, his soulful eyes hard. "He was a sleazy guy, Merry," he said. "I only met him that once, but I knew him. And I didn't like him. He was bad. He didn't belong around here. Maybe not anywhere."

Merry was silent. She looked across the deck to the empty table near the railing where she had practically attacked Spencer Paxton less than a week ago. She took a deep breath and looked back at her friend.

"I know that, Josh. I didn't like him either," she said. "Not one single bit."

Sitting at round tables in the basement of Father Lawrence Northcutt's Our Lady of Safe Seas church, a group of men who called themselves the Men's Association gathered with a dozen copies of the *Sea Harbor Gazette* spread out in front of them. The men met monthly, ostensibly to help Father Larry with the many church projects he had going, but it didn't hurt that Mary Halloran, extraordinary church secretary and manager, had baked her renowned sausage-egg-cheese casserole and brought it hot to each meeting.

On this particular morning, some copies of the newspaper had coffee stains blotting out words or part of a photo. Other copies, those in front of the men who always poured ketchup on their egg casserole, bore red smudges, perhaps more suitable to the story the men were poring over.

Many members of the Men's Association were retired, dressed today in jeans or old denim work pants, but some who still managed bars or restaurants or construction companies or hardware stores, wore slacks and button-downs, dressed to meet a customer or client. And some brought sons, exposing them to community volunteer work and Mary's amazing casserole, with a desire to maintain the group's longevity. Today, perhaps wondering if there'd be some news of the murder circulating among them, the place was full, the oldest members filling in the front tables and the newer generation opting for the back ones and the fast exit they provided if things got boring.

Father Northcutt, pastor of Our Lady of Safe Seas, sat at one of the front tables and looked around the room, pleased at the turnout. It was important for people to be together at times like these. He looked around the group. Gus McGlucken was there. Looking tired, older. But then, weren't they all? Harry Garozzo sat next to Gus, leaving the deli in his wife's capable hands for an hour. Good friends, Harry, Gus, and Mario.

Jake Risso, owner of the Gull Tavern, was talking quietly to some retired lobster fishermen, regulars in his bar where rumors, no doubt, had already taken hold. Even the stately Alphonso Santos, owner of the largest construction company in town, was there. Alphonso didn't often come, though he donated heavily to all of Father Larry's causes, which was an admirable excuse in the kindly priest's opinion.

As he stood and quieted the crowd, Father Larry spotted a straggler. Old Mario Palazola was shuffling in the back door. That was good. He watched him make his way to an empty seat next to Gus and Harry. He still wasn't used to seeing the three men without their fourth, the sadly departed Anthony Bianchi.

The priest pushed back the few white hairs that remained on his head and welcomed the group. Then he bowed his head, blessed the food, the day, and the men, and offered a brief prayer. When he sat back down, the men moved in their chairs to look at Archie Brandley, owner of the Sea Harbor Bookstore and this year's Men's Association president. Archie stood, a serious expression on his kind face. He took off his glasses.

"As you all know, this is a difficult time in Sea Harbor," he began.

Around the tables, voices mumbled and heads nodded.

"Our fine police department is already making progress in solving this case, keeping us safe, but in the meantime, in the midst of the horrible crime, we can't forget that a man died, a man born right here in Sea Harbor Memorial Hospital, and we need to pay tribute to him. Some of you knew his folks, his family. Sea Harbor honors its own."

More mumbles, more agreement. Heads bowed.

Archie crossed himself and then he said, "May you rest in eternal peace, Spencer Paxton the third." At each table voices joined together and said as one: "May he rest in peace."

And then, just one minute before they were released to dig into plates heaped high with egg casserole, a rogue voice from the back of the room followed up the RIP with an invocation of its own.

"And good riddance to you, sir," it said.

Chapter 17

The fact that the murdered man hadn't been back in town for very long changed the tenor of the conversation surrounding his death. Many people hadn't become reacquainted with Spencer, except for a casual conversation here or there. He was, in that capacity, not really a Sea Harbor resident.

And as for the young Spencer Paxton and his early Sea Harbor years? He was reasonably smart, good-looking, and popular, according to a retired schoolteacher who had taught him history. And he was full of himself, she'd added, but aren't all kids at that age?

According to the investigator, it seemed likely the perpetrator had known Spencer Paxton. Premeditated. A "focused crime," he called it. So they could relax that there wasn't a mass murderer in their midst. People needed to get on with their lives and keep things as normal as possible.

When Izzy walked into the yarn shop that next morning, Mae motioned with her head toward the yarn cubbies on the back wall.

Bree stood fingering a bright green nubby yarn, thick and fuzzy.

Izzy walked over. "Bree, you don't need to be here."

"Yes, I do," Bree said, and offered Izzy a smile intended to make her understand.

Izzy only partially did, her thoughts on those she loved and the unbearable thought of losing any of them. The thought of being unable to move. Or breathe. Much less show up in a yarn shop to teach a class. But Bree's situation was different, she knew. Another fact she only partially understood.

Bree held out the skein of yarn. "Just touch this, Iz."

Izzy hesitated, then touched the fuzzy fibers.

"See? It's good for the soul. I need to do what I do, not sit and wonder what's happened, what's ahead."

Izzy nodded. It was something they all needed to do. Put the horrible week behind them. But it took longer than a day or two, even when the person wasn't a part of your life.

The bell above the door rang, and Birdie walked in, with Rose Chopra a footstep behind. Rose had better color today, Izzy thought. A miracle after the amount of questioning she had been through the past couple days.

She was cradling Purl in her arms.

Bree looked over at the sound of Purl's mewing and smiled when she saw Rose.

"Are you teaching a class?" Rose asked.

Bree nodded. "You should come sometime."

They talked for a few minutes, Bree explaining the freedom in working with yarn as an art form, something to hang on a wall. "No patterns," she said. "So no mistakes. And it's wonderful for the spirit."

Birdie and Izzy watched the perfectly normal conversation—between two people living in the middle of anything but normal circumstances.

Bree retreated to the back room to set up for her class, reminding Rose to stop by sometime.

It was so normal it was odd.

"Bree is a strong woman," Izzy said.

Rose looked back toward the knitting room. She frowned. "Strong?"

Birdie realized at once why Rose looked confused. She hadn't made the connection. "You wouldn't have known, Rose," she said. "Bree was married to Spencer Paxton."

Rose's mouth fell open, then shut abruptly. "I . . . no. I didn't know that. Are you sure? I thought . . ." She stumbled with her words. She wasn't sure at all what she thought. Except she liked Bree. She was kind and nice. Artistic. And somehow connecting her in any way to Spencer Paxton didn't seem right.

"Her last name is different, that's the confusion," Izzy said. "She kept her maiden name."

But that wasn't the confusion to Rose. The confusion was that Bree could never have been married to someone like Spencer Paxton.

"You must be right. I guess I was confused," she said.

It pulled her down, somehow. The mix-up in names. The confusion. It led her to another place inside of her that wasn't right.

She tried to shake it all away. She had planned to talk to Stella about her own name confusion the night of their celebratory dinner. But that was the night her world was shaken. The night she saw Spencer Paxton. And the night he was killed.

The conversation had been buried in the days that followed.

She looked at Birdie and Izzy. Her cheeks were burning and she knew she was babbling.

Birdie and Izzy waited.

"It's nothing," Rose went on. "I guess I'm getting people mixed up."

That was the root of the emotion. Suddenly she felt attacked by mistaken identities. But it was her own that was crushing down on her. The confusion in a name, and what it can mean when life takes an unexpected turn. *McIntosh and Paxton. Woodley and Chopra.*

And these kind, wonderful people who had taken her into their lives. They were confused, too. They didn't know who she was, not the whole of who she was. It hadn't been an intended deception. She hadn't lied. And it hadn't really mattered.

But now it did. The things about her they didn't know suddenly mattered a great deal.

It mattered because a man was dead.

She set Purl down on the floor and looked at Izzy and Birdie. "I know I'm sounding a little crazy. And I'll explain it all to you. But I need to talk to Stella first."

She headed for the door, but Birdie stopped her before she got there.

Birdie couldn't explain later why she had imposed herself on Rose the way she had. It wasn't like her. But she had sensed with some certainty that it was what she should do.

She took Rose's arm and said gently, "I'll go with you."

Stella sat on a soft rug on the floor of the Palazola Realty office, trying to distract herself. She was surrounded by yearbooks, her thoughts on Rosie, mixed with a worry that hurt deep down inside of her. The yearbooks had provided a bigger distraction than even she had expected.

Boxes of dusty books had appeared in the office that day, brought in by Gus McGlucken, along with an announcement. "Sorry, Stell," he said. "Like I told Mario, I need that old storeroom. Got a cousin coming in to stay in the apartment for a few months and he'll need some storage room, so I have to get all this junk out of there. Mario told you about it, right?"

Stella had glanced at the boxes cluttering the room. *No, Uncle Mario hadn't told her.*

In a few minutes Gus was back with more—boxes of Mario's

old files, a broken lamp and a couple chairs, a rusted filing cabinet Uncle Mario had stored in the small room. Gus seemed obsessed somehow with getting rid of everything. He'd bring the rest tomorrow, he said. Maybe Mario would give him a hand.

"What about getting Robbie to help?" Stella had asked. She hadn't seen Robbie since the uproar they'd heard through the wall, nor had Gus mentioned anything about him. But Gus hadn't seemed like himself ever since.

"Robbie's moved out," he said, his tone abrupt. "He's been back once—I heard him the next day, stomping around, making a mess of things in the storage room."

Stella didn't ask questions, she could tell Gus wasn't in the mood for it. Nor would he appreciate her asking if she could leave the rest of her things there for a few days until she figured out what to do with them. So she'd piled as much as she could in Uncle Mario's office, pushing his little homemade bar into the corner. Tucked away and hard to get to.

Most of the things should probably be thrown out, including some knickknacks and personal things she'd stored when she had moved out of her mom's and got her own apartment—things she couldn't quite throw away.

She dropped one box as she moved it across the room and a yearbook fell out. "Oh geesh," she thought. She thought she had thrown them away. She picked up another and found a smelly old sock beneath it. Gus hadn't been very discriminating; he'd included one or two of Robbie's old books, too, along with some of his dirty laundry, apparently. There was a whole stack of books, some the flimsy books from grade- and middle school, and then the more substantial Sea Harbor High books.

And then her thoughts turned to Spencer Paxton. She was older than he, but he'd have been in a couple of her books.

Curious, she paged through one of the books on her desk, first quickly, then more slowly, thoughts of Spencer Paxton disappearing as she stared at the dozens of faces looking up at her. Finally she lifted up the whole stack and settled down on the floor, soon surrounded by pages of small square school pictures: grade school, middle school, and Sea Harbor High.

She grabbed a paperweight to hold one page open, then shoved some envelopes in other pages. An old sock of Robbie's in another.

At first she thought it couldn't be. But there, in the fifth grade, was a solemn-looking girl with a space between her front teeth. She didn't have a ponytail—and her face was plump, surrounded by straight, short, dark hair. Her cheekbones weren't defined. But her eyes were the same, those same green eyes. Fresh green, like the color of flowers in spring. Nice eyes.

Rose Ellen Woodley was printed below in plain black type. *Woodley*. Of course. "Rosie had been married," Stella murmured to herself. "Chopra. Prem Chopra who made Indian food for her."

The girl in the photo looked reticent, as if she were holding back. Or maybe afraid. Afraid to have her picture taken?

Stella remembered the goofy photographer who used to come dressed as a clown to take their school pictures. He did it all through grade school. He even did it for the middle- and high school kids. He thought it would make them laugh, but the kind of laughter that he evoked wasn't always what he was trying for.

Rose wasn't smiling at all. Maybe the clown had scared her.

She looked at the small square class pictures of the other students in Rose's class. A few of the kids she remembered—mostly because they had a brother or sister in her own, upper class. It was funny how when you're a kid, three, four years is like a generation. She went back and looked at the unsmiling girl. Rose.

It was definitely her Rosie.

She went back and forth, thumbing pages, pressing some flat. And she finally found a photo of Rose in first grade. Rose with a shy smile. And second grade. But the older she got, the further away the smile went, as if worn away by the years. She followed her through fifth, then sixth, when Stella herself was a happy upperclassman, happy to leave the world of the little kids behind. Happy to drive a car. To feel she had the world by a string. She traced Rosie as she grew, in years and in size, all the way to high school. A freshman. The same year, Stella realized, that she herself had gone off to Salem State and Rose had moved away to the middle of the country. Had she seen Rosie around the middle school–high school campus? Around town or at the beach? She couldn't remember her, not at all. Did she look right at her and not see her?

She thumbed through until she came to an activities section where larger photos filled the pages, highlighting group activities, kids having fun, putting on plays, studying plankton at the Maritime Gloucester museum, being silly. But she couldn't find her Rosie.

And then she did. She picked up the book and looked closer. Rosie looked older, taller, and still pudgy, with braces on her teeth. Two girls were in the photo, Rosie and an older girl, but smaller than Rose. There were adults in the background, lined up on a stage. The two girls in the front were holding a trophy. And Rose Ellen Woodley was smiling. Not big, but it was there.

Math Olympiad Winners, Stella read.

She heard footsteps coming up the stairway, and then a knock on the door. A second later Rose pushed it open.

Stell looked up into Rosie's sad green eyes, the same ones that had been looking at her from the class books.

Birdie walked in behind her.

"Stella." Birdie smiled, looking down at her, sitting in the center of a hodgepodge of books. "Little Miss Muffet."

"But you're not bringing spiders, I hope." Stella's smile was subdued. Her legs were crossed and one book lay open in her lap. She looked down at it, then over to where Rose stood, quietly watching her.

"Rose Woodley," Stella said. And then she smiled, because the girl in so many of the photos had looked so sad.

"I came to explain . . ." Rose began, her voice faltering.

Birdie walked over to Stella and slipped on her glasses, leaning over. She looked down at the page of photos, then one that Stell had circled. *Rose Woodley*. She frowned and straightened up, mentally paging through years of memory.

Stella got up and collected the books, carrying them over to her desk. She turned back to Rose, her hands in the pockets of her slacks. "Rosie—?"

"I wasn't trying to deceive you," Rose said. "I was still using my married name. I never took the time to change it back. Driver's license, IDs—they were all Chopra. Too much trouble. And when I came back here, no one knew me, so it didn't matter. In a way, I liked that. Rose Woodley wasn't happy in Sea Harbor, Stell. I thought I'd give Rose Chopra a chance. But now . . ."

"Now?"

"It's different now. What didn't matter before, matters now. I came over to tell you, to talk to you about it." She managed a smile and walked over to Stella's desk, looking down at the books. "I don't have any of these books. I didn't take them with me. I threw them in the trash."

"How is it different now?"

"It's different because you're my friend, not just Stella Palazola, the Realtor. Birdie, Nell, all of you. But you, Stella. You gave me this job, you've wrapped me in a friendship that already—well, already it matters to me. A lot. Way more than you know.

"It was an accident almost—just a happenstance that no one remembered me or was aware that I once lived here. But it doesn't seem like an accident anymore. It feels deceptive. And I knew I had to tell you because, it's . . ."

Rosie's voice was filled with such sadness that Stella tried to lift her spirits and said with a smile, "What? You were going to tell me first so I wouldn't have the fun of looking at all these goofy little kids' pictures? Never."

Birdie looked over at Stella and blessed her silently.

Stella went on. "Hey, Rosie Woodley or Chopra or whatever you want to call yourself, it doesn't matter to me. You're my Rosie. And that's a good thing."

Rosie bit down on her bottom lip and looked out the window. When she looked back and opened her mouth to say something, Birdie interrupted.

"Woodley, Woodley," she murmured. Then she drew the name out and followed the last *Woodley* with a smile as her memory finally cleared. "I remember your mother, Rose. Yes, I do. Gladys Woodley. She was a lovely woman."

Rose had been holding back the emotion, but at the mention of her mother, her eyes glistened and she smiled as if Birdie was somehow giving her a gift, bringing her mother back to life.

Birdie knew that only too well. People lived on through memories and in your heart. It was good to talk about them. "I didn't know Gladys well, but I'd meet her walking the beach sometimes, and we sometimes attended the same poetry readings at the library. Gladys herself was a poet—a kind of blithe spirit, I always thought. And she loved the water."

Rose's whole face smiled. "Yes, she was a happy, lovely lady. She saw the world differently than a lot of people. She saw it in rainbow colors. And she wanted to paint that kind of rainbow for me, too. It was so important for her to make me happy. Sometimes she tried too hard to do that for me, patching up my life. And it made her so sad when she couldn't fix everything and give me a perfect life, that I kept those hard times from her. Those times that kids go through. Partly I came back here to put my own demons to rest forever, and I knew that would make my mother happiest of all."

Stella listened carefully. And she wondered. She had been a kid, too, and she couldn't remember "hard times," unless Rose meant times like getting her tonsils out on Halloween and not being allowed to go trick-or-treating. But she strongly suspected that wasn't what Rose was talking about.

Birdie listened, too, and knew there was a lot more behind Rose's words. It wasn't a crime for her not to have talked about her past, or not to have mentioned that she had once lived in Sea Harbor. There was no fault there and her explanation was plausible. But there was something pressing on Rose in a terrible way. And it was slowly working its way to the surface.

"And have you done that, Rose?" Birdie said softly. "Have you put those demons to rest?"

Rose looked down at her hands, and then she looked at Stella. Finally she looked back to Birdie, drawing strength from her wise eyes.

"I knew Spencer Paxton when I was a kid," she said. "He nearly ruined my life. I had a chance to tell him what he did to me. So yes, my demons are gone."

Chief Thompson was kind and gentle, listening as if imagining a daughter of his own being bullied mercilessly by some privileged kid who thought he owned the world.

Rose's story came out in starts and stops, but she kept her composure, holding emotion at bay so that her statements were stark naked, unadorned.

It was Stella who found it impossible to keep emotions out of the equation. She had walked those same halls, maybe run right past a young Rose Woodley on the playground. And maybe she hadn't spoken to her, didn't notice her because she was just a young kid. She knew Spence Paxton, too. Everyone did, even the upperclassmen like Stella. She remembered being on a sailing crew one summer that he was on. For sure she'd have seen Rosie during those summer months, wouldn't she? At places they all went to swim and sail?

But that was the problem. She hadn't seen the tall, awkward girl, slightly overweight back then, her shyness making her prey for boys like Spencer Paxton. Rose had been invisible to them.

When the tears began streaming down Stella's face, Birdie stood and walked out of the police station room with her, pulling tissues out of her purse and running smack into Ben Endicott.

"Keys," he said, dangling Rose's car keys from his fingers. "And a wallet and phone."

"You're a lifesaver, Ben." Birdie smiled and pointed to a bench in the hallway.

Ben understood her words to include more than a set of car keys, so he sat on the bench beside them, while Stella blew her nose and Birdie filled him in.

The look of concern on Ben's face didn't escape either of them.

Rose Woodley Chopra had come into the police station on her own accord and handed Chief Jerry Thompson a perfect motive for murder, all wrapped up in a lovely bow.

Chapter 18

Izzy had gone up to the apartment that day, just to be sure Rose was okay.

Rose had come back from the police station earlier and told them about living in Sea Harbor years before, about Spencer Paxton's role in her life. About hating herself, about her near despair, and finally, about growing whole again. Stella and Birdie had helped Rose fill in some of the difficult parts.

Later, when Izzy went up to check on her, Rose was sitting on the couch. Purl was curled up in her lap, purring contentedly. And even Rose looked content. Soft music played in the background and a candle burned on the coffee table.

But her face was flushed and damp from tears. Izzy had sat down for a while, leaning into the soft cushions.

Rose pointed to a familiar quote, framed and hanging on the wall. One she had shared with them before. One Birdie had quoted, too. "You are braver than you believe . . ."

"Wise words," Izzy said.

Rose nodded. "I'll be fine, Izzy," she said.

*　*　*

Izzy parked her car and walked across the lot to the Canary Cove Arts Association building, her thoughts on Rose Woodley Chopra. And on a beautiful little blonde girl named Abby. The daughter whom Izzy's life revolved around. She thought of girls and boys growing up and going through adolescence, and her emotions spilled over, her heart full of Rose and her pain—for what had been.

Yes, she thought now. Rose would be okay. But not without some pain along the way. She checked her watch, and realized she was late. She hurried along the sidewalk.

The Arts building, a small one-story structure, sat on the edge of the Canary Cove galleries adjacent to the main parking lot. It housed an information desk, a business office, and a multipurpose room in the back.

Jane and Ham Brewster were the ones who had suggested the room be used for the fall fiber arts show they were preparing, a more neutral spot than any of the individual galleries.

And it had been a good decision, Izzy thought as she walked through the double doors. Bree was already there, lugging a heavy ladder across the floor. Nell followed behind her with a tape measure and pad of paper. It was too early to mount or hang anything, but time to determine the best way to exhibit all the art.

Izzy tossed her jacket to the side and joined them, looking up at the tall ceiling, the lights, the windows. "I think my sea creatures will swim gracefully from up there," she said. She took the tape measure and climbed up with Nell standing below, recording measurements.

"Jane said anything goes, as long as we don't punch holes in the wall," Birdie called out from a table near the wall.

Bree moved some heavy pieces of mounting materials to the side, then walked over and leaned against the wall, watching the women work.

"Small but mighty," Birdie said to her, and Bree laughed, bending her arm and showing a formidable muscle.

Birdie looked around the room, imagining the colorful pieces hanging from branches, from the ceiling, from the deep window recesses. "It will be just what we need. Magic. We need a bit of that in our lives right now."

Izzy listened from a distance and nodded, imagining the floating jellyfish-looking pieces she was creating from yarn. She'd hang them high so they floated down from the ceiling, catching the light. Silky green and burnt orange, bright pink and purple strands ending in fanciful shapes.

"Magic is always welcome," Nell said. She looked out the window at the darkening sky over the ocean. Inside, the gallery lights were turned on. Maybe they needed more than magic. Miracles, perhaps.

"Count me in on that, too," Bree said, more to herself than the others. "Magic would be super-duper fine."

"And are you?" Birdie asked. "Fine, I mean?"

"Not yet. It's complicated, Birdie. It's a hard time."

"Sometimes we make things more complicated than we need to." She smiled at Bree, hoping to ease the strain she was under. For the past few days Bree seemed to be holding herself together like a small blonde fortress. But tonight there were cracks in the armor, tiny ones, but they were there.

"It's a difficult time, Bree. But complications can come from trying to force it not to be. Leaning into it can be simpler. Things happen. And then they go away."

"Maybe," Bree said. "But it looks bad, doesn't it?"

Nell walked over, listening. Imagining what Bree was going through. It was worse than bad, she thought. She wondered how much detail the police had given Bree. Did she know that Spencer had been bludgeoned, blows that seemed to have come from an angry person, the medical examiner reported. "Yes. Spencer's death was awful."

Bree nodded. "Yes, that was bad. Horrible. But I was being selfish and thinking about myself. It's bad that he and I had a bad relationship. It's bad that the police weren't able to find me that night."

"But you told them why."

Nell's comment hung there, waiting for confirmation as if it were a question. *You told them you were a sound sleeper. You didn't hear the knock or the bell.*

Bree didn't answer.

There was more to her story—they all knew that. They also knew that no one, unless they were drugged or unconscious, could have slept through Bree McIntosh's doorbell. And there was something else.

"Bree, Rose saw a woman with Spencer that night," Birdie said.

Bree looked at her with surprise. And then with regret. "Spence asked me to meet him there, and then he surprised me by dangling keys in front of me. He told me he had bought the place. For cash. Without saying a word to me ahead of time. I was very angry. We argued. And I left in my own car. That was it."

Bree was matter-of-fact. And though liars certainly could deceive people with honest-looking faces, Bree seemed honest to the core. She held things back. But what she said out loud was true.

They'd been surprised earlier to learn that she and Spencer Paxton weren't the happy couple that showed up on society pages. A divorce would happen, she and Spencer had both agreed on that. And she had agreed to wait, she had told them.

"Did you know he was going to be Sea Harbor's next mayor?" Bree asked.

"I heard he was filing," Birdie said. "But we have elections in Sea Harbor. Not only that, everyone votes. We even have protests now and then—I've been known to carry a placard now and again."

Bree smiled. "That doesn't surprise me, Birdie."

"And Mayor Beatrice Scaglia is running again," Izzy said, joining the group. "She'll be difficult to beat."

"No, Izzy. Spencer was going to win, not run," Bree said. "That's what he did. He won. No matter what it was he wanted, he would get it. It's called entitlement. And on the rare occasion that he didn't win, well, we don't even want to talk about that."

"That's an interesting way to approach things, I guess," Nell said.

"You're nice, Nell. It's a terribly arrogant way. But he had it all planned. He was going to be Sea Harbor's next mayor. And after a term as mayor—during which he would make connections, position himself wherever it benefited him—he would move on to the next step—Massachusetts governor or state representative. And then Washington."

"Those were his goals?" Nell asked.

Bree nodded. "Yes, Spencer always had a plan."

"Is his running for office connected to why you were delaying a divorce?"

Bree frowned, as if the question was not easy to answer, not yes or no. "In part," she said finally, "but not because I wanted to be Mrs. Mayor. You know me well enough to know that's the last thing I would want. But Spencer and I had made a deal when I told him I needed to leave him. He had been paying for the nursing home my mother is in. It's a really nice place, and some of them aren't, you know. The nurses there are kind and wonderful to her. But it's very expensive, and Spencer is covering all her costs. My siblings and I couldn't begin to do that. My mom was a great mom, she deserves every bit of the care they give her—and more."

"So if you stayed married to him, he would continue paying?" Nell asked.

Bree nodded. "But not forever. Spencer was practical—and I

was disposable. I don't think it mattered that much to him if I left. But the mayor's race mattered, and getting settled here mattered. He somehow thought that with me at his side, it would all happen more easily, more efficiently. Maybe more effectively. I'd be his pretty hostess, sort of. And then, after two years, I'd be set free, just like a porpoise in the sea. He would give me an easy divorce, and the money I needed to keep my mother in the nursing home for as long as she lived."

Although the circumstance was difficult to imagine, they all knew they'd do unimaginable things for those they loved.

Then Izzy asked the question that had been hovering over them. "Bree. I don't get something. You've become our friend, we've gotten to know you and you're kind and honest. But you married Spencer Paxton. I can't imagine you marrying him unless you loved him."

Bree listened, and looked almost grateful that Izzy had asked, relieved to have permission to talk about it with people she trusted and who would understand. Or if they didn't understand, they would accept what she said because they had accepted her.

"I think I did love him, but I'm not sure who I loved. Spencer and I dated for a year before we married, and it was wonderful, a fairy-tale time for me. I was so young, and had always felt used by men. Because of my looks, I guess. I didn't get that vibe from Spencer. He seemed to take my looks for granted—he had women around him all the time. He treated me well. And sure, I suppose I was taken by the attention. Plus, my mother loved him—he'd come to pick me up for some event but he would bring her flowers. But here's the thing—"

They waited.

"People like Spencer Paxton let you see what they want you to see. And that's what I fell in love with. What he let me see. But that's not a very good foundation for the rest of your life because those other parts are bound to sneak out and rear their ugly heads. Those doors will eventually open."

"Did that happen once you were here in Sea Harbor?" Izzy asked.

"Oh, no," Bree said. "It happened early on."

It was the first time Bree had told anyone the story of how her brand-new marriage had been challenged almost before the ink on the marriage certificate was dry. A sad story about the demise of a marriage before it had ever begun.

The first indication of Spencer's hidden demons, as Bree called them, came very soon after the wedding, and the scars had never left her.

"I can still see it as if it were yesterday. It's vivid. Etched into me. We were coming back from our honeymoon, driving down a beautiful country road. In the distance, I saw a gaggle of geese wandering out from the woods that lined the road. I spotted them right away, their black necks upright, their beaked heads proud. They were so beautiful. I pointed at them, warning Spencer to slow down."

She paused for a minute as if the scene were playing out right in front of her. Then she went on, telling them about the day that sometimes still woke her up in the middle of the night.

Spencer had acted as if she hadn't spoken. And instead of slowing down, he set his sights on the road ahead, on the elegant geese. He narrowed his eyes, and then he wrapped his fingers around the leather wheel tightly and pressed down hard on the gas pedal.

Three geese were left sprawled in a deadly pattern on the highway, the others squawking wildly on the side of the road.

"Spencer drove on," she said, her voice barely audible as she replayed the haunting memory. "He was smiling, as if he'd just won some competition. And he never said a word. Not a single word."

The image left all of the women in silence, thoughts of art shows and floating yarn art forgotten and replaced by something they wanted to forget.

Finally Birdie moved to Bree's side and wrapped the much younger woman in her arms.

Bree buried her head in Birdie's chest, and then she sobbed away five years of marriage.

Chapter 19

Sam was in Boston at a photo exhibit and Izzy couldn't get a babysitter, so they all agreed to come to her. The first ever Thursday knitting night "on location," she said.

Cass appointed herself driver and said she'd pick up Birdie, Nell, and pizza. As long as they were breaking from tradition, they'd give Nell a break, too.

Cass's brother Pete had come to work that day with enough rumors to choke a horse, Cass said. Fishermen seem to be good at that sort of thing. "Dock talk," they call it. She'd bring the talk with her.

Nell was carrying her own load of things she wanted to talk about, but they weren't rumors. At least she didn't think they were.

"And don't forget about knitting," Birdie said. She was about to rip out half the rows in a cardigan sleeve, something Izzy could do for her in a heartbeat.

But the pressing impetus was that they had other things to unravel. Dozens of questions—and concern about people they cared about. By the time they had shared information they were each privy to, Rose's background and history were as known to each of them as their own. And Bree's story as well.

How much the police knew was another story.

"The police have been working nonstop," Nell said as they gathered in the kitchen, bringing out plates and napkins, a corkscrew and glasses. The Perrys' house was one of her favorite places to be. It had been Sam's bachelor pad—open, comfortable, and convenient. The inside had been transformed by Izzy into a white-walled area, with Sam's photographs matted and hung, many ordered by Izzy to bring her favorite Cape Ann places directly into their home: a dramatic black-and-white of a lifeguard chair enveloped in fog; a sunrise over Canary Cove; stormy skies descending on the back bay. And with Abby's birth, a wall dedicated to Sam's photos of the curly-haired blonde who had stolen all their hearts.

But the deck was all Sam's, his nirvana, where he'd bring little Abby on a clear night to visit Mars and Jupiter and the Big Dipper, her big eyes round with wonder.

And that was where Izzy led them all now, carrying trays and bottles.

The evening was cool, but a tall heater near the cable railing rippled the air, sending warm waves across the deck. Izzy passed out blankets just in case, their wooly warmth an invitation to hunker down in the deck chairs beneath the crisp fall sky. And knit. And talk.

Cass came out shortly after reading to her goddaughter Abby several good-night stories and piling her bed with a dozen favorite stuffed bears. She lifted the lid off the box of Garozzo's pizza and passed it around. "I have no idea what's in this or on it, but Harry promised me it will cure all our ills."

"Let's hope," Izzy said, picking up a thin-crusted piece with cheesy lumps of something on top.

"Banana peppers and *capocollo*," Nell said.

"You determined all that with a single bite?" Cass said.

"You're stealing my thunder." She took a large bite of her own, then followed it quickly with a long drink of beer. "Wow. Spicy. But good. It'll keep us awake, our minds sharp." She licked some cheese off her fingers.

"I'm worried about Stella," Birdie began, holding her bite to small nibbles. "She stopped by today and we talked for a long time. I can't remember seeing her this upset."

"That whole house thing must be playing on her. It was her listing—and someone died in it," Cass said.

"Ben has helped her through that part of it. And as you know, Spencer had already bought the house before he was killed. A secret little deal he and Mario Palazola had cooked up. Don't ask me why. Sometimes Mario doesn't make logical decisions. But in the end, he may have been wise. Stella and Mario will get their hefty commissions and the company will be fine. Her major worry now is the mess Rose is in."

"She and Rose have become close," Nell said.

"Yes. And when traumatic things happen, time gets squeezed," Birdie said. "Even though Rose hasn't been here long, it seems like a lifetime."

"Ben said Rose went through the ringer at the police station," Nell said. "Tommy Porter did his best to make her comfortable, but it was a long couple of hours. It was tough. Rose is so central to everything that happened that night."

"I wasn't sure what to make of Rose at first," Cass said. "But as this has rolled out, I understand her better, and why she was reticent that first night. She wasn't there to make friends or confide in us. She was there because she had fixed Izzy's pipe, and that was all. And she probably hadn't intended to stay in town very long, either."

"And she wasn't lying to us about anything," Izzy said. "She introduced herself the same way she would have anywhere. Her legal name. She wasn't trying to hide Rose Woodley. Rose Woodley wasn't the woman who was there."

"There was one thing though," Cass said. "When she and Stella went to the station the morning after, she didn't say she knew Spencer. None of us knew it then. She should have said something right away."

Their silence spoke agreement.

"Keeping something back from the police, even if it isn't important, comes across as suspicious. If you know someone who has been murdered, and you were the last person to see him alive, you mention that," Izzy said.

Birdie weighed in. "I don't think she realized how important that would be. The Woodleys moved away when Rose was a freshman or sophomore in high school. After that, it took years of therapy to help her put what Spencer Paxton did to her behind her. She had to learn how to love herself. And she did. Not all children who are bullied are as successful as our Rose. And no doubt she didn't want to revisit that time."

"Of course she didn't," Izzy said. "He was awful to her. Frankly, I wouldn't have blamed her if she'd killed him. I think I would have, if he'd done that to my daughter."

"But the fact is that Rosie's name is all over this," Nell said. "It's concerning. Pretend you don't know her. All you know is that she was at the house that night, she knew the man who was killed, and she certainly—as you just said, Izzy—had every reason to kill him. Not to mention the weapon was a pipe wrench from the toolbox Rose had left there."

"Fingerprints?" Cass asked.

"None. Rose said she had never used the wrench. Whoever did this cleaned up after himself."

"Or herself," Izzy said.

Their emotions were like the tide below Izzy's deck. Calm and smooth, then swept up and tumultuous, crashing against the shore. At one moment they were playing the prosecutor and in the next breath, the defense attorney.

But in their hearts, they were all defending Rose Woodley.

"She isn't a murderer," Birdie said.

They all looked at her, her short white hair a halo lit from behind.

"The police may disagree," Nell said slowly. "She isn't in a good place right now. Like Izzy said, she'd have every reason to do it. Spencer Paxton nearly destroyed her life. And she never showed up at the restaurant to meet Stella, which the police also know. Where was she after she ran out of the house?"

"Walking, Stella said. She didn't have car keys, we know that, so she had to walk home," Birdie said, an unexpected note of defensiveness in her voice.

"But she didn't think anyone saw her," Izzy said. "And both she and Stella agreed it was late when she got back to the apartment."

"I agree that it looks bad." Birdie put her pizza aside and picked up her glass of wine. "That means only one thing to me. It means we need to put our heads together and think like women. We need to forget about rules and boundaries and find out who really murdered Spencer Paxton. I know Jerry Thompson will turn over all the stones he can. But other eyes and ears are never a bad thing—assuming they are our eyes and ears."

Birdie leaned back in her chair and looked up at the few stars that had made their way into the sky. "Star light, star bright," she said, smiling. But her voice was serious when she continued.

"I had a friend when I was in school a thousand years ago. She marched to her own drummer and some thought her odd. I thought her nice. Clever. Smart. She had a lisp, and her lip was slightly deformed. She was bullied by a group of girls for her looks and for her lisp, way back then. They left mean notes on her desk and painted a caricature of her face on her locker. Bullying's not a new thing, you know. It damaged this girl to the core. She refused to talk in class, and then finally she dropped out of school and ran away. I never knew what happened to her."

The story sobered them.

"Rose was able to repair the damage that was done to her," Birdie continued. "And I can't bear the thought of all that incredible work Rose and her therapist did over all those years being torn down and thrown away. I can't bear the thought of Spencer Paxton—even in death—turning Rose Woodley into a victim again."

Rose mattered. And she mattered to Stella. Her story mattered, too.

Finally Cass spoke. "You were really a kid?"

"Oh, shush, you," laughed Birdie, waving her hand at Cass.

Izzy took a drink of wine and set her glass down a little too hard, red drops sloshing down on the napkin. "Here's a selfish take on it, one that doesn't even take into account the lives affected by this man. I am furious with Spencer Paxton for ruining this beautiful time of year. I didn't like him when I was practicing law, and I didn't like him when he was parading around Sea Harbor these last couple months, and I like him even less now that he's dead. He's messing with us." She sat back in the chair, pulling a striped blanket over her. "There. Now I'm over it. But I want it all gone—the investigation, the finger pointing, the rumors, the sadness in that real estate office across the street and above me, in Rosie's apartment. All of it. I want my autumn magic back."

Cass clapped, they laughed, and the mood lightened. But the resolve was as strong as the ocean currents just yards away.

"We'll do a lineup," Birdie said. "If Rose didn't do it, who else had a good reason? We need to know whom we're talking about. And then we need to get to Spencer Paxton . . . and find out what he did to one of these people that drove them to murder."

The list came easily. Spencer himself helped them out with that. His charming, charismatic veneer was as thin as plastic wrap, and beneath it, he had made plenty of enemies.

"Beatrice Scaglia would be on it," Nell said. "Ben ran into her today. She was walking through city hall looking more chipper than he'd seen her in a long time. 'The happy mayor,' he called her. But later, as he was leaving, he saw her again. The smile was gone and she told him that she'd gotten a call from Jerry Thompson, who wanted to talk to her. *Her*. She was incensed. Someone had told the police about her minor altercation with Spencer at the club."

"It wasn't exactly minor," Birdie said.

Izzy leaned forward, her elbows on her knees. Her face pulled together as if trying to work through a difficult thought. "Spencer messed with Beatrice, too, not unlike what he did to Rose. He bullied Rose into thinking she was worthless. In a way, it was the same with Beatrice—but different."

Izzy shook her head at her own confusing statement. "Uncle Ben called her 'the happy mayor.' That's who she is. Her whole identity is wrapped up in being mayor of Sea Harbor. Everyone knows that. And in comes this guy who was going to strip her whole identity away. Just like that."

"I hadn't thought about it like that. You're smarter than you look, Iz," Cass said. She walked around the deck, picking up empty plates. "He could have done serious damage to our mayor. I agree."

"Yes, he could have," said Birdie. "Beatrice is strong in some ways—certainly in pushing for the things she thinks are important to Sea Harbor. But in other ways she is fragile."

"Perhaps we are all like that. We have a secret place that when touched, can cause other parts to crumble," Nell said.

"Spencer probably didn't know Beatrice well enough to know how important that position is to her," Birdie said. "But then, he probably wouldn't have cared. It's clear he did what was best for himself, no matter what bodies he left in his wake."

"Do you think Spence sent out that newsletter or blog or whatever it was that dug up Beatrice's past?" Cass asked. "It was hurtful."

No one knew.

"Bree said he didn't know much about computers," Izzy said.

"But he knew someone who did." Cass finished topping off the wineglasses and sat down next to Nell, allowing her comment to settle. She looked around, reading their thoughts.

Of course. Robbie McGlucken, who had finally landed his dream job.

"I had forgotten about Robbie. This must be upsetting for him," Birdie said.

"He moved out of his apartment recently," Izzy said.

"Gus said it was his way of letting his old man know he could do it on his own." Birdie stopped, remembering the conversation. And then she added, "But he said it in a peculiar way. The way a father who had had a disagreement with his son might say it. Not pleasantly. But no matter, Robbie liked working with Spencer. Apparently Spence told him that if he helped him win the mayor's race, he'd go places. The sky was the limit. Robbie was thrilled."

"Okay, back to business," Izzy said, shifting attention to finding a murderer. "Motives. Rose. Beatrice. Merry. Dozens of people could attest to Merry's and Beatrice's wrath. They didn't hide it." She took a deep breath and added another name. "Bree."

Bree McIntosh.

"You're right," Birdie said. "Of course. The spouse—"

Nell nodded. How difficult it was to be probing into the psyche and lives of people they genuinely liked, sticking pins into them. She shuddered.

"Bree wasn't in love with him, she's told us that much," Birdie said.

"But she knew there was an end to the marriage—and it wasn't too far in the future," Izzy said. "Soon she'd be free of an uncomfortable marriage, so why do something that could put her in prison?"

But the awful image of the geese lying dead in the road came back to all of them. *Had Spencer pushed the button that made things crumble for Bree one too many times?*

Birdie took a drink of her wine and set it down. "Bree admitted she was there that night."

"But she left after they argued," Nell said.

"She could have come back," Cass said. "Or just parked down the street and waited."

Izzy pulled her blanket up and cuddled into its warmth. "I like Bree," she said.

"But you like Beatrice, Merry, and Rose, too. And you're a lawyer. You know emotions don't count diddly-squat," Cass said.

"Ex-lawyer," Izzy said. "But you're right. Emotions, go away."

"We know Bree had a key to the Bianchi house, she showed it to us," Nell said.

They were all imagining Bree in their heads. A fragile-looking beauty—but that was deceptive. In the short time they had known her they had come to appreciate her strength, both physically and emotional.

"I don't think she'd have brought our attention to the keys if she had used them to go into a house to kill her husband," Izzy said. "Which makes me wonder about Beatrice. How would she have gotten in?"

"Beatrice has ways to do almost anything she sets her mind to. I have come home to find her in my living room several times," said Birdie.

Nell laughed. "That's true. And Stella had a number of keys to the house. Beatrice could have gotten one. So motive and means."

"And then there's Merry, suspecting Spencer—or his company at least—might have had plans for Canary Cove and let-

ting him know he shouldn't even think about it. Not ever,"
Izzy said. "She was a firecracker that night on the deck of the
Artist's Palate." She got up from the chair and headed toward
the deck door.

"Merry?" Cass said. Merry Jackson had adopted all of Canary Cove as her next of kin. Although younger than most of
the artists, she took care of them, pumping them full of organic
vegetables and awful-looking juice drinks. But most of all, to
Cass, Merry was a caretaker, watching over Cass's own husband, Danny, when he camped out on the Artist's Palate's deck,
writing a book, forgetting to eat or drink or go home when the
lights dimmed. Merry fed him, called Cass to come get him
when he fell asleep on the picnic table, or when it was late or
starting to rain and he hadn't noticed.

Cass was forever beholden to the small blonde restaurant
owner. She knew Merry could never kill anyone or anything,
not even the irritating flies that attacked their fries on warm
summer nights.

"No, not Merry," Cass said.

Birdie and Nell looked at her. "We like her too, Cass," Birdie
said.

"Okay. So she had motive. But—"

"The Artist's Palate is closed on Sunday night," Birdie said.
"She wouldn't have been at work. She wouldn't have that as an
alibi."

"I'm sure she's shared that with the police. Ben said she'd
talked to them. She was proactive. She also must have known
her flareup with Spencer was seen by dozens of people."

"Smart, but unfortunately being proactive doesn't prove in-
nocence. So she's probably still on a list. A lineup. A lineup of
women," Izzy said from the doorway. She carried out a ther-
mos of coffee. "That's what we have."

"They are all good women," Nell said.

"Good women," Birdie said. "Do good women . . . do bad things?"

Do they?

The thought floated around the deck, cushioned by the sea breeze, waxing and waning like the moon.

Chapter 20

Nell glanced at Izzy's name on her cell phone and picked it up, setting her coffee mug down next to the morning paper.

"Bree's lecture on fiber art is going to be crowded today," Izzy began without a greeting. "Could you and Birdie come to help? Or just hang out if we don't need help. Or just be here? I need you with me, selfish beast that I am. Cass is working out a computer glitch on a lobster boat or she'd come, too. I know she would."

Although the classes Bree taught before Spencer's death had been well attended, this one—advertised as a talk, not a class—was suddenly an "attraction." "People are curious," Izzy said. "They want to come to see who Bree is. I hate for her to be put on display like this. And the articles in the paper haven't helped."

The *Sea Harbor Gazette* had penned a lengthy article the day before, answering its own headline: WHO WAS SPENCER PAXTON? in some detail. And they had spared Bree little privacy, including a photo they had unearthed from somewhere, a photo of a ravishing woman in a wedding dress, walking down a church aisle on the arm of a man now dead.

"Few people even knew who she was or that she was married to Spencer before all this happened," Izzy said. "Now everyone knows and everyone wants to come and see for themselves who she is. Mae said someone in Shaw's Market actually referred to her as the 'Black Widow,' can you believe it?"

Nell was appalled and had passed the news along to Ben, hoping they could do something to stop such garbage, but neither of them had any idea what that would be. Subtly the article had pointed out something they couldn't argue about: Bree's alibi that evening was very thin. And she seemed indifferent to strengthening it.

"I said I'd cancel the talk or do it myself, rather than put her through it, but she insisted on going ahead. Maybe because she knows she is much better at it than I am. Or maybe because she's strong and what others think doesn't matter to her. It's who you are that matters. That's what I'm going for—and what I will teach my Abby."

"Or maybe she wants to simply get it over with. Gawkers can come and gawk, and then leave her alone. It's rude, sure, but sometimes life is like that," Nell said.

"Maybe. But anyway, I'm just relieved that reporter didn't know more about her marriage, or where it was headed."

Nell hung up, feeling Izzy's strong need to protect Bree. She and Birdie would go to the shop and help out if needed. But mostly, she suspected, they'd simply be there. If nothing else, they could provide friendly, comfortable faces for Bree to look at as she spoke. She and Birdie were bad at gawking. And perhaps they could provide some assurance to Bree that she wasn't alone in the mess that she was working her way through.

They had all left Izzy's deck the night before with more questions than answers, along with an uncomfortable feeling that any resolution to Spencer Paxton's murder wasn't going to be a good one.

Nell had shared the same feeling with Ben when she got

home. He'd been waiting up for her, as if he hadn't seen her for days. It had felt that way to Nell, too. There was too much happening around them, and they were neglecting the together time they both deemed sacred.

So they'd gone upstairs, wrapped themselves in robes and blankets, and sat out on the balcony off their bedroom, a small heater at their feet and their hands cupping mugs of spiced chamomile tea. Surrounded by darkness, their bodies pressed close, they had talked deep into the night.

Nell told Ben about Bree's sad marriage, the marriage plan Spencer was holding her to. And the hateful honeymoon incident.

Ben had listened with compassion, but his voice became practical when he talked about what that story would mean to someone examining the Paxton murder. "Even though Bree could see an end to the marriage, was there more there that she hadn't shared with you? What were the days and nights like? What went on behind closed doors?"

That was true enough—they didn't know everything about Bree and Spencer's marriage. And what they didn't know could be important. Who knew what Bree went through, or what a man who nonchalantly killed innocent birds was capable of?

Could the thought of living even months more of whatever the marriage held be more than Bree could stand? Had something pushed her to the brink?

Nell replayed the late-night conversation in her head as she walked into the yarn shop before Bree's class. Birdie was already there, waiting in the main room of the shop, holding a newspaper in her hand.

"Poor, dear Bree," Birdie said, flapping the folded paper in the air. "And our Beatrice didn't fare much better."

Nell had already seen it. Another article. In a bulleted list the reporter had written what was known so far in the investigation, listing things that left readers free to conjure up all kinds of dire scenarios on their own. It reminded her of the books her nephews and niece used to read out on the Kansas ranch when they were young: *Choose Your Own Adventure.* The thought made her cringe; having her friends tried in a court of public opinion wasn't acceptable.

Beneath the bullet that mentioned Spencer Paxton's plans to run for mayor, the reporter had added a note about a mysterious e-newsletter that had "shamefully denigrated our own mayor"—a detail that sent anyone who hadn't seen the string of articles back to their computers to look them up.

"Awful stuff," Nell agreed, and Birdie promptly dropped her newspaper into a wastebasket next to the checkout counter. "I may finally cancel my subscription."

Mae looked up from behind the computer. "Mary Pisano'd have your hide, Birdie."

Birdie laughed. Mae was right. The columnist's uncles and cousins and siblings owned newspapers up and down the shore—and Mary would surely object if she lessened the subscription list in this Internet age. But not because of the Pisano family's newspapers—Mary liked Birdie far more than she liked her relatives. She'd only be upset because it meant Birdie wouldn't be reading Mary's own "About Town" column.

"Speaking of our good mayor, she's here," Mae said, nodding toward the steps. "She's not her usual Chatty Cathy self. You might want to take her a smile or two."

"Izzy mentioned that she was coming," Nell said as she and Birdie walked through the archway to the knitting room. "And we know it's not to learn how to create yarn art."

Birdie chuckled. Even though Beatrice couldn't knit and wasn't interested in learning, she faked it beautifully by buying yarn whenever she was in the shop, picking out the softest and brightest colors. Mae suspected she had the largest collection of needles in Sea Harbor. Pristine needles, never warmed by a row of knit or purl stitches or polished by the touch and rub of fingers.

They knew the real reason Beatrice had come. It was why she often came to classes and talks in the shop's back room: to listen to conversation that always circulated around the room, to hear people's concerns and issues and fears, something the knitters who gathered in Izzy's shop dispensed copiously. It made her a more fully informed mayor, she believed.

"She's brave to come today," Birdie said. "And probably smart. The mayor in control. That's what her constituents need to see. Not someone who attacked a now-dead man on the yacht club steps."

Although none of them had seen anyone with a phone out during the altercation that day, someone had managed to snap a photo of it, a photo that subsequently appeared in the cryptic online newsletter.

The back room was already crowded with people sitting on plump floor cushions and around the old library table, and on folding chairs against the bookshelf. A few early birds enjoyed the comfortable chairs around the fireplace.

Bree stood on a small wooden platform that Rose had put together for her. Her back was to the alley wall, and a small table holding baskets of yarn was in front of her. She wore old jeans and a T-shirt, her hair pulled back by a giant comb, strands pulling loose and unnoticed.

Birdie and Nell sat on the window seat, marveling at Bree's attempt to make herself ordinary and plain and invisible. She had failed completely.

"Do you see Beatrice?" Birdie whispered as Izzy stood and quieted the group, introducing Bree McIntosh as the incredibly talented artist who had designed the yarn shop window and whose art would be featured in the Canary Cove fiber show.

Nell straightened her back and looked around, finally spotting the mayor on the opposite side of the room. Beatrice looked over at them at the same time, relief showing on her face. She mouthed that she would see them after the lecture, then put a smile in place, and turned toward a screen on which Bree was running a video demonstrating certain yarn-art techniques.

The lecture went well, and the questions asked were courteous. The only thing that Nell took notice of as being out of place were two women who came up to Bree and insisted on taking selfies with her. Bree was clearly uncomfortable with it but rather than make a scene, she looked into the camera, then escaped quickly and came over to Nell and Birdie.

"You were very gracious," Birdie said.

"I kept thinking, are they doing this because they think I killed my husband and they would have some weird sort of bragging rights with the photo?"

"They wanted it because they know you will one day be a famous artist, and they will have legitimate bragging rights with their photo," Nell said.

"It's okay either way. I'm okay. I didn't kill him, although I often wanted to."

Beatrice Scaglia had walked up behind them, catching the end of Bree's comment. "Nor did I," she said. Then added, "Though I wanted to."

Bree turned around. "You're Mayor Scaglia," she said. And then emotion flooded her face. "I am so very, very sorry for what he tried to do to you," she said. "When I found out he was planning to be mayor, I didn't think beyond it. I didn't put real people behind what he would do to get what he wanted. I should have. He . . . he would have done everything he could to beat you."

Beatrice was still. Then she nodded. "Yes, I knew that. He already had made my life sad, and difficult in some ways, and it would only have gotten worse."

Her voice was courteous, but chilly. It would be a while before Beatrice would warm to anyone who had been connected to Spencer Paxton, even someone else who disliked him. Nell wondered briefly who else was on her list.

"I have a question for you," Beatrice said, her voice slightly softer, but not much.

Bree braced herself.

"Was he responsible for that hateful newsletter that was emailed to my constituents? The one meant to destroy me?"

The awful newsletter. Nell had searched her computer the last few days and couldn't find it in her inbox. Not since around the time Spencer Paxton died. It seemed to have been killed along with him.

Bree shook her head no. "I heard about the email from a friend who found it in his inbox with the attachment. I hadn't seen it before that. Spencer was handicapped when it came to computers. He was capable of doing other things to hurt people, but he knew little about computers. I know more than he does."

Nell looked at Beatrice, wondering if she would take it any further.

But Beatrice was unfazed. "No matter who pushed the buttons, your husband was responsible for it," she said, with utter conviction.

Nell stepped to her side. "Beatrice, I think it's all over. People know you. It's over. They will forget."

"Yes," Beatrice said, her face emotionless. "They will. The evil among us is gone."

The tone of Beatrice's voice surprised them. Birdie and Nell looked at each other. It wouldn't have surprised them if Beatrice suddenly started reciting Bible verses, something very uncharacteristic of Sea Harbor's mayor.

But she stopped short of that, put her smile back in place and with a quick embrace of her two friends, she turned and wandered back among the women milling around in small groups, discussing their lives, their children, day care problems. Now and then, an issue being discussed would cause Beatrice to pause and listen more closely—a safety concern near a stop sign or controlling gulls on the streets or school bus problems or graffiti and needles in the village green. Those concerns the mayor would dutifully commit to memory to bring up with her assistant, or the police chief, the city council or school board—wherever it could be appropriately addressed.

"Mayor mode," Birdie said to Nell.

But Nell noticed something different in the mayor's smile. It was dull, injured. Nell felt a pang that was strong enough to make her look away from Beatrice, not wanting to intrude on her private pain.

Beside her, Birdie was looking around, over heads and around bodies. "Did Bree leave?"

Nell hadn't seen her leave either. She walked up the steps to scan the shop and spotted the artist's platinum head hurrying toward the front door. Bree had abandoned the comb holding her hair in place and it floated as she moved, catching the sunlight.

As Bree reached the door, she looked out, and then turned back to wave good-bye to Mae. Nell caught a happy smile flood the young artist's face, as if her world hadn't collapsed completely. As if there might be something good in her life, a light in the darkness, waiting for her just on the other side of the yarn shop door.

Chapter 21

Nell and Birdie didn't wait long before pulling Izzy away from a group of knitters who had already turned the lecture room back into the familiar and cozy knitting haven. They were pummeling her with questions about a complicated pattern, the best cast-on method to use, how to knit a short row, and could she fix a major mistake one of them had made on a lacy shawl?

"It's past lunchtime," they whispered to her, knowing those words alone would make Izzy's stomach rumble. Her lean frame was a constant wonder to all of them.

"We're picking up an order of deli sandwiches at Harry's and taking them down to the dock. Cass is still working on the boat computer and called in for food reinforcements," Birdie said.

The fun of seeing her friend in technological distress was almost as much an enticement for Izzy as the food—but not quite—and in minutes she had squared things away with her customers and with Mae, grabbed a windbreaker from a coat hook, and was happily walking down Harbor Road with Nell and Birdie.

Harry Garozzo was standing outside his deli a block down, his apron stretched across his wide girth, deep in discussion with Gus McGlucken and Mario Palazola.

"We need Sam to get a picture of those three. Norman Rockwell visits Sea Harbor," Nell said, smiling at the three old friends.

"We used to call them the four musketeers," Birdie said.

"And now there are three," Izzy said.

It was something that was almost forgotten in the shadow of a murder. The fact that not too long ago a man lived in that Bianchi house, one who was still mourned by his good friends.

Harry looked up as the women approached, his face breaking out in a wide smile. His arms stretched wide. "*Mie adorabili signore.*"

Birdie walked up and touched his arm affectionately, staying far enough away to avoid the smear of tomato sauce on his apron. She smiled into his eyes, then looked higher, staring at the top of his head. "Harry, dear, you have a piece of pasta in your hair."

His gravelly laughter filled the sidewalk, chasing away two hungry gulls.

Gus slapped him on his back as Mario's laughter outdid that of his friends.

Harry reached up and pulled the strand off his head, throwing it over to the curb, a bonus for a passing gull.

"At least I have enough hair left to hold it, hey Bernadette?" He winked at her, a hundred tiny wrinkles spreading out from his eyes and his affection for one of his oldest friends as thick as his wife's pasta sauce.

"Now that we've cleaned you up, tell me, what kind of mischief are you three up to?" Birdie asked.

"Not nearly as much as we were when our Anthony was with us. He was a dreamer, that one," Mario said.

Gus nodded. "We were reminiscing about the old times. We do a lot of that these days."

"Anthony passed four months ago today," Harry reminded them, making the sign of the cross on his chest. "And not one of us has been back in the Bianchi place since. We miss the place. And we miss the crazy old galoot who lived there."

"Of course you do," Nell said.

"It's just awful what happened over there," Mario said. "It's sacrilegious."

Gus chimed in. "Sacrilegious—sure was. That third-floor room was our sanctuary. Sacred place to us. It was ours. The four of us. We were in and out as free as the breeze."

Harry's face was sad and happy at once, memories flooding his face. "It was the best of times."

"Did you know Mirabella?" Mario asked the women, and a smile broke through with the memory. "You musta known her, Birdie. Sure you did. Anthony's old lady, fussy little gal, skinny as a fence post. She didn't much like our shenanigans," he said.

"I don't think I'd blame her," Birdie said. "You three hooligans in and out of her house."

"We solved that one. Gus here managed a way we could sneak up there, and we had our own little club. For years, right guys?"

"Oh, the things she didn't know," Gus said, shaking his head. "Those were the days."

"Have you ladies heard any more about the Paxton fellow who was offed up there?" Mario asked. "Rumors are flying, but the thing is, no one knew the guy very well. I mean he lived here and we tried to remember him as a kid and all, but who remembers other people's kids?"

Gus was thoughtful. He scratched his chin. "I remember him coming into the store a few times with his dad, mostly buying scuba gear. He was older than Robbie, but maybe just a year or two ahead of my daughter. But he was one of those super kids, you know? *Entitled*, we used to say. Fancy car, vacations. His dad was strict as all get-out, though. Not the nicest of fellows. I remember once when he chewed the kid out in the store, right in front of everyone. Called him some nasty names."

"We gave Mario here a hard time, selling *our* house to the guy. Anthony'd be rolling over in his grave, trying to get out and set it right."

Mario tried to look sheepish, but they all knew selling the house meant a nice retirement for their buddy. And it wasn't the same house without Anthony there anyway.

"I s'pose it should have gone to you, Gus," Mario said. "You put in enough work on the place, fixing things up, if you know what I mean." His bushy eyebrows lifted.

They all laughed at that as if it was very funny, an inside joke. A four musketeer joke.

"Paxton came in here a few times recently," Harry said. "He liked my *vitello* Garozzo. Said it was the best he'd ever had. Left huge tips, too."

"Did he come in with friends? He must have had some local friends, people he knew when he was a kid growing up here," Izzy said.

"Now that's a good point, Izzy," Harry said. "But I don't remember that. He came in with the mayor a few times, but that was before she attacked him."

They all guffawed at that. Apparently, to these men, Beatrice's attack was credible, a woman showing her strength, and not a sign she was getting set to murder anyone. It wasn't a disgrace at all. They liked Beatrice Scaglia. She was a fighter. She'd fight for herself and she'd fight for them.

"Paxton came in with councilmen, some company heads, Rachel Wooten—the city attorney. But I don't remember him coming in to relax or for a good time. Robbie came with him a couple times. They seemed to hit it off good. I was happy to see it because Robbie is usually a loner." He looked over at Gus and shrugged.

"Yeah. Robbie was working for him," Gus said. "That's all I

know. And not from my kid. We don't talk much these days, he doesn't come around. But it seemed to be working. Good thing, since his Harley seems to be eating up all his money. Maybe he'll even buy some shampoo and wash his hair for a change. But who am I to say?"

The conversation lagged some as the unspoken estrangement between Gus and his son seeped into the conversation.

Nell changed the subject. "Harry, how would we know what's going on in this town without you?"

"Ah, Nelly, sometimes that's good, sometimes not so good. Too much gossip can be bad for the spirit. My wife Margaret tells me all the time to block my ears. I shouldn't be listening to customers' conversations, she says."

"Margaret is right," Birdie said.

"Yeah, yeah, yeah. Sure she is. But sometimes the words just get into your ears, like wax, you know? These days I'm hearing things about that poor Rose Woodley—her name is spinning around here like a gerbil wheel. The Monday bridge-club ladies say young Paxton teased Rosie when they were kids. Teased? Who wasn't?"

They listened, nodded, and were grateful the rumors were treated lightly, simple teasing, someone calling someone names—not the desperate bullying that can strip one's spirit naked. Rose didn't need people passing that around.

Harry went on, his opinion about the rumors clear.

"But a nice girl like Rose murdering someone for that or anything else? No way, not ever. I remember her when she was wee. The Woodleys were good people. Came in every Sunday night when kids ate free. Rose loved Harry's deli. She ate like an Italian—a whole muffuletta all by herself. I swear she ate more than her papa. She's a good girl. That's how I see it."

Chapter 22

With Harry's words ringing in their ears, they gathered the white sacks of olive and salami sandwiches, a few soft drinks, and walked along Harbor Road as if it were a normal day. But it wasn't. Nor would the next days be until Spencer Paxton's murderer was found.

Mario Palazola had wholeheartedly agreed with Harry's assessment of Rose. She was a good girl, he confirmed. She was a hard worker. And he'd fight anyone who said differently.

But the fact that Rose had been thrown into the spotlight in such an awful way pained them.

Beatrice and Bree were good women, too. Yet they'd all been pulled into it—into a web of suspicion that could eat away at them little by little. Spencer Paxton was bullying them from his grave.

They walked in silence down Harbor Road and across the village green, passed the white gazebo, now quiet after a busy summer of concerts.

Finally Birdie broke the silence. "How can the dead be so controlling?" She paused and looked up at the sky as the contrails of a plane drew vapor rings across the sky. Perhaps the vapor would loop into letters that would explain it.

"Spencer Paxton is playing with everyone," Izzy said. "Showing them who is boss. I hate it."

"Hate can be powerful," Nell said. "But unfortunately it won't give people back their lives. We need something else. We need to know who did this." She looked over to the rows of pine trees, greening up for the thousands of tiny lights that would brighten their branches in time for Santa's arrival in a few months. The season of peace. For a moment she wished she could fly over the intervening days—Mary Poppins on her broom, watching from above as life in Sea Harbor returned to normal and a murderer was caught.

She dismissed her fantasy and followed Izzy and Birdie down the steps leading to the working pier, toward the sounds of brawny fishermen unloading pots and refilling bait bags. The Halloran slips were down toward the end, adjacent to a weedy wharf area holding stacks of lobster traps and a pile of Styrofoam buoys painted in the Halloran colors: bright green Irish strips with a white-nubbed band at the top.

A black motorcycle was parked nearby.

Nell breathed in the sounds and smells of the demanding, harsh work of fishermen. She felt it every time she ventured into Cass's world. The thick smell of engine oil, the stinging squeal of rope against wood. The constant slap of the ocean against the side of rocking vessels.

"Anyone home?" Izzy shouted out. Then she added the words that were sure to bring Cass out of hiding: "Food is here."

Cass's head popped out of the cabin. "Angels from heaven."

"No, from Harry's. Come."

Cass climbed over the side of the boat onto the dock. "Robbie McGlucken is helping me." She turned toward the cabin and yelled, "Hey Robbie, come out here and take a bow."

An unshaven face appeared, black curly hair falling over his forehead. He lifted a hand, shoved his glasses up his nose, then retreated back inside. Several blinking digital screens were visible through the opening.

"So, Robbie's helping you?" Nell said quietly. "With the computer?"

Cass nodded. "Danny's idea. And he's right. The guy's a genius at all this. We're having some trouble with the navigation system. It's supposed to register the current and topography of the ocean floor, but yesterday the crew ended up in shallow water, scraping a rocky bottom. My pa would be mad as a hatter, wondering why we don't just do it the way he did, remembering what's what by the bend in the land, a clump of trees on an island. A rocky shore. When these gizmos fail, I think he's right."

Izzy pulled one of the wrapped sandwiches from the bag. "It's nice you asked him. He could probably use a diversion. And a job, now that he's lost his. Here's a sandwich for him. Harry always puts in extra."

The mention of food brought Robbie back out of the cabin and onto the pier in record time. He took the sandwich from Izzy and nodded a thanks.

"Cool tattoo," Izzy said, noticing several entwined daisies on his forearm.

Instinctively he picked at the rolled-up sleeve, attempting to roll it down.

Birdie leaned over and looked before it disappeared. "That's lovely, Robbie," she said.

He managed to pull the rest of the sleeve down, then turned and began to walk away.

But Birdie stopped him before his leg went over the rail. "Do you have a minute, Robbie?"

Robbie stopped. He forked his fingers through the mass of curls with one hand, the other grasping the sandwich tightly, as if Birdie might want it back.

"It's so nice of you to help Cass out," she said calmly.

Robbie nodded.

"And the next time my computer shows its mean side, I will be sure to call you. I know it must be hard right now, not only losing a friend, but a job." She continued talking, holding Robbie in place with her calm voice. "We're all terribly sorry about what happened to Spencer Paxton. But it must be especially difficult for someone who knew him and worked with him."

Robbie's eyes narrowed. He looked down at his boots, his glasses sliding down his nose. He pushed them up with one finger, leaving a black mark across his nose.

Nell picked up the conversation, almost as if she and Birdie had rehearsed it. "Ben said you had an interesting meeting at the yacht club the other day. He was impressed with how much you know about computers and the Internet. You were a huge help to Spencer."

Robbie nodded. "He paid me a lot. It was a good gig."

"That's good. You can't say that about all employers. I hope your next one is generous as well. I suspect you are worth every penny," Birdie said. "I have a question about that. You may have known him better than anyone. I know some people in town were upset with him."

Robbie was silent.

"Did you know that?"

"Not really. He was probably upset with them, too. Goes both ways. All's I know is I did my job and he paid me."

"I understand. You were wise. It's probably best not to get in the middle of a boss's feuds. But I have a question. Some of us received emailed newsletters the weeks before Spencer died. No one seems to know who did it. But there was something in it, a photo . . ."

They all watched Robbie's face. He bit down hard on his lower lip, silent. He shifted from one foot to the other. Then shrugged, as if he wasn't sure what Birdie was talking about.

"The photo was of dear friends of ours, Archie and Harriet Brandley." Birdie smiled.

Robbie's shoulders relaxed. "Oh," he said, air releasing from his lungs.

"I would love to have a copy made of the photo," Birdie said. "Could you arrange that for me?"

"Sure. No problem. I'll print it out." Looking relieved, Robbie turned and swung himself over the boat railing and disappeared into the safety of the cabin and the comfort of the computer screens.

"Well, that's that, then, isn't it," Birdie said smugly.

The four women walked toward two old benches at the end of the pier.

"So Robbie is responsible for the newsletter," Izzy said, grinning at Birdie.

"Geesh, Birdie, you're our very own Columbo," Cass said. "I think I'll get you a raincoat and some cigars."

Birdie laughed. "I think if we'd asked him about it outright, he would have disappeared and your computer would never get fixed."

"Or he might have feigned ignorance," Nell said.

"I'm wondering why he did it," Cass asked. "Something to impress his boss?"

"From the number of spelling and grammar errors, I'd say he wrote it," Izzy said. "Spence wouldn't have made those mistakes."

"He probably dug up the old articles, too," Cass said. "He was always good at following directions. He's very exact. He was terrific at Dungeons and Dragons."

"Do you suppose he played a hero or sneaky antihero?" Izzy said.

"Ha, I wonder."

"So would Robbie have thought up the newsletter idea?" Birdie asked.

"No," Cass said. "Not unless he has a mean streak I'm not aware of. My guess he was following orders. No wonder Spencer paid him so well." She glanced over at the boat and Robbie's shadow, working the screen. "I don't think Robbie considers consequences much."

"So it was Spencer Paxton's idea," Nell said.

"In his effort to destroy Beatrice. Geesh. What a horrible man," Izzy said.

"So how does knowing that bring us closer to who murdered him?" Cass asked. "We suspected Spence was connected to the newspaper before. We just didn't know the specifics."

They sat in silence, concentrating on the spicy tang of Harry's sauce, the crispy bun and olive tapenade. They were all thinking the same thing. Bits and pieces of information were piling up, but none of them were pointing in a single direction. None of them were pointing to a murderer.

"I was hoping Robbie might have something to say about the people who were upset with Spence. Surely he was aware of who they are, who was the angriest. Any threats that might have been made," Birdie said.

"Apparently Robbie liked Spencer," Cass said. "And the feeling was mutual. But asking him to come up with people who didn't like his boss might not be something he'd be comfortable doing. He still has to live here."

"That's true," Nell said. "And we've already figured out some of that by ourselves. We know Spencer was a horrible bully—he was as a kid, and he still was as an adult. He was bullying Beatrice. But we don't know him beyond that. What is it you always say, Birdie? We need to walk in the dead person's shoes? That's where we'll find the answer."

"Ugh," Izzy said. "Walking in that guy's shoes is not a pleasant thought. But I think you're right. If we are willing to assume Bree is innocent, even though her alibi for that night is suspicious, and we know she had a key and was even there that night—"

"The same goes for Rose. It's only her word that tells us what happened that night. She was in the room. He was in the room. And she had a compelling reason to kill him," Nell said.

"Okay, they both could be guilty. But I have to think they are not the only people Spencer Paxton has hurt in some way," Izzy said. She wiped a dollop of Harry's spicy mayo from the corner of her mouth.

"Which brings us back to shoes," Birdie said. She looked up, startled by a sudden thundering, rumbling sound, a squealing of tires, and a flash of black as a motorcycle sped off down the pier toward the parking lot.

"Hmm," Cass said. "I hope he bills me."

"Did we drive him off?" Nell asked. "I wonder if our questions upset him."

Cass shrugged. She took a drink of soda and screwed the cap back on. "I doubt if he put it all together. Besides, writing that rag because Spencer asked him to isn't a crime, right? And he was probably finished with my computer fix. Robbie isn't one for long good-byes. Now where were we?"

"Shoes," Izzy said.

They settled back against the benches while Cass checked the last bag for crumbs or special treats that Harry sometimes hid inside the bag for people he especially liked.

"Yes!" she said, pulling out four of the baker's special biscotti—his mother's recipe that he guarded with his life. Crisp, airy, and almond sweet.

"I love Harry Garozzo," Izzy said, snatching one up quickly.

Cass passed one to Birdie and the last to Nell, along with napkins.

"I ran into Rose and Stella this morning," Nell said. "They were headed over to a new listing Stella has. She's trying to keep Rose busy, I think. She is so fond of her. I am not sure which one of them is in more pain."

"I'd vote for Stella," Cass said. "Rose is kind of amazing. She seems to have this ability to zone out, to calm herself down. She's like a Buddha, taking herself to a peaceful, calm place."

"She said it took years of therapy," Izzy said. "She has a spot in the apartment—near that back window that looks out over the water. She sits in front of it on a pillow and meditates every morning. It helps ground her."

"And that leaves poor Stell to do the worrying. She wants so much for this to be over for Rose," Birdie said.

"That brings us back to finding Spencer Paxton's murderer," Nell said.

"Shoes," Izzy said.

"Shoes," Nell agreed. "There's the Spencer who's been walking around Sea Harbor for the past few months, making plans. Doing things. And then there's his past, the preteen and teenage Spence—"

Birdie nodded. "His parents moved away after he graduated from high school. Rosie moved away before that, at the end of her freshman year. Maybe those are the years that we need to investigate."

"Exactly. We know a lot about the here and now. But not the then." Izzy sat forward on the bench, her voice lifting as if they had been in a horrible mess of quicksand and were finally crawling out.

Nell agreed. "That's where we should go, then. Follow him back to his school days. Maybe those are the shoes we need to put on."

"Makes sense," said Cass. "We know people who don't like him now. We need to find out the ones he might have hurt or irritated or betrayed back then."

"Hurt or injured severely enough to murder him all these years later . . ." Nell didn't put a question mark at the end of her sentence. She felt instinctively they were moving along the right track.

And silently she hoped they weren't being blinded by something right in front of them.

Birdie straightened her back and lifted her chin. "That is exactly where we need to go."

"So, what do you say? It's back to school, Peggy Sue." Cass grinned.

Chapter 23

Cass was nostalgic. "It smells exactly the same," she said. "Weird."

"Except you didn't have to walk through metal detectors back then." Nell glanced back at the devices on each side of the door. "I know it's for protection, but it makes me sad every time I walk through one."

And the thought that they were walking through metal detectors on their way to learn about a murdered man escaped none of them.

School had let out, but students milled around, rattling locker doors, grabbing tennis rackets and shoes, talking loudly as they brushed by the three women walking down the hallway. A few looked at them oddly, others ignored them entirely.

"I get the impression no one is mistaking us for new students," Cass said, looking around. She waved at a teacher standing in the doorway of a classroom.

"Are there still teachers here who taught you?" Nell asked.

Cass laughed. "I doubt it. I think most of the staff retired after our class graduated. We were awful. But some kids I went to school with teach here now. That was one of them."

"What about the principal? Patricia Stuber has been here a long time, hasn't she?" Birdie said. "She's a nice lady."

"Oh sure. She's been here since the beginning of time," Cass said. She looked into another classroom as they walked past. "Math. I wasn't very good at that."

Rose, with Stella's help, had gone through every painful memory with them, grade school, middle school, and up through her first high school year. The math contest was central to it all, and they thought of Rose now, this shy, gifted middle school student competing against older kids.

And the awful times that followed her victory.

Cass pointed up ahead. "Ms. Stuber's office is in there."

"She's on the library board with me," Nell said. "The woman has the patience of a saint."

"Which is probably a prerequisite to being a school principal. It's nice of her to make time to see us," Nell said.

The office looked like every school office any of them had ever been in: a windowed wall looking out to the hallway, a counter with a receptionist behind it, and several small offices off to the side. A couple of students sat on chairs against the wall and the young receptionist, headphones on, answered phone call after phone call.

Finally she stopped and looked over, grinning. "Hey, Cass. Hi. I heard you were coming."

"Hi, Peggy," Cass said. "Peg's brother Al is one of our lobster guys," she said to the others. "I thought you worked at MJ's Salon?"

"I was allergic to their hairspray," Peggy said, laughing. "Besides, this place keeps me on my toes. Makes me feel young again."

They nodded and laughed, not mentioning the fact that Peggy couldn't be more than twenty-one herself.

Nell noticed her sweater. "I recognize the sweater you're wearing. Your mom made it in Izzy's shop. It's beautiful."

Peggy grinned again. "You guys are here to see Ms. Stuber, right? I heard her say something about Spencer Paxton, that guy who was murdered over in the Bianchi house. It's really awful what happened to that guy. He went to school here, did you know that? Way, way long time ago, but people remember him. He was sort of a hero." She looked out to the hallway and a wall of glass cases on the other side. "Lots of trophies with his name on them. I guess the trophies are famous now. Kids stop and look at them, point and tell all kinds of stories they heard somewhere, taking pictures with their cell phones. Some reporter was here looking at them, too."

At that moment a tall woman, almost totally gray and with a long, kind face, opened the office door. Her smile was warm and welcoming. "Please, come in, come in. Oh, Nell, it's so good to see you. I've missed a few library meetings lately. Mostly I miss seeing friends like you."

She greeted Birdie warmly, then gave her warmest smile to Cass.

"Catherine Halloran. You are a wonderful sight for these tired eyes. I miss you and your class. And your brother Pete's, too. Warms my heart to see you."

Patricia closed the door behind them and pointed to a circle of chairs around her desk. "Now sit, and tell me what I can do for you. Nell, you mentioned the awful Paxton murder when you called."

Nell nodded. "Have the police been out here?"

"They haven't, although I've talked to Jerry Thompson on the phone. He called as a courtesy, since Spencer attended both the middle and upper schools here. His parents were active in the PTO, and his father was on the sports advisory board that we used to have."

"I've been trying to remember the Paxtons," Birdie said. "I knew who they were, of course, but for a town as small as this, you'd think I would have had more social contact with them. I was on one or two boards with Mr. Paxton, but our contact was minimal."

"His wife was very quiet," Patricia said. "Shy, maybe? I'm not sure. But Mr. Paxton was the opposite." She paused, as if trying to find the politically correct way to characterize the parent of a former student. And then, deciding the circumstances called for simple honesty, she said, "Spencer's father was controlling and difficult to work with."

"In what way?" Nell asked.

"I don't know how he was with the younger children, but he was tough on Spencer. You're all aware of the caricature of the football dad? Clearly unfair to some dads, but Mr. Paxton fulfilled that title perfectly. And not just in football, but as I remember, in everything Spencer was involved in. Maybe it accounted for the fact that his son was one of the most competitive students in my memory. Spencer was bred to be better than everyone else."

"And was he?" Cass asked.

Again Patricia's face was thoughtful. She looked down at the papers on her desk, then at the women sitting in front of her. "I suppose you saw the trophies out there?"

"Peggy pointed them out. She said Spence is kind of a hero now."

"Which would have pleased him. Spencer loved being the center of attention."

"As an adult, he could be charming. Too charming sometimes. We saw that when he came back to Sea Harbor," Nell said.

"That's how he was as a student," Patricia said. "He was one of those boys who knew how to charm the socks off people. At least adults." She smiled. "Like me."

"But other students in the school?"

Patricia paused, then spoke carefully. "He was in that group that every single class has—the popular group. Always in the middle of a big group. And very good-looking, so girls were attracted to him."

"And was he nice?" Cass asked. "There are nice kids in those groups."

Patricia nodded. "You're right, Cass. Spence was calculating, I think. It was important to him that kids liked him, but sometimes at that age, kids think they rise in prestige when others are, well—"

"Teased?" Cass said. "Harassed?"

She nodded. "There was some of that. The thing is, with kids like Spencer, it wasn't overt teasing. Now and then the school nurse got stories, especially from girls, about embarrassing situations—locker kinds of things, notes passed around. Awkward photos stuck on girls' lockers. I'm not saying it was Spencer, but his group. Actions that certainly sound like bullying, although I don't know if it would have been called that then. I don't want to speak poorly of the dead, but Spence, back then, was an organizer and had a whole entourage of kids he hung out with. His place in his social group was important to him. And he'd do what he had to, to keep his place or to win this or that office. To be head man."

"I guess we can all remember some of that from when we were kids," Cass said. "Trying to fit in."

"That's right," Patricia said. "Puberty, adolescence, self-image—it can be a messy, difficult time."

"Difficult on both ends," Nell said. "How easily self-image can be torn apart by teasing and bullying. Did you ever see that kind of behavior in Spence?"

"Well, the thing about him was what I said before. He was savvy. Or sneaky, maybe, although that seems harsh. As I said, he knew what to say to people in authority. And as for students reporting anything, well, you've all heard sad stories about a student—already unsure of him- or herself—who accused the most popular kid in school. Their lives could be made miserable. It's such a difficult thing."

"Sure," Cass said. "I get that. I'm sure there was some of that when I was here, but it's funny that I can't remember it."

"That's because you weren't one of them," Patricia said, smiling at Cass. "You were well liked, popular in a good way."

They all got it. But it was a discomforting thought that a student who truly needed someone to intervene, like Rose Woodley, was denied the help because of her own fears in asking for it.

"You have an amazing memory, Patricia," Nell said. "I am impressed. You have so many students going through here, and yet you remember things so well."

"Some classes, some students, are easier to remember. Like Cass, here." She smiled.

"Do you remember a student by the name of Rose Woodley, by any chance?" Birdie asked. "A lovely young woman who has recently came back to town. She was younger than Spencer Paxton, maybe a few years behind."

"Woodley?" Patricia considered the name. "The name is vaguely familiar, but no, I can't put a face to the name. I guess my memory isn't so amazing after all. It depends, doesn't it? Memory is a peculiar beast. Some years I remember because they carry greater burdens. I remember the years that Spencer Paxton was here, too—they weren't the easiest years by far."

"Because of the students?" Cass asked.

A shadow fell across the principal's face and her eyes grew sad, as if something had crossed in front of them. Something she wanted to forget—but couldn't. And the conversation today was bringing it up in hurtful ways.

She looked out the window, as if collecting her thoughts. Finally she looked back, composed.

"You were saying some years were hard because of the students?" Birdie said gently.

"The students?" she said vaguely, then collected her thoughts. "Not in that way, not what we've been talking about today. But as principal, well, in a way these children are mine for four years. You want to watch over them, to watch them grow into healthy adults. And there were a couple of years back then that were simply . . . well, difficult to get through as a person." She put on a pair of glasses sitting on the desk in front of her, as if changing the temperature in the room. She folded her hands and smiled.

"Now," she said, "is there something else I can help you with?"

"Just one thing," Birdie said. "Did you happen to see the email that circulated recently about Beatrice Scaglia?"

"Oh, Birdie, that was such trash. Poor Beatrice. We spoke afterwards. She was devastated."

"We think Spence might have been behind it," Cass said. Then she corrected herself. Patricia Stuber wasn't her principal anymore, and she wasn't a student ratting on a kid. "He *was* behind it."

Patricia looked surprised. "Beatrice told me that he was filing to run for mayor—she was very upset about it—but I hadn't heard he was responsible for that awful email newsletter."

"You mentioned that he did what he had to do to win," Nell said. "Do you remember how a younger Spencer Paxton reacted when he didn't win?"

"Well, I suppose I'd have to think about it. It probably didn't happen often." She frowned, tugging at a memory. Her head nodded and her face changed, as if she were replaying a video.

"Yes, I do. I remember one time that Spencer Paxton lost."

And though she couldn't remember all of the details, she remembered that it involved a math competition. She couldn't remember who won the competition, but she remembered clearly who had lost.

Spencer Paxton III.

And when the trophy or medal was presented, Spencer's father got up from his front-row seat, looked up to the stage, and called his son a loser. Not a shout, but loud enough for all those nearby to hear. And then he walked out of the auditorium in front of the entire school.

"Yes, now I remember it clearly," Patricia said. "It was an awkward, awful, and unfortunately memorable moment."

They hadn't intended to talk about Rose. They were there to talk about Spencer Paxton. And were getting ready to leave.

But the gate opened with Patricia's memory of the unfortunate moment.

Birdie sat back down and said quietly, "Remember the young woman we mentioned earlier? Rose Woodley."

Patricia frowned for a minute, then sat back in her chair and took off her glasses, setting them slowly on the desk. "The girl who won that competition."

They took turns telling the story, filling Patricia in on a shy student who was gifted in math, and suffered for it.

A story of a quiet student who was as adept at being invisible as Spencer Paxton was at being conspicuous.

Chapter 24

Nell had set everything out on the kitchen island, a nod to the bracing evening air: roasted sweet potatoes, corn on the cob, and sides that Jane Brewster and Danny and others had brought: corn muffins, Jane's coleslaw, gherkins and olives, and a green salad with apples and avocados. All waiting for Ben's tuna steaks and lemon caper sauce to make their entrance. It was going to be an "in or out" buffet, Nell told everyone, something appropriate for the weather and a busy day that began with a class—and ended in a principal's office.

It had been a long, muddled day, but at its end, when Cass, Nell, and Birdie had walked out of the familiar school on the west side of town, they were tired but strangely invigorated. Finally feeling as if they'd found a path. It might be winding or crooked or one that would eventually divide in two, but at least it was a direction. Where it took them would work itself out.

Cass stood at the open French doors, thinking about their long day as Adele sang in the background about "when we were young." She hummed softly along, looking across the deck, her ears tuning in to snatches of conversation, to the comforting sounds coming from the kitchen. Jerry Thompson had stopped by, convinced by Ben that a dry martini and fresh tuna would cure his ills and refresh his spirit. Or at the least, encourage a good night's sleep. He stood at the grill, leaning against the rail, bantering with Danny and Sam about things that didn't matter in the whole scheme of things, like sailing and sports and nice vacation spots, a coffee shop opening in Gloucester. Leaving murder alone and untouched. Out of sight, for a few hours at least.

"He looks older today," Nell said, coming up behind Cass and following her look. "A few more gray hairs at his temples."

Cass nodded. "Do you think Jerry can trace each gray hair to some horrible crime he's had to deal with? To explore and figure out and make right for all of us who demand that he do exactly that?"

"Yes, he probably could, dear man." She touched Cass lightly on the arm, then walked across the room to the kitchen area. Cass followed her inside.

Across the family room, Ham was taking over Ben's martini-making with much direction from his wife. Cass could read Jane's lips: *No, no, just a whisper of vermouth. Don't pour yet, sweetie—give it a good shake first. Both hands now, until your hands are icy cold. Yes, just like that. Hear the crunch of ice against the cold metal.* Jane's long skirt billowed about her legs, a purple shawl slipping from her shoulders as her hands moved with her words.

Cass smiled at the sight of the two well-loved artists trying to turn martini making into its own art form.

She turned away and walked over to the slipcovered couches and comfortable chairs around the fireplace. "She's singing about when we were young."

Birdie looked up, her small stockinged feet resting on the thick wooden coffee table, her knitting in her lap. She'd left the icy-blue cardigan she was knitting for Nell at home, but always had a traveling pair of socks or mittens tucked away in her bag. She pulled out the beginning of a glove, the ribbed cuff strong, the yarn silky soft. *For Rose*, she thought, then confirmed it in her head, and began to knit into the first round of cable stitches. She paused for a sip of the icy martini Ham had put in her grateful hand. Her face was tired. "Who, dear?"

"Adele."

"*When we were young*. That's appropriate for the day."

Nell walked over with a plate of warm Brie, a pot of fig jam, and crackers, her face thoughtful. "I've been thinking about our conversation with Patricia."

"Which part?" Cass asked, looking at the unfinished glove in Birdie's lap. "It's like that glove. All those dangling fibers, in front, in back, everywhere. I know by some miracle Birdie will turn them into a neat cable. But how?"

Nell nodded. "How? I think we take the pieces of Patricia's conversation apart, thread by thread, and see what's there. Not tonight, but we will."

"Iz will bring some perspective to it. She always does," Cass said, sitting on the arm of the couch and watching Birdie's small fingers slip two stitches onto a cable needle and move them to the back, then to the front. It all still befuddled her.

"These are for Rose," Birdie said, looking up. "She and Stella dropped off a sack of apples they'd picked over at Russell Orchards today. Just for nothing, they said. Sweet young women, both of them. I invited them to come with me tonight but they were headed somewhere else—somewhere far away from the troubles that be, Stella said. In the midst of all this crazy, awful turmoil and uncertainty, they are finding a way to get away from it, and even better, a way to find joy. I could feel it."

The front door banged and Izzy came into the family room.

"Where have you been?" Cass asked. "We were about to call out the dogs."

"Working," she said. "Bree and I were making some final decisions about where to hang artwork for the show, and Bree was finishing up her third yarn creation—yes, third! She is amazing. I called Josh over to help figure out some placements. He's a genius at that, and really generous with his time."

"Why didn't you bring them all to dinner?" Nell asked. "Amazing and Genius are always welcome on Friday nights."

"I *did* invite them. Isn't that what we do here?" She laughed and gave her aunt a hug. "Bree looked really tired and was heading home. Josh said something about fixing his bike." She looked beyond the family room to the deck, checking out who was there and not there. "Chief Thompson is here?" She looked at Cass, surprised. "Okay, what did you do?"

Cass gave her *the* look, eyes dark and glowering.

Izzy looked outside again. "It's probably good Bree didn't come."

Ben walked in carrying a tray of tuna steaks and picked up on Izzy's words. He glanced outside. Jerry was still at the far end of the deck, talking with Danny and Ham. "Why shouldn't she come?"

"Tommy Porter wants to talk to Bree again, go over her story—again—get it straight where she was, when, how did she get the keys. What time and why did she leave Spencer at the house." She stopped for breath. "Anyway, it's hard. And maybe she's been spending enough time with the police. She's trying hard to be matter-of-fact about it, but I can see that it's getting to Josh, too."

"To Josh?" Birdie asked. She frowned, looking long at Izzy.

Izzy read Birdie's look. She was quiet for a minute. Then she looked at Nell and Ben. "Okay, Rose told Birdie and me that she thought she saw Josh riding his bike near the Bianchi house the night Spencer was killed. But when I asked her about it later, she said she was sorry she had said anything. She said it was dark, the biker had a helmet on. And she had just had that horrible encounter with Spencer. Who knows what she saw? Those were her words, not mine."

"Has anyone asked Josh about it?" Nell asked.

Izzy didn't know.

Jane Brewster was refilling drinks and listening. Josh Babson was almost like a son to her. "Josh doesn't keep secrets," she said. "Including his feelings for Spencer Paxton. Tommy Porter has been in the gallery talking to him. Josh is up-front. And honest."

"Did he mention anything about riding his bike?" Nell asked.

"Yes," Jane said.

Izzy nodded, a look of relief on her face.

Nell listened as Izzy told Jane what a great help Josh was helping them prepare for the coming fiber show, clearly forgoing her lawyerly neutrality in favor of friendship.

She looked out to the deck as the chief of police walked toward them. Jerry Thompson didn't have the luxury of choosing friendship over duty. It must be a grueling task—questioning friends and acquaintances. And even more difficult if the questioning led to uncertainty, to suspicion even, to more questioning, and to more suspicions.

He had mentioned earlier that Spencer Paxton's body had been released and transported somewhere at the family's request.

Spencer Paxton was out of their town. Gone.

But he wasn't yet out of their lives, not by any stretch.

By the time the dishes were done and Ben had brewed a pot of coffee, the Friday night dinner crowd had nearly disappeared. The Brewsters had taken Birdie home an hour before, and the others followed soon after.

The hour was late, but Jerry Thompson, the lone survivor, seemed reluctant to call it a night. He settled on a deck chaise, his head pressed back against the cushion, looking like he just might not move for another year or so.

Ben and Nell wrapped themselves in blankets on deep deck chairs nearby.

Nell smiled across the fire pit, watching the warm firelight reflect off the chief's face. "It's not easy to relax these days," she said.

"No. But I came close tonight. Thanks to you two."

The vibration of his phone erased that ease in the second it took to check the words on the screen.

He pulled himself forward, his legs moving to the floor, elbows on his knees.

"An emergency?" Ben asked.

"Esther says no. She has sent men out to check on it. It's a simple break-in."

"But you don't think it's simple—"

"Nothing is simple if it touches this case, no matter how weak a touch, fragile a finger," Jerry said, lifting himself out of the chair and shaking away the relaxed vibes he had briefly enjoyed.

"It's the Palazola Realty office. Looks like a human tornado hit it."

Chapter 25

Ben and Nell were at the real estate office the next morning, waiting for Stella to appear. They'd brought coffee and rolls and shoulders to lean on.

Birdie was correct the evening before when she'd given an update on Stella: She had indeed decided to get away, and in doing so had missed the call from the police reporting the break-in at her office.

She and Rosie had headed north to Newburyport, meandering along Route 1A, through small towns with leaves beginning to turn and antique shops luring them in, then a late dinner and night away in a small Newburyport inn with a view of the water. They'd made it a total getaway by sticking their phones in the trunk, right alongside their concerns and the real life they'd come back to early the next day.

Tommy Porter had finally gotten through to her when she'd taken her phone out to check directions early that morning, and she'd immediately called Ben to ask him to meet her at the office. He knew almost as much about her business now as she did, she told him, and Uncle Mario would be no help.

It was Tommy whom Ben and Nell saw first when they walked up the staircase. He was standing just inside the door, its smoky glass insert, or what was left of it, a mass of glittering shards.

"What's going on, Tommy?" Ben asked, looking around at a room that resembled the remains of a four-year-old's birthday party. Drawers were pulled out, boxes turned over, their contents littered across the floor. Filing cabinets open.

"It's crazy. Poor Stella. Wait'll she sees this mess."

A loud clattering on the steps announced Stella would see it soon. She stopped to catch her breath at the top, then walked slowly through the door, smiling grateful thanks to Nell and Ben for being there.

"Oh, geesh," she said, looking around, then pointing to the shattered door. "We just had that tempered glass put in last year. Why would anyone do this?" She looked over at Tommy. "We're not fancy, Tommy. There's not much to steal." She glanced toward the open door to her uncle's office, then the small storeroom, the door also open and the room ransacked, and then looked back at the shattered door.

Tommy assured her he had a guy on his way to board up the door until a new one could be installed, but they all knew that was only part of Stella's grief.

She glanced at the only file cabinet in the room, the drawers open and a few files tossed on the floor as if they'd made the intruder angry. A bookcase next to it was mostly intact, but several books were pulled out. Stella looked over at it and managed a smile. "Do you think he was looking for a secret safe behind it?"

Tommy chuckled. "Maybe," he said. And then he explained the police concern that the break-in might be connected somehow to the Bianchi house up on Cliffside Drive. That maybe the papers, the contracts, the negotiations—might somehow provide a connection to the murder. "We need to follow every lead, and since your company was involved in the sale of a house to the guy who was then murdered there, well, you can see why this break-in raised all sorts of red flags."

Stella gratefully took the coffee Nell handed her and nodded as if she understood, but her face showed that although she understood the connection or coincidence, maybe, she didn't really see how her office could be involved at all. Nor did she want it to be.

"I know, Stell, it's hard to connect the dots," Tommy said, "but it's the kind of thing we need to follow. You never know, and your firm is tied up with the murder for better or worse."

Nell looked at the expression crossing Stella's face. *It was definitely for worse*, it said.

"So we should check the Bianchi files?" Ben asked.

Tommy nodded and he and Ben followed Stella over to the disrupted file cabinet.

"I only keep the most recent listings and active sales in here. We don't have much need for paper anymore because eventually everything ends up digitalized." She glanced over at her desk where her desktop computer sat intact, looking as if it had never been touched.

She confessed with some embarrassment that the file cabinet was the same one Uncle Mario had when he opened the office. Meaning it was very old and wasn't very secure. A fact that was obvious from the ease with which the intruder had pulled it out and dumped it on the floor, popping the drawers right open in spite of a lock.

Stella leaned over and quickly pulled out a thick file. She leafed through it, noticing Uncle Mario's shaky remarks on sticky notes here and there, then handed it to Ben. "You've looked through these Ben. Do you think anything's missing? I can go through them one by one if you think we need to."

Ben took the fat file over to a table and leafed through it.

Tommy looked down at the drawers on the floor, frowning. "The strange thing is, it doesn't look like he went through the files carefully, if at all. It's as if whatever he was looking for would be readily noticed—and it wasn't manila folders."

Ben looked up from the file he was holding. "I think you're right, Tommy. I can't say for certain, but I think everything's here. The important things, anyway. And the papers are neat and clean, no staples or clips disturbed. They look untouched."

Tommy nodded and walked toward Mario's office. "Could you check in here, Stella? Maybe if we go through each room, you'll notice if anything significant is missing. If it's a routine robbery, we can at least make a record of those things for the insurance."

Ben checked out the storeroom, and Stella and Nell went through Uncle Mario's office, replacing drawers, then cramming scattered contents back onto bookshelves.

"This is so crazy, Nell," Stella said sadly. "There's not much here that's worth stealing. Except for maybe Uncle Mario's fancy television. And that's still there. Along with all his whiskey. And my computer. The printer. Wouldn't you think that if whoever did this wanted things to sell or pawn for quick cash, the orthodontist's office across the hall might have been a better bet? He has lots of fancy tools over there. My teeth at one time could vouch for it."

Nell looked around as Stella talked. She agreed. It didn't look like a normal robbery at all. But if not that, then what? Someone had clearly been looking for something.

"Rosie and I straightened everything up a couple days ago—she's good at that," Stella was saying as they went through the rest of the office. "She brought in those plants over near the windows, and updated the bookcase with some great home decorating books, copies of *Coastal Living*, books on buying a home, things clients would enjoy browsing."

Nell could feel Stella's pride and sadness mixed up together. It was more than the break-in. It was how it affected people. Her and Rosie, for starters.

A short while later, Tommy finally conceded that there wasn't anything else for him to check—it seemed to be a random robbery, even though they couldn't account for any missing items. "A mystery," he said. Then added with a touch of sarcasm, "Just what we need right now."

Stella was befuddled, too, but tried to shrug it off. Maybe a homeless person who needed a warm spot for the night or a slug of Uncle Mario's whiskey. His office stash wasn't a well-kept secret.

Maybe. But as Nell and Stella stood in the middle of the ransacked office, saying good-bye to Tommy and Ben, not one of the four believed in Stella's attempted easy resolution. And that left a lingering level of discomfort that would cause Detective Tommy Porter to go back to the station and assign someone to a special patrol of the Palazola real estate office on Harbor Road. "Keep my friend Stella safe," he would tell them.

Stella and Nell were left alone in the office, and Nell started straightening up the bookshelf and collecting papers still on the floor.

Stella stood still, standing in front of the all the framed photos of homes for sale or recently sold. She focused on one directly in the center of the display, the crème de la crème. The listing that shone. An elegant home on the cliff. The Bianchi home in all its seaside splendor.

Stella stood staring at the photo for so long that Nell knew if eyes could truly burn into something, the photo of the Bianchi house would soon be a pile of ashes. She walked over and rested an arm lightly across Stella's shoulders.

Stella turned her head toward Nell, a small, sad smile on her face, but in spite of the smile, tears were collecting behind her glasses, fogging the lenses.

Stella didn't bother to blink them away. Finally she took off the glasses and looked at Nell. "It's that house, Nell. That man. I wish he had never come back to Sea Harbor. Uncle Mario thinks the Bianchi house brought us a windfall. But sometimes, like right now, all I'm sensing is the 'fall' part. And I feel a desperate need for us to land safely."

Nell turned away from the photograph and looked at the desk right next to Stella's, its top polished and a single peach-colored orchid reaching high. Another flower stood on Stella's desk, this one with fuchsia-spotted soft petals that caught the light. Both plants stood tall, the flowers leaning slightly toward one another, proud and alive.

Nell smiled. There were some things in life that Nell hoped for. And there were others she believed with certainty.

"I believe you will, dear Stella," she said. "We will all land safely."

Chapter 26

They gazed at the hanging creations in awe, as if they were in the middle of the Boston aquarium instead of Birdie's den. And right there in front of them, a spectacular jellyfish cavorted in a current of air, performing a ballet.

Even Cass was at a loss for words.

Izzy had woven the fanciful sea creature from sea-silk yarn, knitting the mushroom-shaped top in tiny, lacy stitches. As the eye moved down, silky fibers fell off the underside of the mushroom into long, thin tentacles—purple, bright pink, and orange.

It would join others hanging from the ceiling at the Canary Cove Fiber Arts Show, she explained, where they'd catch the light and move in a slow-motion breeze as people walked by. They'd come alive.

The jellyfish's small poisonous sac that produced a nasty sting in real life was absent from Izzy's work of art.

But not from their conversation.

"Aunt Nell, what else happened? You have that look," Izzy said. She had been standing near the deep, mullioned windows of Birdie's den, holding her art piece in the light for her friends to evaluate. She gently laid it over the back of the chair, content with the accolades and knowing Birdie had texted the invite for reasons other than to compliment her art.

Come at 4 for cocktails, tea or water. And some crazy Moroccan appetizer Ella has dreamed up.

The important part of the message, though, was *come*. Not *if you want to* or *if you have time*. Just *come*. Frustration was building, and somehow they needed to try to pull apart rumor from fact. Crawl inside the mind of Spencer Paxton III. And at the end of it all, find his murderer and get on with life.

Meeting in Birdie's den, high above the harbor on Ravenswood Road, was the perfect place to gain perspective. Removed from town noise but with a panoramic view of all the workings of Sea Harbor. Good and bad.

A tray of gimlet glasses, a lime slice on the side, sat on a low table, and Birdie motioned for everyone to take one. "Raymond Chandler featured them in *The Long Goodbye*," she said. "They will inspire us to untangle this mess and find out who did the crime."

They clinked their glasses in agreement, toasting the mystery writer and inspiration—and the fact that Birdie wasn't leaving room for failure.

They *will* inspire us.

"All right," Izzy said, bringing them back to business. "The *look*, Aunt Nell? You came in here with one." She curled up in a large wingback chair. "What do you think is going on in Stella's office?"

Nell had gone over the break-in quickly when they all came in. It took little time to detail a robbery during which nothing was taken, but they all started talking at once at the thought of Stella's life having another curveball thrown at it. Once those emotions had settled, others took their place.

"What could you possibly steal from a real estate office—photos of houses?" Cass asked, reaching for one of the toasted pita triangles Ella had brought in. They were arranged around a pot of Moroccan-spiced carrot hummus. "It will keep you awake," the housekeeper had said before abruptly walking out of the room.

Izzy wrinkled her nose. "It's so orange."

"She hasn't poisoned us yet," Birdie said. "Don't be finicky, dear."

Izzy dipped a corner of pita into the hummus after seeing the look of pleasure on Cass's face—and the fact that she hadn't choked. "Leaving the electronics behind certainly makes it strange. There'd be little else to steal." She chewed thoughtfully on the pita. "Well, except maybe for Uncle Mario. He's probably wanted in Sicily for a few things."

The thought of anyone trying to steal the portly Italian Realtor lightened the mood for a minute.

"Well," Nell said, "we might not know for sure if anything was taken, but we do know someone broke in and was looking for something. The place was a mess." Nell walked them through what she saw, but it wasn't satisfying Cass, Birdie, and Izzy.

"We're missing something, Aunt Nell. In your head, go back in the office, look around, look at Stella. What did you see?"

Nell held back a smile. She was in a courtroom, being prepped by this very lovely lawyer, to keep her recollection clear and detailed. "Izzy, I think I've told you everything." She picked up her own knitting, the surprise-for-Birdie hoodie that Birdie was watching her knit, making sure she didn't add too many stitches around the bustline. "Stella also seemed totally up-front when Tommy asked her questions. She was genuinely puzzled by it all. She keeps the place neat, and said Rosie is good at that, too. There's little clutter. She would have noticed something missing. My worry for her is that it has to be frightening. It would almost be easier if they had taken the computer or something. That would make sense, at least."

Birdie hadn't said anything. She was sitting in Sonny Favazza's seventy-year-old cracked leather chair, sipping her gimlet. But the disruption in their lives had gone on long enough for her. "It has to be connected to the murder, then. To the house on Cliffside Drive. Maybe not the contracts, but something else. And maybe they didn't find it there. Maybe Stella or a cleaning person or someone inadvertently removed whatever it is the person was after. I think we set that fact aside as a given. And then we will see where it fits into the larger picture."

Everyone agreed.

"Talking to Patricia Stuber was enlightening," Nell said. "I think she helped us understand Spence a little."

"From what you told me, his dad must have been a poor excuse for a father," Izzy said. "A classic bully of a father, begetting—" She paused. "No, I don't think one is born a bully. He was a classic bully of a father *raising* a classic bully of a son."

"Yes," Nell said. "It's textbook."

"So we have a bully. But what we don't have is an adult knowing about the bullying. That was maybe the most interesting thing I learned from Patricia. She didn't deny that Spence probably was one, she just never had anyone reporting him to her. Or few other people, for that matter."

"It's the students who know those things. His buddies," Cass said.

"And don't forget the others," Izzy said quickly. "The kids like Rose, whose lives were made miserable because of guys like Spencer."

Birdie took a sip of her drink and set it down, her face thoughtful. "When we walked through the school and the kids were milling around, I was imagining Spencer and his friends. If someone is inclined toward that kind of behavior, I don't think they would pick on just one person. People develop habits—patterns, like in knitting. Surely Rose wasn't the only one they picked on."

"Has anyone asked Rose if she knew of other kids?" Birdie asked.

"Rose said that when you're the prey like she was, you become as invisible as you can. You don't spend much time figuring out what's going on around you. And she didn't really have good friends that she could have talked to about it. She was one of the kids who sat alone in the cafeteria, studying," Izzy said.

The thought was a sobering one, especially for Cass, who'd wandered through that same cafeteria and been waved over to many tables, invited to sit and laugh and talk nonsense. She shook off the discomforting memory and thought of something else the principal had said.

"Patricia also said something about some years being more difficult than others. And she mentioned that the years Spencer and his friends were in school were difficult for her." She looked at Birdie and Nell. "Did you get that?"

Nell nodded. "It was odd, the way she said it. As if she were remembering something that wasn't necessarily connected to our conversation, but had been triggered by it. Clearly something happened that was difficult. She looked pained as she remembered it."

"And she didn't want to talk about it," Birdie said.

"Do you suppose it was personal?" Cass asked.

"I think it was somehow personal to her. But I suspect it had something to do with the school," Birdie said. "It was in that context that she remembered it."

"Do you think it was connected to the Paxtons?" Izzy asked.

"I didn't get that feeling," Cass said. "I thought she remembered it because we were talking about things that happened around that time."

Nell agreed. "Yes, that's what I remember, too. But even if it didn't directly involve Spencer, it was important enough to affect her, even after all those years. I think it's worth looking into."

"If it was something that happened in town—even a minor thing—the *Sea Harbor Gazette* will have written about it. Anything that caused that sad look on Patricia Stuber's face all these years later was probably newsworthy."

"Stella was a couple years older than Spence. I wonder if there was anything going on that she was aware of?" Birdie said. "I'm taking her and Rosie to dinner. I think we'll have a good old-fashioned talk."

"Stella knew Spence, but he was enough younger that I doubt if she knew much more," Cass said. "She remembers him mostly from summer at the yacht club, this kid who thought every girl—even a college kid like Stell—was in love with him."

"But she might have remembered something traumatic enough that it affected the principal," Birdie said.

Or not. They all knew that high school was the most important time in your life. Until it wasn't. And for some, casting it aside happened very quickly.

"We're doing what we set out to do, following in Spencer's footsteps," Birdie said. "That's a good thing. But I don't think we can totally dismiss some of the others—"

They all looked at her.

"I am not sure Josh Babson has been completely up-front."

Izzy was quiet for a minute. They waited for a protest. But instead, she said, "You might be right. He's holding something back. When I asked him why he was so rude to Spencer that night on the Palate deck, his voice was cold and almost scary, not his usual way at all. I asked him again the other day when I dragged him over to help Bree and me. He said Paxton was truly bad."

"I do like Josh. Jane does, too," Nell said. "And you don't want to believe that people like him could . . ."

"No, of course you don't," Birdie said. "It's that same question all over again. . . . Do good women—or good men—do bad things?"

The room fell silent as a silent vow was made to find out.

Chapter 27

It seemed everyone had plans that night.

"Except for the two of us," Nell said to Ben, quite liking the idea. "Candlelight dinner."

"For two. Not ten."

Nell laughed, then added her choices. "A blazing fire and you to keep me warm. Oh, and tuna tartare."

In minutes they were in the car and headed toward Gloucester, wishing for a spot on the Beauport Hotel's deck, one next to the massive stone fire pit with plates of the hotel's signature tuna tartare in front of them, soft jazz playing in the background. And hoping not to run into anyone they knew.

"We're in luck on all accounts," Ben said, settling into the chair next to Nell. He laid a blanket across her knees and in minutes a tuna tartare appetizer and bottle of champagne appeared.

"So far. My sister Caroline always says the only sure thing about luck is that it will change."

"Your sister is a pessimist."

Nell leaned back and picked up the thin glass of champagne. "Now ... if only we had something to celebrate," she said, resting her head back and gazing into a sea of stars.

"That's not the Nellie I know and love. That's Caroline talking. Please tell her to leave—this is a dinner for two. And we *do* have something to celebrate." He dipped a chip into the avocado cream and handed it to her. "We have this moment. You can't ask for anything more."

Ben sang the last line of the old song and Nell laughed, a cleansing feel-good laugh that loosened her body and soul, the week's events scattering like the sea spray below. They clinked their glasses together and sat in comfortable silence, alone in the world, until the empty tuna platter had been removed and the champagne glasses were nearly empty. A waiter came over and stoked the fire, and Nell leaned over toward Ben, resting a hand on his arm as if anchoring him—and the moment—in place.

The evening passed in a pleasant blur—carried along by tenderloin filets, wine, and an unspoken agreement that talk of murder was not invited.

Hours later they walked down the staircase toward the parking lot, their heads light with pleasure and their bodies full. As they reached the bottom step, Nell pressed her palm against the pocket of her sweater to make sure her phone was still there—something she did with such automatic regularity that Ben teased her about it, especially when she made the motion to her pocket while speaking on the phone itself.

She stopped, then dug through her bag, and then smiled apologetically. "I must have left it on the deck."

Ben offered to retrieve it, but Nell insisted on going herself. She patted her stomach. "Exercise," she said.

A few minutes later, Nell returned, just as Ben was wrapping up his conversation with the doorman, learning where he went to school, what he majored in, and what kind of boat he liked to sail.

She took his arm and walked outside toward the parking lot. "We didn't get all four things we wished for," she said. "Although I suppose three out of four is pretty good."

Ben lifted one brow. "The three we got?"

"A place near the fire pit, tuna tartare, soft jazz."

"All perfect," Ben said.

Nell held up her phone. "Our efficient waiter found it. It was already at the hotel's front desk," she said, holding it up.

"Hmm," Ben said.

"And so were two people we know, checking in for the night."

"Ah, our fourth wish. Not running into anyone we know. Who was it?"

Nell waited a second longer while Ben fished his keys out of his pocket. And then she answered his question.

"Bree McIntosh and Josh Babson."

As had been the case in recent years—ever since Ben Endicott had convinced Birdie that driving Sonny Favazza's old Lincoln Town Car down Harbor Road at highway speed wasn't wise— her groundskeeper, Ella's wonderful husband Harold, drove the big shiny car, stopping at the curb outside the Palazola Realty office while Rosie and Stella piled in the backseat. He tipped his cherished chauffer's hat at them, and then continued down Harbor Road and around the shoreline to the Sea Harbor Yacht Club.

"I was going to come up with a reason for this dinner," Birdie said as they followed the waitress to a table near the wall of windows, "but finally decided I didn't need a reason. Dinner seemed like a good idea. So here we are."

Birdie smiled at Rose. No one talked about Rose staying or

leaving Sea Harbor, knowing the police would have eliminated that option for anyone connected to the Paxton murder until the investigation was complete. But Birdie knew one thing for sure: The more they could wrap the young woman in friendship, the easier that stay would be.

Sitting at the table across from Rose, Stella was beaming brighter than the candles all over the room. Having two of her favorite people together—and then, as icing on the cake, the club's seafood buffet—was a heavenly relief sandwiched in a rough couple of weeks.

Birdie felt it, too. She suggested a bottle of wine and an order of crab cakes for starters, then settled back in the comfortable chair and listened to Rose and Stella talk about a new listing Stella had just landed, and a decaying bathroom pipe that Rosie was replacing. The interplay between the two younger women was comforting somehow, the laughter that came easily a perfect evening tonic. But she especially relished the respect and affection they gave to one another, and the calmness that Rose brought to the table. It was lovely to see what trust and chemistry could do.

And also yoga and meditation, she knew. She and Nell had discussed Rose's practices earlier that day. The conversation was left hanging when Nell suddenly suggested that she and Birdie take a yoga class at the Y.

Looking at Rose now, her calm expression and thoughtful eyes, made Birdie wonder about it all. The young woman had lived through a painful adolescence, an unwitting connection to a murder, and now was caught up in a police investigation, exploring every footstep she took. And she looked happy. Or peaceful, at least. Rose Chopra was a survivor.

Rose was looking around the room, taking in the candles flickering on the tables, a trio playing in the corner lounge, the amazing aromas. "It's even lovelier here at night," she said, and then reminded Birdie that they'd had lunch there together once before—not long ago, or maybe a lifetime.

"It seems like a lifetime anyway," Rose said. "You were here, too, Stell."

"Right over there," Stella said, pointing to a table at the window. "I was getting the Destinos to sign a contract for that big old house on Ocean Spray Road."

"Oh, lordy, I almost forgot that day," Birdie said.

"You probably wanted to forget," Rose said. "I did. It wasn't my finest hour."

"You fainted. It was awful for you. What was it Izzy called it?" Stella asked.

"Vasovagal reflex," Rosie said. "It sounds made up but it's true. It's triggered by different things in different people. In my case it's blood, needles—I could never be a candy striper—and also a sudden traumatic experience."

Birdie listened, revisiting that day in her mind.

Rose looked over at her. "I know, there wasn't any blood that day. But it was traumatic."

Birdie put it together in an instant. How Rose had walked up behind her and had seen Spencer Paxton, just feet away from her.

"That was the first time I had seen Spence since I left here as a damaged kid," Rose said. "I figured it would happen—I wanted it to happen—but I guess you could say I didn't have my sea legs yet."

"It must have dredged everything up in that single second," Stella said. "I don't remember much about Spence from high school—he was an underclassman—though everyone knew him in a superficial way. He made sure everyone knew his name and that he was a successful quarterback. But I have this secret hope that I tripped him or something. I think I did."

Rosie laughed. "Bree told me Spence said you had a crush on him."

That brought a laugh from Stella loud enough to cause several nearby diners to look her way.

Rose chuckled. "That's what Bree and I thought."

Birdie rested her arms on the table, her eyes thoughtful as she remembered the scene at the club entrance. "We never put it together that day, your fainting and the Paxton incident."

"No, how could you have? Besides, it was Mayor Scaglia everyone was concerned about. Her relationship to him, certainly not mine."

"Well, that's true enough."

"My mom subscribed to the *Sea Harbor Gazette* forever," Rose said. "Our Omaha neighbors thought it odd, but Mom liked reading about things going on here, especially regarding the ocean, the tides, fishing. Every now and then I'd scan it. A few months ago, I saw Spencer's name in that chatty column— Mary Pisano's 'About Town,' I think. Something about him coming back to town and a little bit about where he'd been."

"You knew he'd be here?" Stella said.

Rose played with the edge of her napkin. "Yes. That's part of why I came. I knew from years of therapy that seeing him face-to-face was part of the process, maybe the only one left. I didn't know what I'd do or say when I saw him, but I wanted to throw away the whole bad experience that was Spencer Paxton. I wanted to toss it into the sea, gone forever . . ." The sentence drifted off, and Rose turned her head, looking through the windows, into the blackness where the ocean rolled and churned.

When she looked back, her voice had grown soft and faraway, as if coming from another time and place.

"I needed to toss all of it into that same sea that I waded into one night a long, long time ago. I had planned that night carefully. A deserted beach, a gentle tide. I left my shoes at the footbridge and walked across the wet sand and into the dark water, feeling the bottom of the sea move beneath my toes, the salty water circling my ankles, my legs, and then my waist. And on and on into the deeper water until finally the top of my head would be covered. My hair waving like seaweed across the surface, my body relaxing. Dreaming peaceful thoughts. Then sinking down, floating gently. Until I rested on the bottom."

Birdie's breath caught in her chest painfully.

Stella's face had gone pale.

No one spoke.

Rose shifted in her chair, then looked at Birdie and Stella, only realizing in that moment that she had talked too long. Said too much.

"I don't know where all that came from." She tried to lighten her voice. "I didn't get that far, obviously. Just to an outcropping of boulders where the water was shoulder high. Someone called to me from the beach. I don't know who, but I heard my name and I waved back. Then I climbed up on one of the boulders, and I stayed there for a long time, until I'd counted every star in the sky. Finally I slid off into the water, more shallow now because the tide was low, and I walked through the water back to the shore.

"Whoever had called to me was gone. The beach was deserted, except for one small sign of life. A skinny, homeless kitten was standing there, all by itself, meowing and then rubbing against me, needing my body warmth. It was like an omen, you know? Like he was waiting for me.

"I picked him up and we went home."

She tried to put a smile in her voice.

Birdie leaned forward to catch her words.

"It was foolish. I was a kid. Kids sometimes do foolish things."

There was silence, but Rose soon broke it.

"But I didn't drown." She looked at each of them, her eyes locking into theirs. And then she added with equal conviction, "And I didn't kill Spencer Paxton."

The waitress walked into their silence, a welcome distraction. As was the wine that she uncorked and poured for Birdie to taste. After filling their glasses she discreetly disappeared, sensing a special occasion, but one she couldn't begin to understand.

Birdie looked into the candlelight, then lifted her glass, her eyes looking into each of theirs. "To new beginnings, and to new friends," she said.

The glasses clinked. And the single tear that rolled down Rose's cheek did not go unnoticed, nor was it wiped away.

"Let's eat," Stella said, pushing back her chair. "The buffet awaits."

Birdie and Rose followed her across the room to a long table groaning with fresh lobster, oysters on the half shell, grilled fish, and more offerings than one could see standing in one spot.

Rose came back to the table and sat down in front of a plate with a giant lobster staring at her. "Lobster wasn't a staple for us once we moved away from here," she said. "My mom was one of those Catholics who still didn't eat meat on Friday, and when we lived here, we'd have Friday lobster whenever we could afford it. Always drowning in butter and creating the rolls around my middle that caused embarrassment and suffering at the beach. But it made me happy in the moment. I missed it when we moved away." She held the claw of her lobster and tried unsuccessfully to twist it off.

Stella reached over and with one quick movement, pulled it apart. "It's all in the wrist," she said. "I don't suppose you're overrun with lobsters in Nebraska."

Rose laughed. She picked up a tiny fork and began pulling bits of meat from the shell. "Prem—the guy I was briefly married to—did most of the cooking. He said Indians are ambivalent about lobsters. But he'd try to please me, so he'd make something and call it lobster curry, but almost always it was made with frozen shrimp he'd picked up at the market. I knew because I'd find the wrappings in the trash."

"What was he like?" Stella asked. "Prem, not the lobster."

"Nice. Kind. A good friend. We were shy college kids, trying to find our way on a huge university campus and we helped each other navigate all that. Studying, going to movies. I shared a lot with him, including the help I was getting in therapy. Somehow, I can't even be sure now why, we decided to get married. We were nineteen. He was my best friend, maybe my only one back then."

She looked shocked at her own admission.

Birdie was watching Stella, who seemed to be concentrating on de-shelling her own lobster, but she was listening so intently to Rose that a sudden squirt of lobster water onto her chin went unnoticed.

"Anyway," Rose was saying, "we're still friends. We both knew—maybe even before we signed the papers—that neither of us was cut out to be married to each other. We didn't have those feelings, you know?"

Rose went on and added some details about her relationship with Prem Chopra, casual things about their interests, helping each other excel in their classes, and then wrapping it all up in a friendly online divorce. Her voice was conversational, as if she had been talking about a camping trip or a trip to the shore.

Birdie sipped her wine and listened to what Rose was really sharing with them: the story of two lonely people. Good friends. Two people growing into themselves and learning who each of them truly was. Helping each other do that. And then getting on with their lives. It was a sweet story.

A while later the waitress returned with a dessert cart, and the conversation turned to the delicacies. Birdie thought she was about to explode, but she could see the eyes of the two younger women at her table brighten.

Yoga, she thought. *All right, I'll give it a try.*

*   *   *

When they finally walked out of the yacht club and were waiting for Harold to bring over the car, Birdie stood slightly apart, considering the evening and the stories that had unfolded. Considering what Rose Woodley Chopra had told them about herself. Her strength and understanding of who she was had not come easily. But it had come.

The soft string music in the lounge had given way to a more energetic band with a deep thumping bass and words that sounded jumbled to Birdie as they streamed out the open windows.

She looked over at Rose and Stella, talking, their bodies moving unconsciously to the music. Rose's whole face was smiling.

And she thought of a young girl wading out into the ocean.

And coming back.

Her next thought was the one that stayed with her over the next days, teasing and tugging for more attention:

But what if she hadn't?

Chapter 28

Ben had decided he was going to Annabelle's for his Sunday omelet, even if he had to go alone. Three weeks without an omelet at Annabelle's Sweet Petunia restaurant was a bad thing. He'd lost three pounds. Nell thought that was a fine thing, but she turned off the coffee and grabbed her jacket.

The small, out-of-the-way restaurant was the Endicotts' favorite place on Cape Ann. Perched on a hill above the art colony, with trees climbing right up to the deck, it was a secret Sea Harbor residents tried to keep from tourists—their private place with a magnificent view of the century-old artists' galleries and the ocean behind them.

And according to many, Annabelle Palazola made the most memorable omelet on the East Coast. Every week it was different, and every week it was an incredible surprise, the extra ingredients picked from her own garden and never revealed.

Nell waved at Patricia Stuber and her husband who were sitting at a small table toward the other end of the deck. Nearby, Esther Gibson sat alone, surreptitiously slipping bits of bacon to her ancient basset hound, Boyd, who hid beneath the table.

She leaned down to give the police dispatcher a hug and promised with a whisper not to turn Boyd in to the restaurant police. Esther chuckled and promised in return they'd solve this damn murder soon, come hell or high water.

Nell caught up with Ben and Birdie as they walked to the farthest table on the deck, near the back steps and an old maple tree that leaned comfortably against the railing, dropping crimson leaves on the table. A nearby heat lamp defied the end to their outdoor eating.

Cass was pulling apart one of Annabelle's fried biscuits, slathering it with homemade apple butter, when the others walked up. Beside her, Danny was deep into the *NYT Book Review*.

"Sit," Cass said, looking up. She held up a biscuit and grinned. "I saved you one."

Izzy and Sam showed up a few minutes later. Abby had been left behind, much to her great-aunt Nell's chagrin. Izzy's sitter had asked if she could come over that morning. Something about earning a badge for her scout troop. Little Abby was delighted. Playing on the floor with Legos and her favorite sitter was far more fun than sitting still in the middle of adoring adults.

The waitress filled their coffee mugs, added more biscuits to the basket and took orders, although orders were optional, she said; Annabelle knew what would please them. "Sunday specials all around. Got it." She smiled and disappeared.

"Okay," Cass said, her hands moving in the air as she dropped a topic in front of them without a preamble and before they'd had their coffee. "I've been thinking about Spencer Paxton, imagining that I'm walking those halls back at Sea Harbor High—"

"With a letter jacket on, I hope?" Sam asked.

"Quiet, Sam."

"Oh, wait, no. Not Cass. A cheerleading outfit. Short skirt. Skimpy top," Danny chimed in.

They laughed, trying to imagine the lobster fisherwoman doing handstands on a football field.

"Hey, don't laugh," Izzy said, her brows moving up into highlighted bangs. "I did that."

Cass ignored all of them. "As I was saying, there was another article in the paper today. You late sleepers probably didn't see it, but I've been up since five."

"Feeding our chickens," Danny explained.

"Really?" Birdie asked.

"We really have chickens, yes," Danny said, his voice a mixture of amusement and disbelief.

Cass glared at him, daring him to interrupt again.. "It's not a big deal. A neighbor left them behind when he moved. Danny wasn't so sure about it, callous mystery writer that he is. But I couldn't just leave them there. So yes on the chickens—my goddaughter Abby will love them—but I wasn't feeding them at five. I was reading the paper. There was another article today about Spencer Paxton. One of those *Who was this guy anyway?* kind of articles."

Ben nodded. He'd seen it, too. "They still haven't figured all that out. And without more to say about the investigation, reporters are grabbing at things to keep readers satisfied."

"Do you think they're getting closer to solving this?" It was Sam who asked the question. He and Ben had regular breakfast dates with Jerry Thompson, and though the chief had been too busy of late, Sam knew Ben talked to him regularly.

"I don't know. As we all know, they have people with motives and means, and some of those people don't have good alibis. But there's nothing tangible."

"No bloody glove, so to speak," Danny said.

"Right. I presume they need more proof. Or *any* proof. Jerry doesn't look happy."

"In the meantime, the press is trying to solve it?" Nell asked.

"So it seems," said Cass. "This article was one of their investigative attempts. They found a photo of Spence as captain of the football team and then dug up some locals who were classmates and interviewed them."

"Who?" Nell asked.

"A gal who cuts my hair at MJ's Salon and a waitress over at the Gull. A couple of others. Anyway, they all thought Spencer Paxton was one of those high school gods, but admitted that they didn't know him. They weren't in the in-crowd, they said, and he was kind of particular about whom he hung with, unless it was time for some election."

"And then?" Izzy asked. "Wait, I know. Then he'd canvass the cafeteria and roam the quad and charm the 'lesser' students."

"'The little people,' as Leona Helmsley once said," Birdie added.

Cass nodded and took another biscuit. "Students coveted Spence's attention, and when they got it, they'd vote for him. But they made it clear to the reporter they were just impressionable kids and would act differently today. But they also told the reporter that although all schools probably had some nasty kids, they were positive they hadn't gone to school with a murderer. So no one in their class could have killed Spence. Besides, if someone really wanted to kill him, why didn't they murder Spencer Paxton way back then?"

"They actually have a point," Ben said.

"Although there is such a thing as repressed hatred," Izzy said. "It can emerge years later, triggered by something insignificant."

The thought was an ugly one. Simmering hatred. A volcano ready to explode.

"Was there anything said about students who got Spence's attention, but not in a good way?" Danny asked. "I know a little about bullying from some long-ago reporting I did. Where there's one victim, there's usually another."

"If there were others, I think they slipped through the cracks and are probably long gone from Sea Harbor," Cass said. "Kids see what they want to see sometimes and the women in the article never mentioned friends being bullied. Once the reporter decided the women weren't going to lead him to solving the crime, he shifted back to the present. The Spencer Paxton who wanted to be mayor. The man whose wife wasn't happy with him."

Izzy said, "Poor Bree."

"The development angle is interesting—what Paxton Development was planning for Sea Harbor. Folks don't seem to be talking about it much anymore," Danny said.

"I don't think the company ever got far enough. A clerk at city hall told me that once Spencer realized the town didn't want big box bookstores and fancy condos in the art colony, he divorced himself from it and left it up to others in the company," Ben said. "It wasn't the way to win the election. And there's been no sign of the company since the murder."

"Not even to show up personally to claim the body, according to Bree," Izzy said.

"Do people like that really exist?" Cass said. "Ugh."

"Did today's article bring us any closer to who might have killed him? Or am I missing something?" Sam asked.

The question went unanswered as the waitress returned with a tray of Annabelle's golden omelets, served in a bed of chopped tomatoes and fresh herbs. "Guaranteed to cure what ails you," she said, settling a large plate in front of each of them.

Ben immediately forked into the creamy pocket, releasing slivers of spinach and avocado, crisp bacon pieces, and a stream of melted cheese. Flakes of fresh parsley and dill fell from his fork.

"Don't swoon," Nell cautioned while passing a pot of Greek yogurt his way. "It looks bad in public."

Ben took a drink of coffee with a contented look on his face. "So what's the point of the article?"

"Maybe to trigger people's memories," Danny said. "Even though the women they interviewed weren't much help, it might make other people come forward, people who went to school when Spencer did but perhaps knew him better. Or maybe, if not that, people who'd rubbed shoulders with him more recently, at the Gull or Ocean's Edge. Down at the harbor. Spence got around."

"That's a good point," Sam said. "I retract my judgment about the reporting crew."

"I guess we'll have to see," Ben said. "You've been over at his school, what do you think?" He looked at the women around the table. "After all this time, can it be helpful? People change."

"I'm not sure Spencer Paxton changed," Birdie said. "Being in the school building gave us a feeling for how he functioned then, and it wasn't that different. Competitive, aggressive, willing to do almost anything to get what he wanted. And diminishing those who beat him at something, who threatened his ego, like our Rose."

Nell nodded. *The definition of a bully.* She was sitting at the end of the table, slightly apart, doing more listening and thinking than talking, her omelet nearly gone. She agreed that they understood Spencer better after the trip to the school. Even though Patricia hadn't pointed to anything specific, there was something there. Something buried in those old lockers or trophy cases that would bring them closer to the person who killed Spencer Paxton. But saying it out loud made it sound insubstantial. Flimsy. More emotion than fact. So they'd hold it close for now, but each one of them was convinced they were closer to figuring it out.

Find someone who hated him enough. It seemed simple when they had talked about it that way. Find the person who hated him. Collect the facts—the means and opportunity. Case solved. A clear-cut path, and yet not simple at all.

Rose could have hated Spencer enough to kill him. But that was the cruel irony of bullying. What Spencer did to Rose didn't produce hatred for him. Instead—and far worse—it made Rose hate herself.

Nell tuned back into the conversation just as Danny was talking. "My dad said the men's group had a record turnout last week. All because of a murder."

"Curiosity, I guess," Sam said. "Did they think Father Larry would have a scoop?"

"He usually does," Ben said. "But he's also very discreet. I wonder what they thought they'd learn."

"Dad didn't say. But he said they did what they do—especially with Father Larry there. They bowed their heads and sent him off with a prayer."

"But no new rumors ran through the group?" Cass asked. "Those guys say women gossip, but I hear them out on the pier talking about everything from politics to divorces to lobster poaching. Not much gets by them."

"Except the men's club isn't all old guys anymore," Birdie said. "Harry Garozzo tells me they're bringing in new blood. He's got his nephew coming now, and some others, too."

"They come for my ma's casserole," Cass said. "They sit in the back, eat a lot, and get out early, she says."

"Probably true," Danny said. "My dad said there wasn't much discussion about the murder, not as much as he thought there'd be. In fact, the mood wasn't respectful like it usually is when someone dies. When old Anthony Bianchi passed, they spent hours singing his praises, telling crazy stories, then turning the guy into Saint Anthony before the ground was settled on his grave. Not so with Paxton. They got out their RIPs, but it was clear at the end how they felt. Someone even muttered a 'good riddance' from the back of the room, and no one objected."

A touch to Nell's shoulder pulled her attention from the table discussion. She looked up into Patricia Stuber's thoughtful eyes.

"Nell, may I speak with you for a minute?" Patricia said hello to the others and apologized for interrupting. Then she stepped over to the deck's back steps.

Nell followed. "What is it, Patricia?"

"I haven't slept well since you visited the other day," she began. "Thinking about Rose Woodley, and things that might have gone on right before my unseeing eyes."

"You know that isn't how it happened, Patricia," Nell said. "You weren't a part of this. The bullying that Rose suffered often wasn't even at the school. It happened at the yacht club, in a sailing class, and who knows where else?"

"I know that, Nell." She smiled sadly. "But believe me, being principal means you don't forget those students when they leave the school. You go with them, in a way. At least that's how I interpret my job.

"But back to Rose Woodley. I couldn't get her off my mind. I found her photo in the yearbook. I looked and looked, and I saw such sadness in her young eyes. It haunted me. I called together some of the staff who were there when Rose and Spencer were students. We sat around for a long time, talking and pushing ourselves back to those years, that class. That time."

"It must be difficult. So many students go through those halls—"

"Yes, and it was especially difficult those two or three years. There were days when I wondered if I was carrying some kind of curse, something that had tentacles that reached out and affected others in a bad way. Sad things seemed to be happening to our school families at a rate that was difficult to handle." She took a deep breath and exhaled.

"Things in the school?" Nell was puzzled.

"No. But connected to the school because they were our school families. But no matter, the staff and I were responsible for those walking our halls, Nell. They were our responsibility; we were their caretakers during school hours. As we dug back through those years we remembered small things, incidents here and there. Innuendoes. Things that, when added together, equaled bigger things. But they were always covered up somehow. Girls frightened to talk, popular groups with innocent faces."

Nell listened, watching the shadows of memory pass across the principal's face.

"You were right in your suspicions, Nell. Rose Woodley wasn't alone. There were other students.

"And we did nothing to help them."

Chapter 29

"They couldn't have done anything, not if they didn't know about it," Cass said. "Patricia is being hard on herself."

They sat and stood and walked around in the quiet haven of Izzy's knitting room, the casement windows open, filling the room with sea air. The shop was empty of customers, thanks to Izzy and Mae's decision to close the shop on Sundays once the tourists had gone. A decision they all welcomed. It gave the knitters a place to escape to, sometimes to talk or knit and listen to music.

And sometimes, like today, to gather pieces of a puzzle, strewn across their days like uneven rocks on a hiking path.

"Patricia is smart and realistic. She won't beat herself to death over it. But she's allowed that *if only* feeling—for a few minutes anyway." Nell looped a long piece of pink yarn over a pole that she and Izzy had hung in the doorway. Her fiber art in progress.

"And what about *what if*?" Birdie mused. She finished weaving in a yarn end and set her sweater sleeve back in her bag. She moved over to the table where Izzy was scribbling on a yellow pad.

Birdie continued, looking down at Izzy's pad. "What if Rose hadn't been able to leave Sea Harbor? What if she'd had to endure four years of Spencer Paxton?"

What if. A thought none of them wanted to pursue.

Nell took her pole down and laid it across a chair. "Even if we don't find anything directly related to Spencer, it was his world, too. We might understand it better by looking back at that time and seeing if we can find any connections."

Patricia Stuber's evasive comment about difficult years was exactly that—evasive, and they weren't even sure where to look. But something had happened during that time that affected the principal so much that she still thought about it all these years later. When Nell had nudged her for more information, Patricia had said it wasn't anything pertinent to the murder. And she wasn't even sure why it had stayed with her so long. Then she had changed the subject.

"I don't know why or how, but it seems significant," Birdie said. "And if it's not, we'll find another way to connect our dots. I do feel a little bit like I'm flitting back and forth in time. I'm slightly dizzy."

Izzy looked down at her scribbled words. Important words were encased in separate circles, beginning in the middle of the page with one containing Spencer's name.

"I just wrote down random things and people, things that are connected. Or could be. Maybe." She shrugged.

"Your own Venn diagram," Nell mused. She leaned closer. "Clever. You're showing who is connected to whom, to what. Interesting."

Many of the circles overlapped with one or two others: *Elevator keys, Alibi, Beatrice, Rose, Sea Harbor High, Bree*—but Izzy had wisely used pencil, easily erased.

Only one circle floated freely on the page, as if looking for somewhere to land: *Palazola office break-in.*

Birdie pointed to Bree's name. "Why is Bree's circle only intersecting with *Spencer*, and not with *Alibi*?"

"Because Bree is lying," Izzy said matter-of-factly.

The others stared at her.

"She's connected to Spencer, of course," Izzy continued, pointing to the two overlapping circles. "Husband and wife. But she doesn't have an alibi."

"You sound certain of that," Nell said. She hadn't yet mentioned to any of them that she and Ben had seen Bree and Josh Babson together the night before. They had talked about it on the way home, trying to convince themselves that Bree and Josh were both adults. Bree had been through a huge trauma. Perhaps Josh had been there when she was most in need.

But in truth, it didn't matter. Things shifted and took on complicated meanings when a murder was being investigated.

Nell looked around the table at her friends, all of whom cared about Bree McIntosh. They all wanted desperately for her to be innocent of her husband's murder. But before Nell could complicate their hopes further, Izzy went on to explain her earlier comment.

"Bree wasn't in her house when the police came looking for her to tell her about Spencer," Izzy was saying. "No one, no matter how heavy a sleeper they are, could sleep through that doorbell. We know that, and we've been ignoring it, especially me, maybe. But she is vague when she talks about it. Almost muddling her words. It's clear to me she's not telling the truth."

Nell listened, and then it was her turn. She took a breath, and then said, "Bree and Josh were together last night, checking in to the Beauport Hotel in Gloucester."

Izzy's head shot up. "Josh?" And then, as if going back over the days and weeks in her head, she said, "Josh has been around a lot these last few weeks. No, longer, really. Ever since the idea of the fiber show came up."

"We started thinking about the show months ago," Nell said.
Izzy nodded. "Yes, it was . . ." She left her words hanging.

"Jane pushed that," Nell said, wanting to be sure they didn't
jump to conclusions. "She encouraged him to help with planning and preparations. It took some of the load off her."

Izzy nodded, still trying to put it together in her head.

"They're grown-ups. Seeing them together at the hotel doesn't
mean anything, really," Cass said. "At least as far as alibis and
murders go." And then she corrected herself. "But a murder
changes everything, doesn't it—everything means something. Or
could."

But what it could mean for Josh and Bree wasn't clear. "I
wonder how long this has been going on," Izzy said.

They were all wondering the same thing. Had she and
Josh been having an affair—*if* they were having an affair—for
months? Bree had met the Canary Cove family of artists
early on. And she herself said she and Spencer lived separate
lives.

"I suppose it could even have been an agreement between
Bree and Spencer. People do that. Separate lives." Izzy picked
up her pencil and stared at her diagram.

"But if not, Spencer's death would certainly be freeing for
them," Cass said. "But we're conjecturing all over the place
here."

"That's what we do, Cass. We conjecture all over the place . . .
until we know." Birdie put on her glasses and looked at the diagram again, watching Izzy add information to the page.

The new circle had *Josh* printed in the middle. "I don't know
how I forgot him. He should have been on here all along." Her
voice was tight, as if she herself had somehow been betrayed by
people she cared about.

Josh's circle overlapped with *Spencer*.

And *Bree*.

But Josh floated free of *Alibi*.

"He doesn't have an alibi?" Cass asked. "The police must have talked to him. Even Jane and Ham talked about him disliking Spence."

No one knew for sure.

So his circle remained connected to *Bree* and *Spencer*. And not intersecting with *Alibi*.

Exactly the same as Bree's.

"So," Cass said, stretching out the word. "She and Josh were having an affair. Maybe. What do we do with that?"

Sometimes, they decided, a question worth its salt simply had to go unanswered. At least for a while. Until it ripened.

The drive from the yarn shop to the small building that housed the *Sea Harbor Gazette* was a short one. Knowing a columnist at the paper helped, and as they piled out of Nell's car, the back door of the building opened and Mary Pisano, the energetic columnist and their friend, poked her head out.

"The morgue is ready for you," she said happily, then sobered. "That's not a good word to throw around these days, is it?"

She ushered them past a couple of reporters who barely looked up, then down a hall to a room in the back with MORGUE printed on the door. Mary flicked on the light. "Help yourself, my friends. The machines are in here. I pulled out the microfiche you asked for, Nell. There are soft drinks and bad coffee out front. Have a good time. I'm off."

She grinned and waved, and in an instant, all five feet of Mary Pisano had disappeared, leaving them in a dusty-smelling room that felt entirely like the word that was printed on the door.

"Spooky," Cass said, pulling out a chair behind one of the machines. She turned the machine on. "Okay, ladies, step into my time machine."

Izzy laughed and turned on the machine next to her.

Nell and Birdie pulled up chairs between them, adding their eyes to the scanning process.

In the space between the machines sat a pile of microfiche, something none of them had used in a while.

"It takes me back to graduate school," Nell said.

Izzy and Cass agreed.

"Even the smell is the same," Izzy said. "The law library. It's all coming back, strangling me. File after file, case after case." She clenched her throat with one hand, then settled back and inserted the first roll of film. "Okay, to work."

Since they weren't sure what they were looking for, or the exact year, Izzy and Cass took separate years of newspapers, starting with Rose's freshman year and ending with Spencer's graduation.

"We don't care much about weather or sports or obits," Cass said. "But let's keep eagle eyes out for the name Patricia Stuber or Sea Harbor High."

"Or the Paxton name," Birdie added.

Soon the room echoed with the sound of film sheets sliding beneath glass, buttons pressing, and an occasional reminder to go faster.

"One year done," Cass said, taking out the film and inserting another. "Apparently the Math Olympiad didn't make the city paper. But my hairdresser's wedding did. Pretty dress."

The next year started quickly with several months going by in a flash. A nor'easter captured the news, including school closings for two days, then a schooner festival. But in May, Izzy paused, then rolled back a page. "Oh, geesh."

They leaned toward the screen. The photo took up the front page. A car smashed against a guardrail on the highway. The headline looked huge on the screen. FOUR SENIORS AT SEA HARBOR HIGH KILLED. It was a month before graduation. "School and town reeling," the caption read.

"I remember that. My ma tore it out and sent it to me. Four kids in a town this size is huge. Everyone knew at least one of the kids or a relative."

Birdie remembered, too. "Esther Gibson's granddaughter Sandy died in that car accident," she said. "They were so young. It was terribly sad."

Cass named two others who were in the accident—her dentist's daughter, and a son of the accountant who handled the Halloran Lobster Company books.

Patricia Stuber was quoted in the article, and when Izzy enlarged a photo, she was visible at one of the memorial services, standing in the back, looking as if she had lost her own child.

"Do you think this is what was clouding Patricia's mind during that time?" Nell wondered out loud. It was awful and tragic, and must have been challenging to deal with at the school. But it was one day, one year . . .

When Cass began moving through the next year, they could feel Patricia Stuber's presence in the room, mourning her students. "They were her family," Birdie said.

Cass paused during a week in July. Another accident, another death. A freshman at Sea Harbor High was in a fatal sailboat accident. And just a few months later, a young man who looked like everyone's next-door neighbor, fell asleep while driving home from his homecoming dance.

"Jimmy Northcutt," Cass said, her voice unusually husky. "He crashed into a tree over near Canary Cove. Jimmy was related to Father Northcutt and hung around the church. My ma loved that kid. She made him cookies."

Everyone was related to someone else, someone's neighbor, and someone's friend. And they realized with overwhelming certainty that this was, indeed, what could have clouded the principal's life for months and months. In ordinary life, when one wasn't scrolling through years on microfilm in minutes, the events, though tragic, would only have been tumultuous to those directly affected. Family, loved ones, people who cared. Like Patricia Stuber.

Things she could do nothing about.

Izzy inserted another year of newspapers and paused for a minute, her hand on the knob, not sure what a new year would bring or if she wanted to read about it.

She also wondered if they were on a wild-goose chase.

Then she started the last film, slowly moving through winter, then spring. She stopped in April, when a small article reported the death of a long-time and beloved math teacher, who had died peacefully in his home. It had occurred the same week as a young student at Sea Harbor High had died unexpectedly from an undetected heart abnormality.

They moved on, slowly, as spring morphed into summer, then fall, along with articles on football games, homecoming games and dances, and apple picking. Halloween costumes and Thanksgiving food drives. Happy events.

"It looks like the curse Patricia Stuber felt was finally lifted," Nell said.

"And the dear woman was right," said Birdie. "There was nothing she could do about it but ache for the sadness people suffered."

It wasn't about anything malicious. It wasn't a conspiracy. It was simply a tragic, sad time in the life of the principal of Sea Harbor High and all the families and townspeople who were touched.

Izzy continued to slowly roll through the newspaper images as they talked, the print beginning to blur into one long, hazy image.

"Wait," said Birdie. "Would you please go back one? There, at the bottom of the page."

Izzy rolled back, then enlarged the headline running along the bottom:

A Long Journey into Light at Sea Harbor High

They smiled. "Happy news," Izzy said, and began reading about happy times at Sea Harbor High. The article elaborated on student awards and school accolades and social outreach programs, honors convocations and award-winning faculty. A school awakening from "a seemingly endless winter," the reporter wrote.

It was a human-interest article that went to an inside page, filled with photos that highlighted the school, its staff, and students in the nicest of ways.

It was an uplifting, pleasant article.

Until the end.

In rounding out his article, the reporter had brought the reader back to the tragedies that had burdened the school in the preceding years. Sad times that were now a part of the past. And at the end, he had tied it all together by paying tribute to those they had lost.

Across the page, filling the entire width, were photos of those the community had lost. One after another.

It was odd and slightly jarring, reading it from the distance of time. Seeing all those faces together as one would in a mass tragedy, which it hadn't been.

Cass reached over and enlarged the photos, faces of some people she knew. And then she paused on one.

"Look at this," she said sadly.

Birdie's face grew sad, too. What she remembered was the sadness of those left behind.

The face wasn't familiar to Izzy or Nell. But the name was.

Nell leaned closer. A disturbing sensation moved through her. Perhaps it was the power of distance that sometimes brought clarity. The fact that the years they'd just journeyed through reflected a town she hadn't been a part of. She wasn't as close to the events as Birdie and Cass. She didn't have the emotional tug that sometimes colors logic.

She looked at the article again, and noticed Izzy staring at the same page.

In that moment she realized that going back to Sea Harbor High may have been the wisest thing they had done.

Then she asked Izzy if they could make a copy of it, but Izzy was already at work.

Chapter 30

Izzy and Cass ran hard, sand spraying up beneath their shoes, as if the sweat and punishing jog would purge them of thoughts of murder and death.

They ran along the curve of the shore, then up the hilly road into the Cliffside neighborhood, the wind against their cheeks, their legs running the familiar route on autopilot. Finally, where the road divided and went off in different directions, they slowed, then stopped and leaned down near a fence, hands on their knees, pulling in gulps of sea air.

Izzy pushed back a handful of hair that had escaped her baseball cap and stretched out one leg, then the other, her body welcoming the movement.

Beside her, Cass wiped the perspiration from her face and neck. "Do you feel you've just been brought back to life?"

Izzy made a face, looking behind Cass to the house across the street. "Funny you should say that . . ."

Cass turned around and they both stared.

The Bianchi house stood tall and imposing behind the low wall, and looked anything but alive. The iron gate was closed across the drive and bushes crowded the sides.

"Have you ever been inside?" Izzy asked.

"No. I'm not sure I'd want to, although they say the Bianchis used to have some wild parties up here. For some reason the Hallorans and the Bianchis didn't run in the same circles." She laughed and leaned her head way back, looking all the way up to the third floor as she stretched her back, her hands on her hips.

Izzy followed her gaze and for a long time they both stood there, imagining the people who once lived there, and the four old men who'd made the top floor their own private club.

And the man who died there.

The sound of a car coming up the road distracted them and they looked down the street. The car slowed down, and then a few yards before reaching them, the engine idled and Izzy and Cass watched as the electric gate at the Bianchi house began to open. The car moved into the drive and parked. Stella Palazola climbed out.

"Hey, Stella!" Cass shouted and waved.

Stella shielded her eyes against the sun, and then waved back. "Hey, guys, come on over," she yelled. "Come see what I have."

They picked up their water bottles and walked through the gate, looking again at the house, which seemed to have grown ten feet higher at close range.

"Yeah, it's big," Stella said, following their gaze.

"We run by here all the time," Izzy said. "But it's different now."

"More foreboding?" suggested Stella. "I definitely get that."

"What will happen to the house?"

"Good question. Ben suggested that we wait for things to settle before talking to Bree, but the house is hers. I don't know if she's even looked at Spencer's will, but I know this was to be hers. He added it in after he bought it."

"That's almost cruel. She doesn't even like this place."

"I know a good Realtor who could sell it for her." Stella laughed. Then she turned back to her car, excitement lighting her face. "But forget about that for a minute. Come see what I have." She motioned to the back door window and stepped aside, letting Izzy and Cass look in.

A grocery store box sat on the backseat, its floor cushioned with an old towel. And inside the box sat two kittens looking curiously at the eyes staring in at them.

"What?" Izzy and Cass shouted in unison.

"I know. Crazy, right?"

"Where did they come from? They're adorable," Izzy said.

"Yes, they are," Stella said. "I found them in the garage of a new listing I got. They were abandoned, meowing up a storm, waiting for me to save them. So I did."

"What are you going to do with them?" Cass asked.

Stella looked at her as if she were crazy. "Do with them? They're for the office. They're for Rose. For us." Then she smiled enigmatically and said, "They're an omen."

Stella smiled at her own words and repeated them. "That's what they are. An omen."

Cass and Izzy smiled, not sure of how to respond. But Stella was clearly happy, so they were too. They turned away from the car and looked over at the house.

"So what are you doing here?" Cass asked.

"I came to remove a couple photos that the Bianchi kids forgot. Want to come up with me? The house still spooks me a little when I'm alone. I didn't want to ask Rosie to come with me, though. That third floor isn't her favorite place."

Cass and Izzy were happy to fill in for Rose, and in minutes the elevator was taking them up to the top of the house to a room that had been rambling around in their imaginations for days.

Izzy looked at the brass key ring Stella held. It was just like the one she had seen in Bree's house. "How many keys are there to this place, Stell?"

"I've been asked that a lot lately. Eight of these rings. And they're all like this one, with numbers on the dangly doodad. Only five, though, had elevator keys in addition to the house keys. My uncle says Anthony Bianchi had an obsession with keys and was very particular about who had access to the elevator. He had grandkids and worried about them getting on it and pressing buttons. We got all the key rings when we got the contract on the house. My uncle forced me to give two to Spencer—he wanted to present the house keys to his wife as a special surprise apparently. Some surprise, right? I had a full set. Rosie had the fourth, because she was working up there. And I gave the fifth to a security guy I hired to check the house. That's it. And I have recorded each one dutifully. None ever went missing. So it's a mystery how someone got up there. Unless . . ."

"Unless Spencer let the person up. Maybe he was expecting someone?"

"Someone who killed him? A possibility maybe, but it doesn't seem likely. Rosie took the elevator down, so Spence would have to press the button to bring it up, then get in and take it down again, then bring the person up," Stella said. "If Spence had been expecting someone, why didn't he just wait downstairs for that person?"

"Could someone have made a copy of the key?"

"It's an unusual key. Only the elevator company could have done it and I think the police have looked into that. I wondered if there was a key we never knew about, but Uncle Mario thinks that's highly unlikely. The room was Anthony's haven—well, his and his three buddies—and it would have been a betrayal—Unc's words—if Anthony had not told them about extra keys."

"So the other men didn't have keys?"

"No. I guess that's odd, isn't it? But maybe not. Though they claimed the room, it wasn't their house, and the guys wouldn't have come over here unless Anthony was home, right? So they wouldn't have needed keys." The elevator bounced slightly, then came to a stop, and the doors opened.

"Welcome to the tree house," Stella said as they walked into the sun-soaked space.

"Wow. What a place. Unexpected for sure. From the outside and entryway, I expected something more formal." Cass walked over to the large back windows and looked out over the ocean, then down to the patio below. "This is where Rose saw him that night?"

Stella nodded.

Izzy joined Cass and looked down, imagining how Rose must have felt when she realized who it was, standing on the patio.

Stella took several framed photographs off the wall, wrapped them in bubble wrap that she pulled from her bag. "That's it for me. Anything else you want to see? I don't think the owner would mind."

"We've seen more of the place than Bree has already," Izzy said.

"Oh, there is one thing you have to see. Rosie and I had a good laugh over it. Okay, first, imagine Gus, Mario, Anthony, and Harry Garozzo up here—four good-hearted geezers." She waved for them to follow her and walked to a bookcase not far from the pool table. She moved a fat book aside and pushed a button.

And the mirrored bar appeared like magic. "Some private club, right?"

They laughed and decided the four friends had the right idea. It wasn't totally unlike the yarn shop's back room, although without the bar. But it was the same. It was about being friends, sharing life. A much nicer image to carry away than a man being murdered on the smooth cherrywood floor.

They walked over to the elevator and Stella pressed a button to open the doors.

"Stella, what spooks you most about this place, about being here alone?" Izzy asked. She looked back into the room while Cass kept the doors from closing.

Stella looked at the tall ceiling, the windows, imagining the old men playing cards and drinking whiskey. And then her face turned serious and she looked around again, then back to the elevator.

They all stood there for a minute, Izzy's question hanging in the air. But each of them shared one single image: It was of Rose Woodley, standing in front of the elevator, waiting for it to come up, to stop, for a man to get off. And having no way out.

"It's this elevator," said Stella, her words echoing ones Bree had uttered without ever having seen the inside of the Bianchi house. "I mean, who does this? Who just has an elevator to take you up and down? What if there was a fire or something? There'd be no escape."

Once outside, Stella offered them a ride home. Cass and Izzy answered in unison.

"Great," said Cass.

"No thanks," said Izzy.

A minute later they climbed into Stella's SUV. "For giving in, Iz, I'll let you ride shotgun," Cass said. "Besides, I want to sit back here and love these kitties."

"Such a magnanimous person," Izzy said to Stella, buckling herself in.

Stella laughed and turned her head. "Hey, Cass, sorry for all the junk back there. Just shove it aside. Tools of the trade. But treat those little kittens with care."

Cass put the kitten back in the box and looked over her shoulder at a trunk full of FOR SALE signs, piles of posters and pamphlets, a camera and some tools.

"I know, I know. It's a mess," Stella said, pulling out of the drive.

"Hey, you should see mine. At least there aren't any lobster traps back here." Cass looked at a stack of thick, familiar-looking books scattered across the backseat and the floor. A sock was stuck to one of them. She picked up the top one and pulled off the sock. Sea Harbor High was embossed across the top in a fancy scrolled font.

"Yearbooks, Stella? What is this, a trip down memory lane?"

Stella laughed and Izzy turned and craned her neck, one elbow across the seat as she tried to see what Cass was talking about.

"I love yearbooks," Izzy said. "But why are they in your car?"

Stella gave them an abbreviated version of Gus cleaning out a storeroom and dumping it all in her office. "Most of what we were storing over there was disposable, but I had taken these books from my mom's home when I was moving, intending to take them to my apartment, but somehow they didn't get further than the office and ended up in storage. Gus was frustrated that day—he and Robbie had had a blowup a few days before, and I think he was still kind of upset about it. Anyway, he kind of dumped the books on the floor. And you can't see an old yearbook lying on your floor and not open it, so I did.

"And that's the day I found Rose Woodley. It was a good day, finding Rosie." Stella smiled, her voice catching. "And they're in my car because I hate messes in the office. I know, my car doesn't show it, but I do like to keep things in the office organized. Rosie does, too. Uncle Mario? Not so much. But I didn't want to throw these out, so I threw the boxes in the back of my car. Let's say they're in transit to my apartment. I'm just not quite as fast a delivery as UPS." She laughed, then honked and waved as she spotted a friend at the next corner.

"The sock is a nice touch," Cass said, picking it up with two fingers and dropping it back to the floor.

"Not mine. We all used that storeroom and Gus was in such

a frenzy that he got some of his and Robbie's things mixed in with mine. Like dirty socks. A torn necktie. Treasures," she said.

"I bet you're going to use those books to secretly target all your old classmates and put them on a mailing list. Prospective home buyers," Cass said, leafing through one of the books.

"That's not a half-bad idea, Cass." She stopped for a red light and looked back at her. "I could use a thinker like you. Want a job?"

Izzy spoke up. "I'll give you Cass if you let us borrow these yearbooks for a couple days." Her voice held excitement, an idea forming in her head. "And would you mind dropping us at the Endicotts'?"

Cass looked down at the book in her hands, their hour in the morgue rewinding in her head. She smiled at the back of Izzy's head, and wished she had made the connection herself.

Nell curled up in one of the cushy chairs near the fireplace. Ben and his friends were sailing for the day, and inside, the house was quiet. Reflective.

She stared through the large windows facing the deck. There was still a little sunlight left in the day, but what she saw instead were twisted shadows falling across the decking.

And playing across her mind was a photo in the old *Sea Harbor Gazette* article. A face that stared back at her. Unblinking.

But she wasn't sure yet what to do with it.

Birdie walked over from the Endicott's kitchen carrying glasses of tea and a plate of banana bread. They'd gone over the article Izzy had copied, knowing that they'd discovered the reason for Patricia Stuber's difficult years. But what they were really looking for was a murderer.

There was more to learn from those years. There were lives that had been profoundly affected during that time. Families that were changed forever. And there was a student from those years who had been murdered. And the reason for that was there in that high school. Someplace. Just around a corner.

The article Izzy had printed out sat on the coffee table.

Birdie glanced at it, and then looked away. "We're close, but the bridge isn't quite there." And they weren't even sure they wanted to get to the other side.

The noise at the front door was a welcome diversion.

"We're here." Izzy's voice preceded her into the family room. She and Cass came in, still in running gear, still sweaty, and carrying two boxes of books.

"Yearbooks," Birdie said, her face lighting up. "Where did you get them?"

"From Stella. How did you know what they were?" Cass asked, setting the box down next to the coffee table.

"At the morgue, after we looked at all those pictures of young people, I was reminded of the yearbooks I saw in Stella's office that day. More faces. And somewhere behind all those faces, we're going to find out why Spencer Paxton was murdered. I feel certain of it. I was going to ask Stella to drop them by."

It was one of those moments. They'd had them before, those times when their thoughts, unspoken, came together without the need of texts or emails or phone calls. They were just there.

"Well, here they are. That's good, then," Izzy said.

Nell had also taken out Izzy's Venn diagram, and positioned it in the middle of the table. She looked at the yearbooks. "I feel a little bit like I did that day at the high school. We are so close to something, it's all around us, but we don't know exactly what to ask, what to look for."

"We're closer now," Birdie said. And Nell admitted she was right.

Cass pulled out Rosie's middle school book, then the yearbook for her freshman year at Sea Harbor High, when Spencer Paxton was a couple years older.

They found Rosie's class picture, so small the sadness was almost hidden in the black-and-white photo, but not quite. The activity section was active, but not for Rosie. "One photo in the whole yearbook," Cass said sadly.

"Is there a photo of the Math Olympiad competition?" Nell asked. "It'd be the year before she was a freshman, but it was a high school competition, so there should be a photo somewhere."

"The competition that humiliated Spencer Paxton," Cass said. She found the correct year and searched through the activities section. Then she looked again. Finally she found it, a small picture in a collage of many others. It was a picture of the three finalists, so small the faces were barely distinguishable. And the names unreadable. It was clear there were two girls and a boy in the photo, but that was all. It wasn't even clear who the winner was.

"That doesn't make sense," Nell said. "Look at the page before it. There are plenty of awards, plenty of large pictures of happy kids in their moments of glory."

They were silent for a moment. And then Birdie wondered aloud. "The Paxton family was powerful and it was unacceptable for Spencer to be less than perfect. I wonder if this was manipulated somehow."

Izzy picked up on the thought. "Sure, it's a high school yearbook and a puny younger kid who wasn't even a real student in the school, and a *girl* no less, won the competition that Spence had lost. So they buried it."

Cass flipped to the list of yearbook staff in the back and pointed to the activities editor. *Spencer Paxton*. She shuddered.

"I think we need to concentrate on something we've glossed over," Izzy said. "People like Spencer don't just bully once, and they don't just do it to one person. Rosie left Sea Harbor High a year later, after her freshman year, but I don't think her leaving town would have changed who Spencer was."

"So we need to look for others who might have been targeted," Cass said.

But how much can we learn from photos in a yearbook? Nell wondered. "I wonder how the other girl in the competition fared. Rose left a year later, but the other girl might still have been there."

"I asked Rose about her. She couldn't remember much, except that she was nice," Birdie said. "And this photo isn't telling us anything."

But they continued to look, paging through and moving on to the next book.

Izzy dug through the second box that held earlier books, the grade school and middle school annuals, thinner and flimsy. "I wonder . . ." she said, and then stopped talking and started looking.

Nell checked a text from Ben. "The sailors have landed," she said. "They'll be by shortly to give rides to the needy."

They looked at the boxes and the books and then back at Izzy's diagram. And then the article from the *Gazette*. They'd only begun.

Moments later Nell heard the cars outside and took the article and Izzy's diagram off the table, tucking it back inside a folder. Later she wondered why she'd done that. It had been instinctive. Like a puzzle that was being solved, but until a few more dots were connected, showing it would be premature.

Possibly wrong. Possibly dangerous.

Ben walked in and stopped just long enough to tell them that Danny and Sam were waiting in the drive. Danny was taking Birdie home, too.

And he was heading for the shower.

Cass put the books back into one of the boxes and set it next to Nell's bookcase. "To be continued," she said, and Nell nodded.

Izzy was still sitting on the floor, the middle school annual in her lap, ignoring the activity around her. When she looked up, her eyes were huge.

"What?" They gathered around.

"The high school didn't make much of Rosie's math win,

probably like we guessed—because she wasn't a student in the school and was only in the Math Olympiad competition because she excelled at math. That and Spencer Paxton wanting it buried. But Rosie was still in middle school then. And her middle school teachers were very proud of her accomplishments."

"And?" Cass asked.

"And they didn't ignore it." Izzy flattened the page in the middle school annual and they all gathered around her, looking down at the activities page. The Math Olympiad event took up half of a page, including a short description of their own student, Rose Woodley, winning a high school competition, and a photo of Rosie with the two high school finalists, the trophy held high in the air by the two young women who had defeated Spencer Paxton.

Three young people. And they knew each one of them.

Chapter 31

"You like him," Nell said. She was sitting on the Artist's Palate deck with Jane Brewster, cofounder of Canary Cove Art Colony, but the conversation wasn't about the art colony. Nor was it completely comfortable.

"Yes, I like Josh very much."

"Do you think he's honest?"

"How can I judge that, Nell? We believe our friends. But sometimes even they feel compelled to shade the truth for whatever reason. It happens."

Jane was Nell's oldest friend in Sea Harbor, and speaking frankly was an integral part of their relationship. Even though sometimes it led to disagreements. Today was bordering on that.

"Rose thought she saw Josh outside the Bianchi's home the night Spencer was killed."

"*Thought*," Jane said.

Nell acknowledged that was true, and also Rose's coating her statement with descriptives that nearly disqualified it from being taken seriously: it was dark, he had a helmet on, she didn't really see his face, only his hair. And more.

"Neither he nor Bree had an alibi for that night," Nell said. And then she shared with her good friend that she'd seen the couple together at the Beauport, checking in for the night.

Jane's expression didn't change.

Nell could tell she wasn't surprised.

"What they do isn't our business," Nell said. "But getting to the bottom of Spencer's murder is our concern, all of us, especially when innocent people like Rose and Beatrice are living under a shadow."

Merry walked over and refreshed their coffee, then walked on. Nell watched her walk away and thought about the restaurant owner's own dislike of Spencer's company. People had overheard Merry speaking in strong terms about anyone trying to alter the small artists' colony that was their home. And Izzy and Cass had seen Merry almost attack Spencer Paxton.

Nell shook her head. Even in death the man was upsetting Nell's town. And she wanted it over.

"Yes," Jane said, bringing Nell back on topic. "You're right. Someone killed Spencer Paxton. And we're all floating suspicions all over the place."

A shadow fell across the table and they looked up.

Josh Babson and Bree McIntosh stood hand in hand, their faces solemn.

"We just came to grab coffee, but we saw you two over here," Josh began. "From the expressions on your faces, we figured what you were talking about."

"Would you like to sit?" Nell asked.

Josh checked his watch. Then nodded and straddled the picnic bench. Bree sat close beside him.

Merry spotted them immediately and came back with coffee, then patted Josh on the back as if offering some kind of comfort.

He looked at Jane. "I wanted to talk to you anyway, so I was glad when I saw you here. You're like, I don't know—you and

Ham are real important to me," he said. "I'd never deceive you or put you in a bad spot. Never. You know that, right?"

Jane managed a smile, although neither she nor Nell liked the serious look on Josh's face.

He rested his arms on the table, his large hands playing with one another. "The chief has requested my presence again," Josh said. He smiled, attempting to make it light. "Bree and I are headed over there shortly."

Nell tried to read their faces. Her breathing stopped for a minute. No matter how overwhelmingly she wanted this over with and wanted Rose and others to be able to walk freely through this town, she didn't want this.

Josh looked over at her. "I talked to Ben late last night. He gave me good advice."

Nell hadn't known. Dear Ben. When things were confidential, Ben kept them that way.

Bree was silent, but her eyes hadn't left Josh's face.

"I went out for a bike ride that night. The night he was killed. The police know that. But I rode over to the Bianchi house for a reason. Bree told me she was meeting Spencer over there, and I couldn't get it out of my head that the guy might hurt her. It just took over everything. So I went, to make sure he didn't, to get her out of there. I hated the guy. And when you hate someone, it makes you think bad things. When I got there I saw that Bree's car was gone and I was relieved. Then I spotted Rose walking along the sidewalk, so I rode away from her, down the block and in between a couple parked cars. But as Bree knows, I didn't go back home. She knows that because she was there at my house, waiting for me. For hours. She was there when the police went looking for her at her own house to tell her that Paxton had been killed—but of course they couldn't find her. And she was still at my house when I finally came back in the wee hours of the morning."

He paused and swallowed a long drink of coffee.

"Clearly I didn't share all that with the police, nor did Bree. She was trying to protect me. And herself, too. An affair before the guy gets murdered? It doesn't look good, does it?"

"It's not an affair," Bree said quietly. "Josh and I fell in love a long time ago. Maybe another life, who knows? But for sure when Canary Cove adopted me months ago and I met this fine man—and fell in love with him."

Josh let her speak but didn't look her way, and when she finished, he continued.

"Janie, I see the worry on your face. But here's the truth. I didn't kill Paxton. I didn't touch a hair on his head. Didn't knock him out. But I wanted to. I saw the lights on in the Bianchi place so I figured he was still there. And I had a key—Bree's key. But what I did instead was force myself away from that place. I thought of you and Ham, and this town, and mostly of Bree. So I got on my bike and I rode the darn thing around the whole coastline of Cape Ann—twice. I pedaled my way through Rockport, Annisquam, along the back shore in Gloucester, you name it. Until I finally exhausted all those bad, hateful feelings, and I went back home. To Bree."

And somehow, during Josh Babson's long ride, Spencer Paxton was murdered.

A nor'easter of relief passed through Nell, surprising her in its intensity. But after another drink of Merry's strong coffee, she realized why Bree and Josh weren't celebrating.

They were innocent, and would reveal everything to the police. But in so doing, they were handing Chief Jerry Thompson a scenario that revealed an earlier lie, a powerful motive, a bike rider out in the middle of the night, and a couple desperately wanting to go on with their life.

She thought briefly of Izzy's Venn diagram and the multiple circles with which Josh's circle was now intersecting.

It was messy indeed.

*   *   *

The thought had come to Cass in the middle of the night. Fortunately for those whose friendships she valued, she had waited until morning to share it. The text she sent out suggested they meet her at Coffee's.

Cass had bought a plate of cinnamon rolls, several rolls already gone before the others crowded into the booth, cradling large mugs of strong coffee.

"It's this thing about someone breaking into Stella's office," Cass said. "It kept niggling at me last night, maybe because we hadn't been able to connect it to anyone or anything on that chart of Izzy's. It was just floating around by itself. Nothing was stolen. Why not?"

Izzy was nodding. It had bothered her, too. It didn't fit.

"When did that break-in happen?" Birdie asked.

They all thought back. In memory and on cell phone calendars, in random texts.

Izzy spoke up first. "We're all in a time warp. This murder has done something to our minds. The break-in was just a few days ago. It was Friday night while we were at your house, Aunt Nell. Jerry got a call, remember?"

"Of course." Nell shook off the feeling Izzy had just described. They were definitely out of sync with whatever time the world was using. "Ben and I went over to the realty office Saturday morning. Stella was perplexed because nothing was gone. The office was a mess."

"Nothing was missing except the yearbooks," Cass said.

"The yearbooks," Birdie repeated. "Yes, they were there a couple days before that when Rose and I went over and found Stella looking through them. Gus had cluttered the office with lots of things."

"And then they were gone," Cass said. "Stella said she had tossed them in her car later that day just to get them out of the way."

"Who would want those old yearbooks?" Nell said.

"That's the question," Cass said. "Maybe someone who is also trying to figure out what happened to Spencer Paxton."

"Or someone who knows what happened to him," Birdie said quietly.

"We need to look at them again with that in mind," Izzy said. She checked her phone calendar again. "My afternoon class is canceled. I can be out of the shop by three or four." She looked around at the others.

The time was good for everyone, and in minutes they'd finished their coffee and moved out of the crowded coffee shop and into the start of a new week. A productive week, they hoped. And if they looked long enough and hard enough in a pile of dusty old yearbooks, they would find the answer to a murder.

Nell was sure of it. Or at least she wanted desperately to be.

Nell had a half hour before her library board meeting. She had planned to skip it, but remembered that Harriet Brandley would be there. Like Cass, she had been bothered the night before, too. A different question. The same murder. And maybe Harriet would be able to shed some light on it.

She walked down Harbor Road, away from Coffee's and toward the harbor pier. The wind was bracing enough to bring color to her cheeks, warm enough to be pleasurable. And the double jolts of coffee she had already consumed that day added some pep to her step.

She crossed the street on impulse, realizing she had little in her refrigerator and she hadn't been in the new cheese shop that had opened next door to Garozzo's Deli. One thing she knew for certain was that searching for a murderer in old yearbooks could be made more pleasurable with cheese and a glass of wine.

"Nellie!" Harry's bombastic greeting seemed to come from nowhere, until the baker followed his voice out of the deli, his arms stretched wide.

"Harry," Nell replied, happy today for the hug, even if it left some tomato sauce in its wake.

"So how are we doing?" His face grew serious.

"We're fine, Harry. And you and Margaret?"

Harry glanced over his shoulder, then looked back to Nell. "I'm hearing bad things, Nellie."

Nell frowned. "About the Paxton murder?"

"It's moving so slow that it has people worried. Thinking that maybe our mayor might have had something to do with it. And there's talk that the Canary Cove group had it in for Paxton, too." He looked over his shoulder once more, then up and down the street. "And that pretty wife of his?" Harry nodded his head slowly. And then he said to Nell in a hushed voice, "That poor little thing is being talked about from the ladies' bridge club that meets in here to you-name-it. An affair, some say."

"Oh, Harry," Nell said.

"I know, I know"—he held up his large hands in dismay— "she's a sweetheart. Quiet and shy but with a big heart. Margaret says she helps her take all our extra deli food to the shelters. That little thing, no bigger than a fly, but always there to help. And Margaret says the next time the bridge club meets here in the deli and says a word about her, there're getting something in their chowder they didn't ask for."

Nell laughed at the thought of big, generous Margaret standing up to Sea Harbor's premium bridge club. "I'm with you and Margaret on this one. We have no business prying into people's bedrooms, and I happen to like Bree McIntosh, too."

"People are all talking about our special tree-house space, ever since that reporter snuck in and took a picture of it. I suppose we're sort of famous."

"I haven't seen the room," Nell said, relieved to have moved on from the subject of Bree. "But I hear it was the best of the best. Izzy says it had the same vibe as our knitting room. A place for good friends to be together."

Harry nodded, his face reflecting exactly that. A place for good friends.

Nell usually loved Harry's stories but suspected today he was about to launch into ones that might make her miss the library board meeting after all.

He surprised her. Instead he simply said, "We were at our best when we were together."

And then he got a twinkle in his eye and added, "And old Anthony—with Gus's help a'course—made it easy. Anytime. Any night. Our tree house welcomed us. And if Anthony was off to Sicily or somewhere, we were still welcome. It was our haven."

Nell frowned. "So you all had keys to the elevator? To the house? I can't imagine Anthony's wife liked that very much."

"Keys? Mirabella?" Harry laughed so hard he had to put one square hand on Nell's shoulder to steady himself. This time a look over his shoulder wasn't enough to be sure no one was listening.

He pulled Nell over to the side of the store and whispered his sacred secret to her, one the Tree House Four had solemnly kept from Mirabella, Anthony's finicky little wife, for nigh onto forty years.

Nell was late. She snuck in the back door just as the treasurer was finishing up the business report. She found a chair against the wall and looked around, finding Harriet Brandley immediately. Danny's mother was sitting near the front, taking dutiful notes and listening carefully.

More carefully than she was, Nell chided herself. The day wasn't half over and her mind was nearly full to capacity. She forced herself back to attention, and kept her mind on fundraising events, activities at the library, and a new project they were initiating to bring authors in to speak.

The meeting was organized, without controversy, and ended

early. She was seeing and feeling good omens everywhere today. And this was another one, confirming that indeed, things were coming together.

"Nell, hello," Harriet said, coming over and sitting down in the empty seat next to her. "I've been wanting to talk to you."

Nell smiled into Harriet's intelligent eyes. "We must be keyed into one another. I've been wanting to see you, too. How is Archie?"

"Fit as a fiddle. He's a dear, even when he isn't."

Nell laughed.

"I wanted to tell you that sweet Rose Woodley came into the shop the other day. She mentioned how you and the others had taken her under your wing, and she has a job with Stella. She's a dear girl, Nell, one of my special ones, and I wanted to thank you for being caring. This is such an awful time. And she's been through so much."

"I didn't realize you had a connection to Rose."

"She came in to the store all the time when she was young. I loved watching her mind open as she sat curled up, reading Ray Bradbury and others. Danny was in when she stopped by and he remembered her, too, much to her surprise. And she was even more surprised when she learned that Cass and Danny were married. There's something special about that girl."

"I think you sense those who need to be protected, Harriet."

"Maybe so. She was so quiet when she was young. So shy. And I'd see her almost cower when some of the louder kids came into the store. But I had no idea how badly she'd been treated. Not then. And I should have." Harriet's smile drifted off, and her mind, too, as if she was remembering things that pained her deeply.

For a moment, Nell wondered if she, too, had suffered as a child. And then she remembered why she had wanted to talk with Harriet. "I know others came in here, too. I think you created a safe place for them. Books and cookies."

Harriet smiled. "Many came in and out. A few were very special."

Nell suspected Harriet knew the question before she asked it. Another little girl seeking a safe haven or a warm cookie. Or Harriet's smile.

Harriet nodded and thought back to those sad days, then remembered the things that had made the teenager smile.

"She died too young," Nell said. "She was ill?"

Harriet looked at Nell for a long time, and then she said with a slight, sad smile, "We're a small town, Nellie, you know that. But we can keep our secrets."

She asked Nell to sit. And seemed almost relieved to have shared one of them.

Chapter 32

Nell had the yearbooks spread out on the coffee table.

Ben and Sam had gone out to the Northshore Mall for some sailboat equipment and the house felt empty.

She had made it back to the cheese store and arranged a few rounds on a tray, a bowl of crackers. But her heart and stomach weren't in it, and she suspected the tray would go untouched.

Cass and Birdie walked in, their moods matching Nell's. "If only it were Thursday and we were sitting down with food and yarn and a fire," Cass said.

Izzy showed up a few minutes later and headed for the books, but before she could begin, Nell took out the chart and the article, and then she shared Harriet Brandley's sad story.

They were quiet for a while, moving around the island carrying their own thoughts.

Izzy went back to the yearbook, finding it difficult to think about.

There was no happy ending here.

The middle-school yearbook didn't tell them much more than what they now knew. The three students who competed in the Math Olympiad, the one who lost. The one who survived. And the one who didn't.

Cass picked up a book they hadn't looked at before and frowned. "I wonder why Stella has this one. She had already graduated." She checked the year again and then opened it up, checking the name in front. It was written in the familiar scrawl that teenager girls adopt. "This isn't Stella's, that's why. Stella said Gus dumped these in her office quickly and had accidentally included some of his own things." She looked at the name in the book again, and passed it around.

It was Gus's daughter's book, her junior year. The year Hallie McGlucken died.

Cass found Hallie's photo in the junior-class section and looked at it for a long time. When she finally passed it along, she reached for a tissue, and then asked if there were more books that weren't Stella's.

Nell had already found one. It was the year Rosie was a freshman, and Hallie a year ahead.

And Spencer Paxton, a senior.

Nell turned to the back of the book, where she found more comments—not too many, but enough to know that Hallie McGlucken had a few friends who loved her and who hated the taunting and pain she had suffered from a boy who seemed to have everything. And every single one mentioned the initials SP along with a pencil sketch of a devil, and nonsensical things about him that they thought would make her laugh and help her survive.

They were huddled around Nell now, reading along with her.

Cass suggested going to the class page, where they all hoped to see a smiling Hallie. But she wasn't smiling. The photo was circled with a permanent marker, a giant heart with an arrow leading to the bottom of the page.

"I will love you forever, Sis. And I will see you soon."

Cass held the book up to her face and smelled the ink. "This is new," she said. She flipped to the senior page.

Spencer's picture was there. Only it wasn't. The same marker had effectively erased his face from the page.

"The attempted robbery," Nell said softly. "He needed to get these books back."

But the bigger concern was the note and heart around Hallie McGlucken's class photo.

Nell called the police, while Birdie called Gus, wondering how she could reach Robbie. Nothing important, she just wanted to chat with him. Gus was busy, and quickly rattled off a cell phone number, but said he hadn't seen Robbie in a week.

Detective Tommy Porter didn't answer Nell's call, but he returned her voice message almost immediately. She quickly relayed the information they'd gathered. It fit into their own investigation, he said, but expanded it, filling in some important holes, for which he was grateful. Yearbooks hadn't factored in.

Then Nell read him the note that they thought Robbie had written, and he shared her concern. And her urgency.

Sea Harbor was small. It should be easy to find someone in a leather jacket on a motorcycle. They knew the police would have better methods, but none of them could sit still, so they piled into Nell's car and drove down Harbor Road. But it had been days since anyone had seen Robbie McGlucken tearing up the road.

About to give up, Cass suggested one more place they should try. "It's where I would go," she said. The cemetery.

Birdie remembered where the McGlucken plot was, and that's where Hallie would have been buried. A plot in St. Mary's cemetery, close to the Favazza plot, near an old oak tree at the top of a hill. A beautiful spot that overlooked the ocean.

They knew it was a long shot, but worth the short drive to the edge of town.

No one knew Robbie McGlucken very well, but they knew one thing. He loved his sister Hallie more than life itself—and he hated what had been done to her.

And now they were worried about what he might do to himself.

Nell had left a message for Ben, filling him in and leaving Izzy's diagram on the kitchen island. Finally completed.

And Izzy had texted both Sam and Ben from the car to tell them where they were.

They drove through the cemetery entrance, then up a small hill to the office. Nell pulled into the small parking lot beside the stone building while Birdie pointed farther up the hill to a stand of pine trees. "If memory serves me, it's right near those trees."

She got out of the car and turned toward the office door. "I wonder if Henry Staab is still around. He was the caretaker out here for a hundred years. Absolutely devoted to the families."

"And to you, if I remember correctly," Nell said.

They laughed, and Birdie explained to the others that "a thousand years ago" Henry Staab had proposed to her. Out of the blue. And while she was engaged to her Sonny.

They all looked toward the office, liking the diversion and thought of a young Birdie being chased by not one, but two men.

As if lured outside by their memories, the door opened and a small, gnome-like man walked out, more hunched over than the last time Birdie had seen him. Tiny wisps of white hair, scattered willy-nilly across a nearly bald head, flew in the breeze. He hobbled over to them, supporting himself on a gnarled cane that matched the shape of his body.

"I knew you'd come back to me," he said to Birdie, grinning.

"Henry, you're still here," Birdie said, allowing his thin, bent arms to wrap around her in an unusually vigorous hug.

"Where else would I be?"

"Well, out there somewhere." Birdie waved toward the winding rows of well-tended graves.

Henry gave one short laugh, and then pulled nonexistent eyebrows together, squinting at her. "You're looking for the boy," he said, his gravelly voice barely audible. "He knew you'd come."

It was then they noticed a motorcycle parked around the side of the stone building.

"Is this where he's been staying?" Birdie asked.

"He's come up here every day of his life since the day we put his poor sister in the ground. Every day. When he and the dad had a fracas, I told him, sure, he might as well blow up one of those newfangled beds and move in. Stay close to her." He nodded toward the pine trees. "So he did."

They walked together toward the top of the hill with Birdie, and old Henry leaning on his cane, leading the way. A soft wind tugged deep red and orange leaves from tree branches, scattering them like offerings over the graves and granite head stones.

At the top of the hill, Henry nodded to the right. They saw the leather jacket first, the serpent on the back protecting a hunched-over Robbie McGlucken. He sat cross-legged on the ground, leaning forward, absently pulling strands of grass from the ground, and speaking softly. Without turning around, he held up one arm to silence the footsteps behind him.

Then, for minutes that seemed like hours, he continued to talk to his sister, soft affectionate words, an occasional laugh, as if Hallie had said something in response.

In the distance, Nell heard another car, then glanced at her phone and a message from Ben. Jerry Thompson was waiting at the stone house. He and Gus were there, too.

Finally Robbie pushed himself off the ground and turned toward them, acknowledging Henry first, and then the others.

"He was a bad man," was all Robbie said, and he began walking slowly down the hill to the cemetery office.

"It was almost as if Robbie had rehearsed his confession," Nell said. They were gathered around the kitchen island, a pan of Harry Garozzo's lasagna heating in the oven.

Robbie had held nothing back, even after the police chief suggested they wait until they got back to the station to talk. It was as if once he got started, he couldn't stop. He just kept talking.

There was little in what he said that the women hadn't imagined or hadn't known for a fact. He'd found his sister's old yearbooks in the storage room and read the notes from Hallie's friends, and he put it all together.

The same yearbooks his father had mistakenly dumped off in the real estate office.

Finally, with the yearbook messages ringing in his head, Robbie had confronted his father, who for all these years had protected Robbie from how Hallie had died. There was no heart condition—unless you counted a broken heart. Robbie had demanded to know everything, and Gus explained how she'd waited until he was safe in school—then taken a rope and hung herself in the garage.

Birdie pulled back thoughts of those days. She remembered bits and pieces, but mostly she remembered how the town had wrapped Gus close, how his friends Mario and Harry Garozzo and even Father Northcutt had managed to celebrate Hallie's life—and how they had buried the painful secret of her death along with her.

"Did Gus know why she did it, I wonder?" Izzy said.

"I don't think so. Hallie left a note that said she loved them. And she was sorry. That was all," Ben said. He checked the oven and pulled out the pan.

"I know it was the yearbook note that got him thinking. But I wonder . . ."

"What?" Nell asked.

"I wonder if Robbie didn't have some idea in the back of his head somewhere that Hallie had taken her own life. And maybe he blamed himself somehow?"

But Robbie hadn't touched on such personal things.

"Hopefully a good prison psychiatrist will be able to help him sort it out," Danny said.

"I don't think it was premeditated," Ben said. "Spencer had told Robbie where he was going that night. I think Robbie went over to the Bianchi house for answers."

Izzy agreed. "Imagine how tangled his thoughts must have been. He read the yearbooks and all the references to someone with the initials SP, along with Hallie's friends' comments about what she'd been through."

"It's exactly what Patricia said—reporting bullying is disastrous," Cass said. "So Hallie had kept it silent, and even her friends were afraid to step up."

"And not reporting it can be deadly," Birdie said.

"I can't imagine the thoughts that ran through Robbie's head," Nell said. "Questions and confusion—and all that he really wanted was to find out he was wrong, that this man he trusted would tell him it had never happened. None of it."

"And he had perfect access to the Bianchi house," Birdie said. "Mario was so proud of their secret entry. They all were."

Sam laughed. "I can't believe Anthony's wife didn't know about it. Those four guys were something else."

"Gus built the secret staircase," Ben said. "But Robbie had helped fix the door a couple times. Getting up to the third floor was no problem. That was one of the things that had the police stumped. Stella had been meticulous about who had the keys. But someone had obviously made their way up."

"And it was also one of the reasons the police couldn't let go of Rose," Ben said. "She had access, not to mention that she had been up there that night."

Robbie had told them at the cemetery how, when he got to the top of the stairs that night, he heard voices. So he waited, hidden from sight. And he listened as Rosie calmly laid out her story about how Spencer Paxton had nearly destroyed her.

And that's when he knew. When he heard Rose bring up Math Olympiad, something that had brought so much joy to his sister that he could still remember it, even though he was just a kid. He remembered her smile, her excitement at winning. How he'd sat with his dad and they'd clapped and clapped.

As soon as Rose left, Robbie confronted Spencer. It took one harsh laugh from Spencer—and his proud, detailed description of how cleverly he'd gotten even with the two stupid ugly girls—to send Robbie over the edge. He grabbed one of Rosie's tools and once he started, he couldn't stop.

Not until Spencer Paxton was dead.

"It's sad. The whole thing is so terribly, horribly sad," Stella said, her eyes filling up.

They all agreed. There was no happy ending. Only sadness.

Nell looked across the island at Rose, sitting on a stool next to Stella, her lasagna untouched.

Rose was the saddest of all.

She'd wanted to walk in that ocean and not come back. But she had come back.

Hallie McGlucken hadn't been able to walk herself back.

And it filled Rose Woodley with enormous sorrow.

Chapter 33

Ham and Jane Brewster were wandering through the crowd, welcoming friends and neighbors and perfect strangers to the first ever Canary Cove Fiber Arts Show opening.

Jane looked lovely, her colorful flowing caftan a Kandinsky painting come to life, her graying hair pulled back in a loose bun. Ham stood next to her, his white beard trimmed for the event, hundreds of wrinkles spreading out from his great blue eyes, welcoming folks with handshakes and hugs.

The crowd moved among Izzy's sea urchins floating down from the ceiling, Bree's enchanting cavern, and dozens of pieces of fiber art hanging from branches and wires and framed on the walls.

In a far corner, Pete Halloran's Fractured Fish band was set up on a small stage, playing old covers that would give way to rock and hip-hop, indie, and more as the evening went on.

It was a happy mood. The art colony was aglow.

And the Brewsters were loving it.

"It's a fabulous party," Beatrice Scaglia said, doing a slight dance step as she came in the door. Ben laughed and offered her an arm to keep her balance.

"We did it," Izzy said, coming up and giving Jane a hug. "Everyone is here. It's amazing." Bree was behind her, a glass of champagne in one hand and Josh Babson close to the other.

Even Josh had spiffed up for the show. A new pair of jeans and an emerald-green shirt that Bree had found for him were garnering him attention he was trying hard to ignore.

"It's not my thing," he whispered to Nell.

Nell smiled and stood tall, kissing him on the cheek. For a minute, he was startled. Something else that wasn't his thing. Then he allowed a slow smile.

"Fall is here," Nell said. " 'A second spring when every leaf is a flower.' "

"Let us rejoice in it," Josh responded solemnly. And then laughed along with her.

It was a smile and laugh Josh didn't often let out.

Perhaps they'll come more readily now, Nell thought.

Stella and Rose were manning a table filled with cheeses, crackers, creamy dips, and baskets of fried clams. "I'm a kitchen kind of person," Rose said to Nell with a grin. "I like being behind the scenes."

Stella laughed. "It's all a façade, Nell. Rosie likes crowd watching. Me too." Then she pointed to Pete's band, where a microphone was being tapped to quiet the crowd.

The crowd hushed, and Jane Brewster walked up, waving and blowing kisses. She thanked everyone for coming, for their huge contributions to the artists' foundation, and for their love of the arts.

"And I've one more person to whom we need to give thanks. She wouldn't come up here with me, I even had trouble getting her to approve this announcement. But this is the perfect time, the perfect night to get you all to celebrate with me. So raise those champagne glasses high."

The crowd clapped and Jane went on with a flourish.

"One of our very own talented artists has gifted—yes,

gifted!—to the Canary Cove Arts Association its very own retreat and educational center. A beautiful home our artists will help renovate and make our own. A place we will share with the community, fill with children and adult classes and shows and celebrations and all sorts of marvelous things." She paused for a minute, her smile so big it was difficult to talk, but Jane continued, her eyes moist.

"The Bianchi home on Cliffside Drive will forever more be known as the Canary Cove Art Haven. Our deep and overwhelming thanks to one of our own—Bree McIntosh."

No one knew quite where Bree was—and some didn't even know for sure who she was—but the crowd cheered and clapped, congratulating anyone who happened to be standing nearby as they raised their champagne flutes in the air.

Nell and Birdie had looked for the most obscure corner, knowing they'd find Bree there. And they did, standing with Izzy and Cass and Josh, her cheeks as red as her dress, and her eyes moist.

"Sometimes it all works out the way it should," she said, and she hugged them all tightly.

The party would go on for hours, they knew, but a short while later, Birdie whispered to Nell that she had one more stop that night, and she needed to be on her way.

"You are double partying? Or on a Birdie mission? The latter is my guess." Nell smiled down at Birdie and suspected she knew exactly where Harold would be driving her friend.

Birdie answered her with a hug and a finger to her lips, then walked out the front door to her waiting Lincoln Town Car with Harold at the wheel.

It was a short drive and Harold found his way easily, driving through winding streets on the east side of town, then turning into a quiet neighborhood with tree-lined sidewalks. He slowed down and pulled to a stop in front of a white frame house, a driveway beside it, and lights blazing inside. The light from old-fashioned street lamps brightened the walk.

Several cars were parked at the curb and Birdie smiled when she saw them. They were all there, just as she had hoped.

Gus McGlucken opened the door, a bottle of beer in his hand, his face worn and looking older than a few weeks ago. He wrapped Birdie in his arms and pulled her inside, into the living room with its portable bar, its big-screen television, and a bookshelf groaning with the history books Gus liked to read.

Mario Palazola and Harry Garozzo pushed themselves out of their recliners and walked over, beers in their hands, too, and their faces filled with sad smiles that held love and friendship and grief all together in one tight bundle.

"Ah, our sweet Bernadette," Harry said, his gravelly voice wrapping her up in it. "You came. We knew you would."

And then Mario chimed in. And Gus.

And in a minute or two, with the beers helping them along, the three men had linked arms and were weaving back and forth, their voices harmonizing with bass and baritone, Harry trying hard to be a tenor.

"Bernadette, sweet Bernadette . . ."

They were their own barbershop trio. Loud and clear they sang all the way up to the rafters, the words of their own making, until Birdie's tears came, and then Gus's, too.

They collapsed in the chairs that circled around the TV, with Old Blue Eyes crooning "Fly Me to the Moon" in the background.

"Anthony loved Frank," Mario explained to Birdie. "We knew he'd wanna be with us, to be with Gus here, so we're channeling him down through Frank."

"Music," Birdie said, smiling up at wherever Anthony Bianchi was, along with a salute to Frank's voice coming from a corner speaker. "It helps us grieve and love and laugh. It helps us live." They sat together for a while, telling old and worn stories, talking and crying and laughing a little, too. Three old friends, with the woman they loved "like one of them."

Birdie shared a single beer with them, and when they walked her to the door, the four old friends hugged long and hard, each one wiping away a tear or two.

Birdie walked slowly back to her waiting Lincoln Town Car with Harold at the wheel. Quiet and patiently waiting.

She felt the stillness of the night surround her, comforting her, and then she stood for just a moment, looking back at the well-lit house.

And she knew that Gus McGlucken was going to be okay.

Acknowledgments

My thanks to Suzan Mischer for graciously allowing us to use a pattern from her book, *Greetings from Knit Café*. The slouchy cardigan is one of my favorites. I've spent time wandering through the book, and Suzan's shop was one of the inspirations that helped me create Izzy's yarn shop in the Seaside Knitters Society Mysteries. Not only has Nell used some patterns from this book, but I have, too, and I have loved them all.

Thanks to my Kensington family, an amazing group of people who have nurtured these mysteries in new and wondrous ways. I am grateful to my editor, Wendy McCurdy, and Norma Perez-Hernandez, Michelle Addo, Lauren Jernigan, Karen Auerbach, and all those behind and in front of the scenes who support this series from draft to print.

As always, my thanks to Christina Hogrebe, Andrea Cirillo, and the whole amazing Jane Rotrosen family who have supported me for more years than I can count. I love them all and am in their debt. Without them, I might still be a frustrated 1980s writer, sitting in a den, piling up unused manuscripts in a dusty drawer.

To my readers and friends, who seem to know exactly when an encouraging email or call or invitation to lunch is what I need to write the next chapter in a book. You never fail me. And to Sister Rosemary Flanigan and Mary Bednarowski—charter members of my invaluable "sounding board."

To Jane and Mary Sue, world's best sisters, whose hugs and support (and marketing efforts!) are dished out effortlessly and endlessly.

To Nancy Pickard, who is always there.

And to my family, for everything else.

This wonderful pattern, designed by Helen Roux, appears in *Greetings from Knit Café*. The book's author, Suzan Mischer has generously granted permission to share it here.

Slouchy Cardigan

ABBREVIATIONS

CO—cast on

BO—bind off

K—knit

K2tog—knit 2 stitches together

N—needle; N1—needle #1

P—purl

P2tog—purl 2 stitches together

R—round / row

RS—right side

Sl1—slip 1 stitch purl-wise

Ssk—slip 2 stitches individually knit-wise; knit these 2 sts together through back loops

St/Sts—stitch / stitches

WS—wrong side

YO—yarn over

MATERIALS

One pair straight needles, size US 8 (5 mm). Change needle size if necessary to obtain correct gauge.

Stitch markers, yarn needle

Gauge—19 sts and 25 rows = 4 inches

Size—Small/Medium (Medium/Large) to fit women's bust, size 32"–34" (34"–36")

INSTRUCTIONS

BACK
CO 84 (88) sts

R1—(WS) *K1, p1; rep from * across.
Change to St st—work even until piece measures 4" from
beginning, end with a WS row.

SHAPE SIDES
(RS) Decrease 1 st each side on this row—82 (86) sts remain.

Work even until piece measures 8" from beginning, end with a
WS row

Decrease 1 st each side on this row—80 (84) sts remain.

Work even until piece measures 16-½" from beginning, end
with a WS row.

SHAPE ARMHOLES
(RS) BO 3 sts at beginning of next 2 rows, 2 sts at beginning of
next 4 rows—66 (70) sts remain.
Decrease 1 st each side every row 3 times—60 (64) sts remain.

Work even until armhole measures 9-½" from beginning of
shaping, ending with a WS row.

Shape Shoulders
(RS) BO 5 sts at beginning of next 4 rows, 4 (6) sts at beginning
of next 2 rows—32 sts remain. BO remaining sts.

RIGHT FRONT
CO 84 (88) sts.
R1—(WS) *K1, p1; rep from * across.

Change to ST st and AT THE SAME TIME, shape center front
as follows:
BO 2 sts at beginning of next row, then every other row 4
times. Work 1 (WS) row even. 74 (78) sts remain.
(RS) Decrease 1 st at beginning of this row, then every other
row 23 times 50 (54) sts remain, then every 4 rows 9 times,
every 6 rows 6 (8) times—and at the same time, when the
piece measures 16-½" from the beginning, shape armhole.
End with a RS row.

Shape Armhole
(WS) At Armhole edge, BO 3 sts, 2 sts twice, then decrease 1 st
every row 3 times—24 (26) sts remain.

Work until armhole measures 9-½" from beginning of shaping,
end with a RS row.

Shape Shoulder
(WS) at armhole edge, BO 5 sts twice, 4 (6) sts once—10 sts remain. Work 1 row even. BO remaining sts.

LEFT FRONT
Work as for Right Front, reversing all shaping.

SLEEVES (make two).
CO 61 (64) sts.

R1—(WS) *K1, p1; rep from* to last 1 (0), k I (0)across.

Change to St st; work 4 rows even, end with a WS row.

SHAPE SLEEVE
(RS) Decrease Row—[K10, k2tog] twice, k13 (16), [k2to, k10] twice—57 (60).
Work 7 rows even, end with a WS row.

Decrease Row—[K9, k2tog] twice—53 (56) sts remain.
Work 7 rows even, end with a WS row.

Decrease Row—[K8, k2tog], twice, k13 (16), [k2tog, k8] twice—49 (52) sts remain.
Work 7 rows even, end with a WS row.

Decrease Row—[K7, k2tog] twice, k13 (16), [k2tog, k7] twice—45 (48) sts remain.
Work even in St st until piece measures 14 (13)" from beginning, end with a WS row.

Shape Sleeve—(RS) Increase 1 st each side on this row, then every 6 rows twice, every 4 rows 2 (4) times—55 (62) sts.

Work even until piece measures 18" from beginning, ending with a WS row.

Shape Cap—(RS) BO 3 sts at beginning of next 2 rows, 2 sts at beginning of next 4 rows, then at each side decrease 1 st every other row 10 times—21 (28) sts remain. Bind off remaining sts.

HOOD (optional)
CO 124 sts.

R1—(WS) *K1, p1; rep from *across.
Change to St st; work even until piece measures 9-½" from beginning, end with a WS row.

Divide Hood and Shape Top—(RS) Work 62 sts, join second ball of yarn, work to end. Working both sides at the same time, work 1 (WS) row even, turn, and then decrease 1st at beginning of this row, then every other row once.

Work 2 rows even, end RS row.

<u>Decrease Row</u>—(RS) decrease 1 stitch, each side, as follows:
For right side of hood, work across to last 3 sts, k2tog, work 1 st; for left side of hood, work 1st, ssk, work to end—61 sts remain each side. Work 1 WS row. Repeat Decrease Row once, then at each center edge, BO 2 sts twice, 3 sts once, then 4 stitches once, AND AT THE SAME TIME, at each outside edge, BO 7 sts twice, 8 sts once. BO remaining 27 sts each side.
BO 28 sts for each side of hood.

FINISHING
Sew shoulders together. Set in sleeves; sew side and sleeve seams. Sew center back seam of hood. Sew hood to neck edge, lining up center back seam of hood with center back neck edge. Using yarn needle, weave in all loose ends.

For more information about *Greetings from Knit Café*, visit http://www.abramsbooks.com/ or your favorite bookseller.